SHIROBAMBA

SHIROBAMBA
A Childhood in Old Japan

BY YASUSHI INOUE

translated from the Japanese
and with an introduction by Jean Oda Moy

NEW YORK · WEATHERHILL · TOKYO

Published by Weatherhill, Inc.
420 Madison Avenue, 15th Floor
New York, N.Y. 10017
by special arrangement with
Peter Owen Publishers

First English edition, 1991
First Weatherhill edition, 1993

Printed in the U.S.A.

ISBN 0-8348-0269-4

Library of Congress Cataloging in Publication Data

Inoue, Yasushi, 1907–1991
[Shirobamba. English]
Shirobamba: a childhood in old Japan / by Yasushi Inoue ;
translated by and with an introduction by Jean Oda Moy. — 1st.
Weatherhill ed.
p.   cm.
ISBN 0-8348-0269-4 (pbk.) ; $12.95
I. Title.
PL830.N63S44513   1993
895.6'35—dc20   92-42956
                                                            CIP

INTRODUCTION

In *Shirobamba*, the distinguished Japanese novelist Yasushi Inoue looks back on the second decade of this century to re-create the innocent world of his own youth. The novel opens on a dreamlike scene of children chasing the gauzy white insects they call shiro-bamba, which in summertime appear in swarms and float in the twilight air until night closes in. As the first chapter ends, the children are called home one by one until the last child left on the darkened road is Kosaku, the protagonist of the novel, who is the young Yasushi Inoue. It is a poignantly nostalgic scene, haunting in its evocation of long-ago pleasures, and it also gives a hint of the loneliness and anticipation of loss that will be recurring themes in the boy's awareness even when he is most socially engaged.

Shirobamba was originally published in serial form in the magazine *Shufu no Tomo* between January 1960 and December 1962. Almost immediately thereafter it appeared as a book, in two volumes. This translation is of Volume One, which covers the boy's second and third years in elementary school. There are no great peaks and valleys in the story; it is more like a horizontal scroll slowly unfolding to reveal a vivid cast of characters involved in daily comings and goings and in seasonal festivals and special events. Some of the characters grow and wax strong and others wane and die. The action is set against the scenic backdrop of the Izu Peninsula, about eighty miles southwest of Tokyo. In addition to its accuracy as to time, place and events, *Shirobamba* is a true *roman à clef* in that all its characters represent persons who actually lived; only the names have been changed.

In order to appreciate the intricate kinship relations within

5

Kosaku's family, the reader needs to understand something of the Japanese adoption system. In the past, the Japanese placed such importance on the survival of family names that a childless person or couple commonly adopted a blood-related child, or even a young married couple, to ensure that their own name would not die out. In this case Kosaku's (i.e., Inoue's) wealthy but childless great-great-uncle adopted Kosaku's maternal grandfather and grandmother as his children. But later he also arbitrarily (and quite unconventionally) arranged to have the eldest daughter of the adopted couple, who was Kosaku's mother, adopted by his mistress Onui. Thus Kosaku's mother, Nanae, became obligated to look after Onui in her old age, even though the two women shared no blood ties. This latter arrangement explains much of the animosity between the inhabitants of the Upper House, where Kosaku's grandparents live, and the household of Granny Onui. The Upper House bitterly resent the fact that Nanae, one of their number, should have been adopted by a woman of much lower class – especially one redeemed from the pleasure quarter and elevated to the role of mistress by the adoptive patriarch – and that Kosaku, another of their number, is being raised by such a woman. Granny Onui, for her part, is deeply stung by their resentment. And Kosaku is caught in the crossfire between the two factions.

Of the many characters populating this novel, three women play crucial roles in Kosaku's life: Sakiko, the young aunt whom he idolizes; Nanae, his mother, a proud, exacting woman, at once magnetic and forbidding; and Granny Onui, his guardian, who is by far the most fully realized character in the story. Her contentiousness, her braggadocio and her loud disparagement of all whom she considers inferior to 'her' Kosaku do not endear her to the village at large any more than to the Upper House, but on balance she comes across as a spirited, resourceful and endearing person. She is an engaging mixture of innocent and jade, by turns spiteful and sagacious, outrageously opportunistic and tenderly self-denying, hypocritical and sincere, vulnerable and domineering. For all her self-serving ways, there is never any doubt that her love for Kosaku is genuine or that she is his prime reliable source of emotional security.

In addition to the characters and events portrayed in these pages, the Japanese countryside serves as a pervasive and sublime presence. Here in particular the author's considerable poetic skills are everywhere evident (Inoue began his writing career as a poet), with the result that a journey through the book is like a real-life excursion of the senses to another realm.

Shirobamba of course suggests a great deal about the forces that moulded the author's career. It is clear that Kosaku's early separation from parents and siblings and his uncomfortable status as protégé of an elderly and idiosyncratic woman in conflict with his own family, combined with the young child's natural desire to please, have fostered a painful uncertainty about just where his loyalties ought to lie. What is more, although he has been told that his placement with Granny Onui is temporary, he may well feel abandoned by his mother. In any case, he more than once declines to return to his parents when the chance is offered. It seems extraordinary that so young a child should be allowed to make such a major decision. In the novel we see that Kosaku's relationship with his mother is ambivalent; he longs to be close to her but he expects and fears her rejection. This apprehension of only qualified acceptance extends to all members of his family. Obviously, childhood stresses can find many outlets in later life. It is my belief that the unusual domestic circumstances experienced by the young Inoue encouraged above all a sense of isolation in the sensitive and intelligent child, and that this sense of isolation in turn enhanced the habits of introspection, detachment and close observation so important to any writer's craft.

Shirobamba has been used as a textbook in Japanese schools for many years and still enjoys a large adult readership in Japan. Inasmuch as most of the simple demands and pleasures depicted in the novel are no longer familiar to children of the present generation, part of the book's value lies in its record for posterity of a lifestyle that seems as remote to most of today's children in Japan as it does to readers in the West. Conversely, it should be noted that some cultural characteristics have not changed all that much. Vis-à-vis outsiders, for example, a strong vein of the insular mentality seen in Kosaku's village still lies beneath today's veneer of modernization, a prevalent 'us-versus-them' type of thinking. For this reason, then, *Shirobamba* may yet provide some helpful glimpses into the contemporary Japanese mind.

I believe that *Shirobamba* is destined to occupy a place in Japanese letters akin to the American *Huckleberry Finn* or the English *David Copperfield*. Like those two familiar classics, it deals with a boy's adventures while growing up, in a lucidly portrayed time and place amid memorable characters. As in the earlier works, a sparkle of humour, in this case often subtle but occasionally boisterous, frequently lightens the narrative. And finally, like Twain and Dickens, Inoue is quite simply a master storyteller.

Jean Oda Moy
Sunnyvale, California. 1990

1

When twilight fell back then – that is to say about the fourth or fifth year of the Taisho Era,* which makes it more than forty years ago – the village children shouted, 'Shirobamba! Shirobamba!' as they ran to and fro in the street, chasing tiny pale creatures that floated like bits of cotton in the darkening air. Some leaped to catch them with their bare hands, others waved cedar branches, hoping to snare them in the leaves. The term 'shirobamba' probably meant 'white-haired grannies' originally. The children had no notion where the insects came from, but they did not think it particularly strange that they appeared at twilight time. It wasn't clear whether they came because it was dusk or whether dusk fell because they appeared. The creatures were not always white but at times had a slightly bluish cast; that is, during the lighter hours they looked white, but as the twilight deepened they seemed to take on a bluish tinge.

And about the time the shirobamba began to look bluish, the parents' voices could be heard calling the children home.

'Yuki! It's dinner time!'

'Shige! Time to eat!'

'If you don't hurry, we won't let you eat!'

These voices carried over great distances. Then Yukio would disappear. Next Shigeru would be gone. And in this

* 1915–1916

9

way their numbers dwindled: first one child, then two, and so on.

The children did not exchange goodbyes. In the twilight where the shirobamba hovered, some skipped and hopped their way home while others ran energetically, carrying cedar branches, holding them high like banners, each drawn to his own home as if by some magic spell.

Kosaku always played to the very last. Dinner was late at Kosaku's home, and Granny Onui seldom came to call him. Therefore, Kosaku still played in the street when every single friend had left. Only then, after the street was silent and the darkness nearly complete, did he start walking home.

Before Kosaku reached the storehouse where he lived with Granny Onui he passed many homes along the road, all brightly lit for dinner. After he reached the area where the children played in front of the main gate of the Amagi branch of the Imperial Lands and Forestry Administration Bureau (referred to by the villagers as 'the Bureau' or 'the Office') there were fewer distractions. Only a few houses lined the road from there to the storehouse. Just beyond the Office was the home known as the Upper House, where Kosaku's main family lived: his grandmother, his grandfather and his mother's young siblings, in other words, the boys and girls who were Kosaku's aunts and uncles. The youngest, Mitsu, was the same age as Kosaku.

Even though Kosaku knew his maternal grandparents were in the brightly lit main house, he never looked in after dark. He might go there to play with Mitsu; for some other reason or no particular reason at all he might enter as freely as he did his own home . . . during the daylight hours. But at dinner time something alienating emanated from that lamplight. An element in the atmosphere seemed to say, This is *not* your home. You belong in the storehouse.

If it happened that Kosaku had to go on an errand to the main house during dinner time, Grandmother Tane invariably invited him to stay.

'Ko-cha,* eat with us.'

---

* Diminutive for Kosaku

10

'Uh-uh. I'll eat at home.'

'But this is your home, too. Don't be so standoffish, and please come and eat with us.'

'Uh-uh. I don't want to.'

It was always the same, no matter what Grandmother Tane said. Kosaku always refused the invitation. At such times his grandfather and the others usually ignored him and continued eating. Kosaku could not help feeling antagonistic towards them. At any other time of day he could behave just as he would in his own home, but at meal times the Upper House clearly turned into a home of strangers and a part of Kosaku said, If this is not my home, I will not accept your food.

Just across the narrow alley from the main house was a general store, the only shop of its kind in the village. Hardware items and an array of sundries were crammed so tightly within its walls they looked as if they might overflow the earthen floor and spill out the entrance. All the villagers came to shop there when they needed wire, nails, pots and pans, kitchen knives and the like.

Next to the general store was a smallholding known as Sadoya where, in addition to a main house, there stood a shed in whose dark interior two cows perpetually wrinkled their noses. Across from Sadoya was a little house where Bunkichi, a forty-ish bachelor and day labourer, lived. The land adjoining Bunkichi's house belonged to Kosaku's family and boasted the only truly garden-like garden in the village. The main house on that property was rented to a doctor from Tokyo who served as the village physician. He was a married man but he had no children. Moreover, although he was a doctor, he had hardly any patients because unless they were seriously ill, none of the villagers ever sought medical help. Therefore the doctor's house was always quiet. And at the rear of the property, behind the doctor's house and built on slightly higher ground, was the storehouse where Kosaku lived with Granny Onui.

Coming home for dinner, Kosaku would typically cast a few last glances at the light streaming from the homes along the old highway before entering his own yard, then he would make his way past the side of the main house to the storehouse. Around the time he returned, whether in summer or winter, Granny Onui was usually to be found outdoors, still preparing the evening meal, like as not working in near darkness with the only light coming from a lamp inside the storehouse. It would seem that cooking for one old woman and a child should be a simple matter, but for some reason dinner was always late.

'Tadaima.'*

No other child in the village ever used this salutation, but Granny Onui had trained Kosaku to greet her in this manner whenever he came home, and he had grown accustomed to it.

Every evening just the two of them, Kosaku and Granny Onui, sat down for their late dinner under the lamplight.

'How many times did you go to the Upper House today, sonny?' she would ask.

'Twice.'

'It's better that you don't go too often.'

This exchange invariably took place at dinner time. Kosaku always gave a noncommittal answer. He couldn't promise that he wouldn't go. The area around the Upper House was the centre of the boys' play activities, and many times a day they had to go there for water or to sample delicacies.

'Nothing good will come from going to the Upper House. That brat Daigo is so aggravating. He ignores me even when I meet him in the street. As for that Mitsu – she used to be such a sweet child, but now she's learned from the others and looks sulky whenever I see her. The grown-ups are probably filling her head with bad talk about me.'

Granny Onui's remarks were always in the same vein. For three hundred and sixty-five days of the year Kosaku had to listen while she criticized the members of his main family who lived in the Upper House. Although she concentrated her attacks on the children, there could be little doubt that her real resentment centred on their parents, Kosaku's

---

* A polite salutation used to announce one's return home

12

grandmother and grandfather. She never mentioned the grandparents' names, but even to a child like Kosaku her feelings were obvious.

At times Kosaku might say, 'I don't like Grandfather at the Upper House.' Then Granny Onui would narrow her eyes with pleasure and pull herself close to him, as if to stroke his head.

'But Ko-cha, he's your real grandfather. There may be things you can't stand about him, but no matter what he says to you, you mustn't say bad things about him. Do you understand? Those folks in the Upper House are a narrow-minded bunch, but they really are good people at heart.' It seemed Granny Onui might be trying to convince herself rather than Kosaku.

Sometimes Kosaku deliberately disparaged those at the Upper House just to see the look of pleasure on Granny Onui's face. And indeed when he felt so inclined, there was no lack of material. Kosaku played every day with Mitsu, who was his own age, but his grandparents made it clear they loved their daughter more than their grandson. And simply because he was living in the care of Granny Onui, whom they detested, there were times when they seemed to regard Kosaku as an ally to the enemy.

Even Kosaku's great-grandmother, Granny Oshina, who also lived in the Upper House, was inclined to regard him with hostility. Granny Oshina was the foster mother of Kosaku's grandfather, and although she claimed no blood ties she was treated with great consideration by everyone. Because of her advanced age, she lived so quietly confined to a back room that her presence in the house was barely noticeable. Once, however, when she happened to see Kosaku, she said, 'Poor thing. Taken hostage by that terrible woman. Now this child is getting stranger and stranger.'

Kosaku had stared for a long moment at the quivering mouth framed by a mass of wrinkles that was her face. Then he said, 'Granny, you're so old, aren't you going to die? When are you going to die?' It did in fact seem remarkable to Kosaku that this almost seventy-year-old woman, with her back bent to such an angle it looked as though it might break

13

and with her sagging skin so deeply etched with wrinkles, should still be alive and speaking to him.

Granny Oshina, obviously shocked and at a total loss for words, had simply glared at him. And he, having taken his revenge for her slurs – calling Granny Onui a bad woman and himself a strange child – had left Granny Oshina sitting motionless like a wizened statue.

Granny Onui had been the mistress of Great-Grandfather Tatsunosuke. Tatsunosuke had been a physician. As a young man he had held such prestigious positions in Shizuoka prefecture as Director of Kakegawa Hospital, Chief of the Nirayama Medical Bureau and Director of the private Yowa Hospital in Mishima. Had he been ambitious, he might have soared to even greater heights. But as it was, for some unknown reason he gave up all public activities at the peak of his career in his mid-thirties and retreated to his native home in the mountains of Izu to spend the rest of his life as a country doctor. Even there he attained distinction and led a busy life. His career as a private practitioner in the countryside flourished to the extent that he sometimes travelled by palanquin to see patients in Mishima at the base of the peninsula and in Shimoda at its tip.

Granny Onui was a woman whom Tatsunosuke redeemed from the pleasure quarters of Shimoda, and for this reason she became the target of considerable gossip in a region where people were in any case prone to be busy-bodies. She had served Tatsunosuke with devotion in every aspect of his life until his death at the age of fifty. Thereafter, the fact that she was of such strong character that she chose to remain in the village even after his death was apparently reason enough for all the villagers to shun her.

Tatsunosuke had lived apart from his legal wife, Oshina, after his middle years. Shina, a daughter of Chief Retainer Yamamoto of the Numazu feudal clan, was a woman who had never set foot in the kitchen since her arrival as a bride. Charitably speaking, she was a naive, gentle person; negatively speaking, she was totally useless. At the time of her wedding she brought with her a vermilion-lacquer bath basin and a pair of halberds, which samurai daughters were trained to use. And that had been the talk of the village for quite some time.

As Tatsunosuke had no children either by his legal wife or by his mistress, he adopted Bunta, his elder brother's child, then gave Bunta the house in which he himself had been living – that is, the Upper House. He thereupon built another house nearby, where he established his private practice and lived with Onui. Finally, during his last years Tatsunosuke made Bunta's eldest daughter the head of a branch family, to which he willed the home in which he practised, and entered Onui's name on the family register as this woman's adoptive mother. Thus did Tatsunosuke reward his mistress and provide for her support in her declining years. Bunta's eldest daughter, whose name appeared on the family register as the adopted daughter of her grandfather's mistress, was Kosaku's mother, Nanae.

Kosaku's father was a military doctor who was now living with Nanae at Toyohashi, his current post. Kosaku was too young to understand exactly how he had come to leave his parents and be placed in the care of his great-grandfather's mistress. With greater maturity and understanding he might have detected a grain of truth in Granny Oshina's assertion that he was 'taken hostage by that terrible woman'. To some extent Granny Onui must certainly have regarded Kosaku as a valuable pawn in her efforts to consolidate her precarious position within the family.

The true reason for the present living arrangement was that after Kosaku's mother gave birth to his younger sister, Sayoko, she was unable to find help with the raising of two young children: because of this hardship she had placed Kosaku 'temporarily' in Granny Onui's care. Granny Onui had undoubtedly made up her mind, once this unexpected treasure fell into her hands, that she would never give him up. Meanwhile, after living with her for a year, Kosaku had become more attached to Granny Onui than to his parents and now resisted going home.

So it was that from the age of five Kosaku had been living

in his family's home in a mountain village at the foot of Mt. Amagi on the Izu Peninsula in the care of woman with whom he had no blood ties and whom his main family at the Upper House heartily despised. To Great-Grandmother Oshina, Granny Onui was the harlot who had stolen her husband, and to Kosaku's grandparents she was the schemer who had so ingratiated herself with Great-Grandfather Tatsunosuke that she ended up not only owning a house and land larger than that of the main family, but also in the role of adoptive mother to their own daughter and captor of their grandson.

The Upper House was a place of constant comings and goings. Just five people lived there full time: Kosaku's grandparents; Mitsu, who was Kosaku's age; Daigo, three years older; and Great-Grandmother Oshina. But two others were frequent visitors. They were Daizo, who attended a middle school in Tokyo, and Sakiko, who was enrolled in a girls' high school in Numazu. These two came home for all school holidays and for every long weekend. To Kosaku they were actually uncle and aunt, but since Mitsu addressed Daizo as 'elder brother' and Sakiko as 'elder sister', Kosaku imitated her and addressed them in the same way.

When the Upper House was filled with people during the New-Year celebrations and during spring and summer holidays, their meal times appeared to Kosaku to be very festive. Even Granny Oshina, who usually stayed cooped up in her back room, came to the dinner table in the family room – her body doubled over as if she were trying to lick the tatami mats on the floor – and the eight-mat room was filled. The family members alone – the great-grandmother, the grandparents, Daizo, Sakiko, Daigo and Mitsu – numbered seven, and a few servants were generally present as well.

Grandmother Tane and Grandfather Bunta had been blessed with many children. Four others besides Daizo, Sakiko, Daigo and Mitsu still survived. Nanae, Kosaku's mother, was the eldest; after her came Daiichi, who had gone to America; then Daiji, who was in Manchuria; and

16

Suzue, who had been adopted into the Matsumura family, important farmers on the west coast of the peninsula. Although Kosaku had never met Daiichi or Daiji or Suzue and had no idea what they looked like, he referred to them, in imitation of Mitsu, as 'Elder Brother Daiichi', 'Elder Brother Daiji', and 'Elder Sister Suzue'.

Sometimes Grandmother Tane corrected him on this: 'You must call them "Uncle Daiichi", "Uncle Daiji", and "Aunt Suzue". They aren't your siblings. They're your uncles and your aunt.'

But Kosaku paid no attention. If he had, he would also have had to say 'Uncle Daizo' and 'Aunt Sakiko', and the mere thought of that was ludicrous. How could he possibly address Elder Sister Sakiko as 'Aunt Sakiko'?

Once, however, on a mischievous impulse, he tried it just to test Sakiko's reaction. 'Auntie Sakiko!' he piped innocently.

Sakiko, who wore the long plaited hairstyle currently in favour among high-school students, impatiently flipped one braid over her shoulder. 'Don't you call me that. I won't stand for it,' she admonished.

'But you *are* my aunt, aren't you?'

'Even if I am, don't you *dare* call me "Auntie" again!' And she glared at him.

Ah. So Sakiko felt as uncomfortable with 'Auntie' as he did. Kosaku usually called Daigo 'Go-chan'. He called Mitsu 'Mit-chan' unless he was angry with her; then it was simply 'Mitsu'.*

Except on the rare occasions when she spoke to them directly, Granny Onui almost always called the children from the Upper House by their plain names. Not only that, she usually added a disparaging adjective. 'Sulky Omitsu', 'Unruly Daigo', 'Stubborn Sakiko', and 'Good-for-nothing Daizo'. Among all that generation she singled out only the fourth son as a recipient of praise, and he had died shortly after birth.

---

* To call a person by name without an honorific or diminutive is considered rude.

17

'That baby had such an intelligent look about him. If he had survived, the Upper House would probably be in better shape. But life doesn't work out that way,' she concluded spitefully.

For all the bustle and chatter of the Upper House, Kosaku felt no particular envy. He was quite content with his life in the storehouse with Granny Onui. Not a single thing about its firmly established routine was displeasing to him. Every morning when he wakened, he called from his bed as though it were his morning greeting, 'Granny!'

Then, wherever she was, whether downstairs or even outdoors preparing breakfast, Granny Onui would hear. For although she had become hard of hearing, her ears were remarkably keen in response to his voice.

'Granny! Granny!'

At the second or third call, he could count on hearing Granny Onui's panted 'Dokkoisho, dokkoisho',* as she made her way up the stairs. Then she would appear on the landing, stretch her back, take a deep breath and say, 'Yes, dear. Yes, dear. I've come.'

Next she would open the cupboard where she kept a little store of inexpensive paper-wrapped sweets and bring some to Kosaku.

'Here. Have your wake-up treat now.' She either placed the sweets in his palm or pushed them under his bedding. 'Breakfast won't be ready for a while, so you just stay in bed,' she'd say.

Then she would go downstairs again. She never said, 'Hurry up and get up,' or 'Get up and wash your face.' Usually the wrapping contained a boiled sweet made with brown sugar. Kosaku would stay in bed sucking the dark-coloured balls until he finished eating the two or three pieces given him.

The people at the Upper House disapproved of these morning treats.

'Even before you wash your face, you're sucking on those

---

* A rhythmic vocalization expressing an expenditure of effort, something like 'ooh-la-la'

18

black hard balls. Your teeth will fall apart soon,' Grand-mother Tane often warned.

Granny Onui was indignant whenever Kosaku reported such a remark to her. 'You don't have the kind of teeth that will fall apart. You're different from Omitsu. You go and tell her that.'

In any case, Kosaku continued to suck his boiled sweets in bed almost every morning. At times the treat was a single, large chunk of hard crystal candy, which was made of white sugar and had a slight minty flavour. Now and then he was treated to some other cheap confection, such as sweet-bean candy or candy twist. After he had finished his morning treat, he would call out to Granny Onui again.

'Granny! Granny! Can I get up now?'

'Yes, dear, you can get up now. I've made some hot, hot miso* soup for you.'

As Granny Onui dressed Kosaku in his kimono, drawing the sash tightly as she smoothed out the wrinkles and then tying it in front, Kosaku always gazed out the small north window with the iron lattice. A pomegranate tree grew directly in front of this window, its leaves pressing against the panes so that he had to peer between them to see the world beyond. What he saw between the pomegranate leaves was a paddyfield. In summer it was green with growing rice, in winter dark with withered stubble. It was one of the fields tended by the family across the way, and it lay at an elevation level with the storehouse window. It was about three feet higher than the land belonging to Kosaku's family, and a streamlet served as the boundary between the properties.

Almost anywhere Kosaku stood in the room on the second level of the storehouse, he could see only this paddyfield; but if he went right up to the window and looked out, he was able to see numerous fields gradually sloping down-wards, and beyond a depression in the land, part of the neighbouring hamlet. He could see hills, farmhouses, groves of trees, the white highway, and in the far distance, the

---

* Soya-bean paste used for soup or as a condiment

beautifully shaped, tiny, toy-like Mt. Fuji.

When Kosaku was dressed he would go downstairs to wash his face at the wooden platform by the bank of the stream that flowed along the edge of his family's land. There Kosaku would scoop water into his mouth, swish it around a couple of times, then scoop up more water and dab his face. It took little time to wash. But in winter when ice crusts formed on every blade of grass on the embankment, he would dawdle for some time, pulling them off and dashing them to the ground, wholly caught up in this pleasure until Granny Onui came to fetch him.

Meals were taken near the landing on the second floor, by the window on the south side. This window was framed with an iron lattice, just like the one to the north. The breakfast menu seldom varied. If it did, the change took the form of radishes, aubergine or melons cooked in the miso soup or used as pickled vegetables, depending on the season. Besides the miso soup and regular pickles, pickled ginger root, pickled scallions and Kinzanji miso* were always placed on the table. This menu held not only for breakfast; it was the same for lunch and dinner. Granny Onui was not one to put a lot of effort into cooking, and as she didn't care for fish or meat, about the only difference between breakfast and lunch or dinner was that for the later meals some cooked cabbage would be added.

'Now, dear, do you want to pour some of the hot miso soup on your rice?'

'Do you want to make tea rice with Kinzanji miso?'

Granny Onui had bad teeth and poured something hot on her rice at each meal; in the course of time she began to push this practice on the boy.

Before they finished breakfast they were likely to hear the voices of neighbourhood children – Yukio, Kameo and Yoshie – calling Kosaku.

'Ko-cha, time for school. Ko-cha, come to school,' they chanted in unison in front of the storehouse.

---

* A type of soya-bean paste with aubergine or melon marinated in it, eaten with rice

The chanting usually began about a full hour before school started, sometimes almost an hour and a half. From where Kosaku lived, if one ran, it took less than five minutes to reach the school. Even so, whenever Kosaku heard his friends calling he would rush to wrap his textbooks and lunch in a furoshiki kerchief and, bundle in hand, make a mad dash down the stairs.

'Sonny! Sonny!'

Granny Onui was always right behind him, running after him with either a handkerchief or some tissue paper. Handkerchiefs and tissue paper were foreign objects to the other children in the village. Kosaku himself never made use of them, even though he carried them. But Granny Onui always chased after him as if he had forgotten something of vital importance. She knew full well that her little boy was different from the other village brats, and she felt if he carried a handkerchief or a few tissues it served as evidence of that difference.

The children went from house to house in the village rounding up other classmates, then all gathered by the Bureau or near the strawstacks in the paddyfield next to Kosaku's house. There they played happily until it was time to go to school. The children's gathering places changed from time to time. It was not as if anyone gave an order, rather that changes took place according to some natural force. And once the children started gathering at a new spot they would continue at the same place for two or three months. The boys gathered with the boys, the girls with the girls, and their assembly places were separate.

In similar fashion, once the children began to play a certain game they continued with it for a long time. They would play that game until they were totally bored with it, and only then would they become absorbed in a new game. Then the new game would in turn become popular with all the children and played to the exclusion of all others until complete boredom set in. In this way they developed a passion for menko cards,* became absorbed in trapping birds, made daily

---

* Flip-the-cards

rankings of sumo wrestlers, and so on and so on.

And each day just about the time everyone had grown somewhat tired of playing, someone fortunately remembered it was time to go to school and they formed a group and moved off the meeting ground. About the same time, other children from hamlets one or two miles away, also in groups, would appear on the new and old highways heading for the main gate of the school.

Each of these groups showed hostility towards all the others, sometimes subtly, sometimes not so subtly. All wore fierce expressions and glared at those from other hamlets. No conversation passed between groups, but sometimes rocks were thrown for no apparent reason. This animosity continued until everyone had entered the school gate and the groups broke ranks.

The small schoolhouse had eight classrooms. There was one room for each form from the first to the sixth, one room for the senior classes,* and one used for sewing. Each form had about thirty pupils. All the pupils wore the uniform vertical-striped kimono. In addition, all wore sandals, brought lunch boxes containing pickled radishes or riceballs with salted plums inside, and all had dirty faces and lumpy heads.

There were as many teachers as there were classrooms, one teacher to a room. Because the teachers often slapped or rapped heads, the students fell quiet as soon as they entered their classrooms. The first-form teacher was strictest of all; therefore the first-years were usually pale from the tension of trying to avoid blows.

When classes were over for the day the children raced home to toss their school bundles indoors, then gathered at the assembly place. Because school hours were longer for the upper than the lower forms, at first only the younger children could be seen in the play area; then the older ones appeared to swell the ranks. And there they played until the shirobamba fluttered in the dusk.

---

* Special classes for those who did not go on to secondary school but wanted more education. Many children ended their schooling after completing the compulsory sixth year.

2

In the spring when Kosaku entered the second form, Sakiko, who had graduated from Numazu Girls' High School and had spent some time learning domestic arts at a relative's home, came back to the village to stay. Kosaku was overjoyed. He now took pleasure in going to the Upper House. Sakiko had always come home for winter and summer holidays, but now her permanent presence completely changed the atmosphere of the Upper House. For him, she added all the brightness and gaiety of a big arrangement of roses, even to the back rooms of the house where the sun never reached.

One thing that made her different from the other young women of the village was the big-city air she brought back with her from Numazu Girls' High School. In her pompadour hairstyle, in her choice of kimono, in her manner of speech, and even in the way she walked, she was 'refined' and 'high-class' to use two terms of that era. After Sakiko came home, Kosaku went to the Upper House many times a day.

But Granny Onui disliked Sakiko and habitually disparaged her: 'Such an affected young woman. She'll come to no good one of these days.'

Likewise, Sakiko had no use for Granny Onui. When the two women met on the road, even a child like Kosaku could sense how cleverly Sakiko ignored Granny Onui. Granny Onui, for her part, simply looked away in an exaggerated

23

manner on these occasions. But Sakiko did not turn away or otherwise alter her usual demeanour. She simply neither greeted nor spoke; she acted as if Granny Onui was not there.

Because of the strained relationship between Sakiko and Granny Onui, Kosaku often felt uncomfortably caught in the middle, even though he was just a child. He tried to mediate between the two women, but his efforts were futile.

'Just now, Granny Onui . . .' Kosaku would begin, but Sakiko would quickly interrupt.

'She is *not* your grandmother. She is "Old Onui".'

'She is too my grandmother.'

'She certainly is not your grandmother. She's an outsider. Now listen to me and remember this well. You may be living with that person, but she is not your grandmother. She is not part of the family. Let's see now, what should you call her? I've got it . . . "Baya".'*

Kosaku would have considered such a remark unforgivable coming from anyone else, but in Sakiko's case for some strange reason he did not even get angry. That's just the way things are, he thought.

After Sakiko returned to the village Kosaku started going with her every day to Nishibira, where natural springs bubbled forth in a ravine. When it was about time for her to start off for the communal bath, Mitsu would stop by to call him. Because Kosaku felt somewhat embarrassed at going alone to the bath with two members of the opposite sex, he asked neighbourhood friends to accompany him. Yukio from the general store, Kameo from Sadoya, where the cows were kept, and Yoshie, from the sake brewery and related to Kosaku's family, were three who always accepted his invitation. Yukio and Kameo were a class behind Kosaku, while Yoshie was in the same class as Kosaku and Mitsu.

Bathing preparations were very simple for Kosaku and his friends; all they did was hang a towel from their kimono sash,

---

* 'Baya' is a term used for an old woman servant, as opposed to 'bachan' which means 'granny'.

24

and they were ready to go. Granny Onui tried to get Kosaku to take along a tin soap container, but he refused because it would interfere with his play.

The boys always waited in front of the Upper House for Sakiko and Mitsu to come out. As Sakiko came down the two or three stone steps that led to the road, she held out the furoshiki kerchief, containing her towel, soap and a small metal basin, to the boys.

'I want you to take turns carrying this,' she said.

It was a somewhat demeaning task, but Kosaku was always the first to accept the bundle. Then, feeling as if he had been entrusted with something of great importance, he held it high above his head with both hands like an offering.

About fifty yards from the Upper House, the old road merged with the new road. The new road was lined on both sides with houses interspersed here and there with shops. Among the latter were a wooden-clog shop, a barber's shop, a pharmacy, a post office, a sweet shop, a tinsmith and a dressmaker. The shop owners were seldom in their stores, and customers had to go to the back doors to be waited on. Because of these various shops, the new road appeared uncommonly lively to the children. Coming from the old road to the new one was like going from the country to the big city.

The houses and shops lined the new road for a little over a hundred yards, and this cluster of about twenty buildings was called Shuku. The group of twelve or thirteen homes where Kosaku's home and the Upper House were located was called Kubota. In addition to these two hamlets, three others – called Nishibira, Arajuku, Sekonotaki – nestled in the ravine where the hot springs bubbled forth, while on the mountainside were the hamlets of Nagano and Shinden. These seven or eight hamlets were collectively called Yugashima. In addition to Yugashima, a number of small hamlets scattered about in the ravine in the mountains along the Kano River counted in the village cluster known as Kamikano. The total population of Kamikano was not large, nor was the number of homes, but the village covered quite a large area. Yugashima was its largest component; the others

25

were smaller, ranging from two or three houses to ten or so.

Kosaku and his friends always grew a little tense as they passed through Shuku on the new road. Sakiko walked ahead with Mitsu, Kosaku followed a short distance behind carrying the bundle, and still further behind came Yukio, Kameo and Yoshie. Sometimes the children who lived along the new road jeered at them.

'Ko-cha lo-oves Mitsu!'

The mocking words were always the same. Kosaku was mortified at the implication of something going on between Mitsu and himself. True, they were in the same class at school and constantly together like siblings, but they fought more than they got along. When the teasing started, Kosaku always lost his composure and roughly transferred the bundle he had been carrying high overhead from one hand to the other, deliberately swinging it in a wide arc as he passed his tormentors. Thereupon, they would transfer their taunts to his companions.

'Yuki-cha wet his bed last night!'

'Running a-round with la-dies!'

These sallies were delivered in a jeering sing-song. Then the humiliated boys, Yukio and the others, would break into a run. At school Yoshie was quiet and somewhat slow and usually off in a corner by himself, but Yukio and Kameo were high-spirited boys who seldom lost to anyone in a fight. When they left their own hamlet, though, and went on to the new road, for some strange reason they lost their spirit. It was partly because they were outnumbered, and probably the fact that they accompanied two females weakened their position.

Once through Shuku, the boys would come together, eyes sparkling from the excitement of having trespassed in enemy territory. To reach the hot springs at Nishibira they had to turn off the new road at the edge of Shuku, then take a trail that led down into the ravine. From this point their spirits revived. They sometimes walked down ahead of Sakiko; at other times they carried on following her.

'Well, Yukio. It's your turn now, so take the bundle from Ko-cha,' Sakiko might say. Then, as he accepted the furoshiki bundle from Kosaku, Yukio's face would stiffen as if he had received orders from a high command. Kosaku, on the other hand, felt himself released from a major duty, and freed to romp with Kameo and Yoshie. The task of carrying the bath items would be assigned similarly to Kameo and Yoshie until the party had reached their destination. The boys took great interest in carrying this sweet-smelling bundle. Although the true nature of the feeling was unclear, there was something about it akin to mild intoxication.

Natural hot springs gushed forth at three locations in the ravine, and near them a large villa, three inns and two public baths had been built. These buildings were scattered some distance apart along the river, each belonging to a different hamlet. The two bath houses were in the hamlets of Nishibira and Sekonotaki. Since Nishibira was closer and the interior of the building brighter, Kosaku's group usually went there.

Although it was called a bath house, the Nishibira structure was no more than a simple roof with a dressing area in one corner; but the hot water was abundant and the big tub, divided into two sections, was always brimming over. There was a wooden partition between the two halves, presumably to distinguish the men's bath from the women's, but there were no fast rules as to which was which and no one paid any attention.

There was another reason why Kosaku and his friends preferred the Nishibira bath. Right next to it was a horse-bathing area, and they often watched horses being washed in the rectangular tub there. Naturally, the tub for the horses had no roof and was much shallower than the tub for people.

As soon as Kosaku and his friends reached the public bath they raced to undress, jumped into the tub, and set about splashing and rough-housing and sending up sprays of water. Often as not, Mitsu joined in. A river flowed near the bath house, and the children would dash out naked for large stones to carry back and toss into the tub. As a rule, no one else was around during the daytime; the villagers came only in the evening after their day's work. No matter how much

Sakiko scolded, Kosaku and his friends continued their boisterous play, while Sakiko's fair-skinned, buxom nakedness shone through the curtain of spray.

'Ko-cha, you brought your towel, didn't you? Bring it over here! I'll wash you.'

At this order from Sakiko, Kosaku would go to the dressing area to fetch his towel. Sakiko then soaped him, first his front then his back. She scrubbed only Mitsu and Kosaku, not the other children; but she rinsed out all their towels, which invariably looked as though they had been boiled in soy sauce.

On one such day Sakiko said to the children, 'Beginning tomorrow, I'm going to be a teacher at school. If you don't listen to me, you'd better watch out. I'm going to be very strict!'

At this announcement, the rough-housing stopped.

'That's a lie,' Yukio said.

'Of course it's not a lie. If you don't believe me, just listen to what the principal has to say at morning assembly tomorrow,' Sakiko replied.

By no stretch of the imagination could the children picture Sakiko as a schoolteacher. Her whole aura was totally different from that of a schoolteacher. Kosaku in particular simply could not envision her in that cold staff room at school.

The next morning, however, Kosaku and his friends learned that Sakiko had not lied. During morning assembly Mr Ishimori, the principal, announced that the young third-form teacher was leaving and in the near future Sakiko Igami, a graduate of this school and a member of the Upper House, would become a teacher at her alma mater. When the principal spoke Sakiko Igami's name, Mitsu and Kosaku stood stiffly and blushed.

Although Kosaku was pleased that Sakiko was to become a teacher, he was also worried about her reputation among the students. And what concerned him most was that because of his close relationship to her, the other students might think she favoured him. Speaking of relatives, the principal, Morinoshin Ishimori, was Kosaku's uncle, his father's elder brother. The Ishimori family were farmers in the hamlet of Kadonohara about two and a half miles away, and Morinoshin, the eldest son, had taken over as head of the family. Kosaku's father, the second son, had been adopted into the Igami family as the husband of the eldest daughter. There were several other siblings, all of whom had been married or adopted into families in nearby hamlets and villages. Therefore Kosaku had many relatives on his father's side in the vicinity, but for some reason he had little contact with most of them.

Principal Morinoshin Ishimori was a man of about fifty whose thin face always wore a stern expression. He seldom spoke unless there was something he needed to say, and he never laughed. He was known even to the villagers as a difficult man. Therefore, although he was Kosaku's uncle, Kosaku rarely spoke to him. On the contrary, Kosaku never harboured any special feeling whatever towards this man who was his uncle, but only saw him as a frightening principal, one who would never under any circumstances show partiality. None of the other students even thought of this intimidating principal as Kosaku's uncle.

Indeed, whenever the man and boy happened to meet outside the school, Morinoshin Ishimori would purse his moustachioed lips and glare and say, 'Kosaku, are you studying?'

'Yes, sir, I am,' was Kosaku's reply as he shrank back like a frog eyed by a snake.

'Come and visit us sometime.' His uncle always made it sound like an order.

Kosaku had in fact been to his father's ancestral home only once before. That was when his grandmother from the Upper House took him to visit his father's father, Grandfather Gintaro, when the old man was ill.

Two days after the principal made the announcement about Sakiko during morning assembly, she appeared at school for the first time as a teacher, and Kosaku was nervous that whole day. One of the older boys poked Kosaku's forehead in the playground and said, 'That girl from your main family is just a substitute teacher. Go and ask her.'

'Uh-uh! She is too a teacher!' Kosaku protested.

'I know she's a teacher. But there are two kinds of teacher. Sakiko is not a real teacher. She's a substitute teacher – you go and ask her,' the student repeated.

For some reason, Kosaku took all this as a personal affront and was sharply irritated. He met Sakiko during the lunch break that day in the corridor in front of the staff room.

'Ko-cha!' Sakiko called from behind. Since there were a number of students nearby, Kosaku was annoyed that she used his familiar name. Pretending not to hear, he walked briskly away.

'Ko-cha!' her voice pursued. There was nothing he could do now but stop. 'Will you go home and get my lunch?' she asked.

Kosaku did as he was bade, but all the way to the Upper House he felt self-conscious at having his schoolmates know he had to fetch lunch for Sakiko, a woman teacher. When he returned bearing the lunch bundle to the staff room, he found the atmosphere there completely altered by Sakiko's presence. A red flower arranged in a slender glass vase stood on Sakiko's desk by the window, and the maroon of her hakama* skirt brightened the whole area around her, providing a sharp contrast to the rest of the dingy room. Outside the window, clusters of children peered in to watch the activities within.

Sakiko was assigned the third form, so Kosaku and Mitsu were not taught by her. Even so, now that she was a schoolteacher she seemed different to Kosaku from the former Sakiko. Somehow the look in her eyes was changed. He could no longer be mischievous or use rough language in her presence. Nor was Kosaku the only one to sense the difference; Yukio, Kameo and Yoshie also showed a new deference in her company.

After Sakiko became a teacher Kosaku and his friends gradually stopped going to the Nishibira hot springs with her. She continued to invite them but they did all they could

---

* A pleated skirt worn over a kimono reaching the wearer's ankle and tied at the waist. This garment was often worn on formal occasions during the early part of this century by both men and women, and sometimes by children from higher-status families.

to avoid going. Still, they felt that they had to accompany her perhaps once in ten times.

Now when they accompanied Sakiko on the new road, the children of Shuku no longer mocked them. Groups of children still played on the road, but as soon as one of them spotted Sakiko and shouted, 'Here she comes!' the others abandoned whatever game they were playing and took off towards the mountain side of the road as if fleeing a most terrifying thing.

'She's coming! She's coming!' they shrieked as they scrambled away. Sometimes a first-year failed to escape in time and stood paralysed with fear.

'What's the matter?' Sakiko might ask such a child with a smile, at which the child, believing himself reprimanded, usually began to wail at the top of his lungs.

Sakiko was by no means the only person who occasioned this reaction. The children, especially those in the lower forms, commonly believed that all schoolteachers were ogres, for the reason that whenever they misbehaved, their parents were apt to threaten, 'I'm going to tell your teacher on you.' The mere thought of such a trauma was usually enough to make them obedient.

Truth to tell, the school was not a hospitable place for children. The eight-room schoolhouse was extremely austere in appearance, both inside and out. Inside, the wooden doors to the classrooms had shoji-paper covering rather than glass panels, and should someone put a hole in the paper, there was a thorough investigation. The culprit, in addition to being rapped on the head a few times by his teacher, had to bring paper from home and repair the torn area. The doors were completely repapered annually by the girls in the senior classes at the beginning of the second quarter, right after the summer holidays ended.

Every day after classes the students cleaned the halls outside their classrooms. After they had finished sweeping, they brought buckets of water and wiped the halls with damp rags. Since their teachers stood by supervising, they kept busy to avoid punishment.

Kosaku disliked clean-up more than any other period in

the school day. From time to time, he had been known to stop working and stand absent-mindedly, unaware of what he was doing, and each time his teacher had shouted at him mercilessly. The second-form teacher was an elderly man who arrived each day on foot from his mountain village about three and a half miles away. Not only was this man the oldest of all the teachers, he was also the one who never, but never, overlooked the smallest infraction.

Kosaku would not soon forget how when he had entered school as a first-former and sat at his own desk for the first time in the little classroom, a thunderous 'Hey, there!' had descended upon him and the next thing he knew he was being dragged by the ear and told to stand in the hall outside the classroom. He never did learn why he had been punished in this way. On the same day three other children had their faces slapped and in that way learned for the first time in their lives how cruel the real world could be.

As if the building and the teachers were not punishment enough, even the playground was a cheerless place. Rocks protruded from the black earth all over the place, making a trial of physical-education classes and spontaneous play alike. When one fell down it was likely to be extremely painful. Because there were few trees it was unrelentingly hot during the summer, and in winter it was extremely cold on days when the wind blew out of the north. Apart from the fact that a small, beautifully shaped Fuji could be seen in the distance, there was not a single redeeming feature in the playground. But the children had been taught by their elders that this view of Fuji was the grandest in all of Japan and of course they believed it.

After Sakiko became a teacher the first quarter seemed to end in no time. Report cards were always given out on the last day of the first quarter, and for this occasion Kosaku was dressed in his best kimono and hakama skirt, and also given a large handkerchief to wrap round his report card.

For Kosaku the last day of the quarter would be a trying day. Only two students in the whole school had to wear

32

hakama skirts, and they were always the same two: Kosaku, and Mitsu of the Upper House. If the director of the local branch of the Imperial Lands and Forestry Administration Bureau happened to have children, they also might wear hakama, but when Kosaku was in the second form the director had no children.

Although Kosaku and Mitsu both hated wearing hakama, they had been instilled with the notion that they were the type of people who ought to wear it. Thus, despite their reluctance, they accepted their lot. The other pupils also seemed to take it for granted that Kosaku and Mitsu were of that special breed who wore hakama, and for that reason the girl pupils usually gathered at Mitsu's house and the boys in front of Kosaku's storehouse.

Kosaku wakened that morning enveloped in a complexity of mixed feelings – joy at knowing the long summer holiday was about to begin, annoyance about the hakama. As he rose, he found the garment, neatly folded together with his kimono, already beside his pillow.

While he washed, children began to gather in front of the storehouse. He wolfed down his breakfast and Granny Onui dressed him.

'I don't like this – wearing a hakama,' he complained feebly.

'Sonny, when you grow up, you're going to be a great man. You're going to be your great-grandfather's heir.' Granny Onui's tone told him there was no room for further discussion.

In such situations Granny never brought up Kosaku's father or his grandfather. This was because she harboured resentment towards both. Only in his great-grandfather, who had been her protector and who had determined the course of her life, did she perceive greatness, and she seemed to have decided on her own that only Kosaku was worthy to be his successor.

'Only Mit-cha and I have to wear these,' he lamented.

'That sulky Omitsu certainly shouldn't wear a hakama. You're the only one in the village good enough to wear one. But never mind. Mitsu's hakama are probably just hand-me-downs from that good-for-nothing Sakiko. Get up close to her today and have a good look. They're probably faded and worn out,' Granny Onui said.

Even though she knew it to be customary, Granny Onui was still irritated that the Upper House dressed Mitsu in a hakama.

The children's current gathering spot just before the trek to school was under the cherry tree at the side of the village office, just inside the main gate. There a fairly large clearing, part of it lawn, made for a perfect play area. The cicadas had been chirping since early morning. As they spotted the insects, the children climbed the tree, but that morning Kosaku, hampered by the hakama, had to wait quietly on the ground.

When he arrived at school he felt the eyes of all the students on him. Mitsu, apparently feeling similarly self-conscious, went directly into her classroom and did not return to the playground. The time remaining until morning assembly seemed endless to Kosaku. When a group of pupils from Nagano hamlet came through the school gate, he had an uneasy premonition that something bad might happen because he was wearing a hakama, and he knew the older boys from that hamlet were all unruly.

His fears were soon confirmed. Three fifth-formers approached and surrounded Kosaku as he stood under a cherry tree. One of them sneered, 'Take off that funny-looking thing and put it on your head.'

'No, I won't.'

No sooner had he spoken than someone shoved him in the chest and he staggered backwards. Simultaneously, someone poured sand down his back. Kosaku kept his mouth tightly pursed and glared. Since he was no match physically for three bigger boys, he decided he had no choice but to take whatever they handed out without fighting back.

Just then shouts rose from one corner of the playground. Another student had just come through the gate wearing a hakama. Many students ran towards the gate. It was Koichi Asai, Kosaku's classmate from Shinden, the hamlet closest to Amagi Pass. Koichi was a reticent boy who usually did

34

nothing to attract attention. Kosaku himself had rarely spoken to him, even in the classroom. This was the first time Koichi Asai had worn a hakama to school.

When the boys surrounding Kosaku spotted this new prey, one of them said, 'Bring Koichi here too.'

The other two grabbed Koichi as he neared the centre of the playground and soon returned with him.

The three now turned their attention from Kosaku and demanded of the newcomer, 'Tell us why you came here wearing that thing.'

Koichi cast his eyes down and said nothing. Then one of the boys shoved him in the chest, just as he had done to Kosaku, and when Koichi reeled back the other two grasped him from behind and tried to pour sand down his collar. Still Koichi said nothing; but he struggled fiercely and finally broke free. He then picked up a handful of sand and threw it into the face of one of his tormentors. The three bullies flinched at this unexpected show of rebellion. But Koichi looked around, found a rock the size of his head about two yards away, and ran to it. He picked it up with both hands, raised it above his head and came back towards the three bigger boys. There was an ominous tension in Koichi's movements just then. Startled by his menacing look, the three older pupils scattered in all directions. The next instant Kosaku saw the large stone leave Koichi's hand and land near the feet of one of the fleeing boys. The rock did not hit him, but had it struck him the consequences would have been grave.

Kosaku continued watching Koichi, who stood panting as he glared at the three boys. As this incident took place before the morning assembly, many witnessed it. Just then the bell rang and two or three teachers appeared. The three older pupils walked towards the assembly lines, but Koichi continued standing there as if waiting for his agitation to subside.

Kosaku was filled with admiration for Koichi's actions. As he continued to watch Koichi, he forgot all about the morning assembly. Gradually the impact of what he had just witnessed penetrated deep into his soul until he experienced

35

it as an occasion of beauty, this one young boy taking his bold stance against injustice and violence. Certainly the attempt to strike out with a stone was reckless, but the mere fact that this reticent classmate had dared to do it was magnificent. Kosaku felt fully aware of his own timidity for the first time in his life.

During the first hour after morning assembly the pupils received their report cards. After all the cards were distributed, the elderly teacher announced that for the first quarter Koichi Asai was top of the form, and Kosaku was second. Mitsu was eighth, and Yoshie of the sake brewery was third from the bottom. Most of the students didn't care at all about their ranking in class. They sat with blank expressions, each repeating over and over the number given by the teacher so that he could remember it and tell his parents. The woodcutter's son from Shinden, who had been told he was at the bottom of the class, could not understand why he was the only one who had not been given a number.

'What's my number? What's my number?' he wailed as he peered at those who sat at desks in front of and behind him. Finally the quick-tempered teacher pulled him up by his ears and slapped him twice on the cheek.

Kosaku felt dejected as he wrapped his report card in the white handkerchief provided by Granny Onui. In the first form he had been top for all three quarters. Now for the first time he was surpassed by the boy from the mountain hamlet. He was no match for this Koichi Asai, either in school work or in courage. Today was the first time he had even recognized the existence of this unobtrusive, reticent lad, and now he could not take his eyes off him.

Kosaku went straight home, carrying the cloth-wrapped report card. Since the other children also had report cards, they too went directly home without their usual dawdling.

As Kosaku neared the storehouse he was startled to see Granny Onui standing at the entrance. 'Tadaima,' he said and held out the package. After receiving it, Granny Onui, her body bent nearly double, went up to the second storey and placed it in front of the household shrine. Then she helped Kosaku remove his hakama.

36

'Koichi-chan from Shinden wore a hakama too,' Kosaku reported.

'Someone besides sonny wore a hakama?!' Granny Onui asked with an expression that said that such nonsense should not be allowed. 'Whose brat was that?'

'Koichi-chan of Shinden.'

'Hmm.' Granny Onui sounded almost hurt. 'If people don't know their place, nothing good will come of it! The only one who looks right in a hakama in this village is you, Ko-cha.'

She folded the hakama carefully and appeared to take great pleasure in the task. And as always when she folded the hakama she spoke of his great-grandfather. 'Whenever your great-grandfather had important guests he went to the living room in his hakama, and because of that I don't know how many times a day I brought out or folded that hakama.' Now, after putting away the folded garment in the old chest of drawers, she picked up the handkerchief placed on the shrine altar and said, 'Well now, I'll have to go round and tell the neighbours about how well you did, sonny.'

Kosaku cringed as he watched her untie the handkerchief. When she finally took out the report card she carried it to the iron-latticed north window and peered at it for a long time. At last she said, 'Sonny, it says you are number two.'

'The teacher said Koichi-chan is number one.'

'Well, then, does that mean Koichi is first and you are second?'

'Uh-huh.'

'That can't be possible.'

'The teacher said so.'

'Is Koichi the brat who wore a hakama?'

'That's right.'

'Hmm. Well, well.' Granny Onui stood up, still holding the report card in her right hand. 'I won't stand for such stupidity. He's putting us down.'

To Kosaku, Granny Onui's grotesquely distorted, wrinkled face seemed terribly frightening as he watched her.

'I'm going to your school for a short while,' she announced.

37

'Granny!' Kosaku clung to her legs. He couldn't bear to have her go to the school.

'There's a limit to such nonsense,' she snapped. 'Just because the teacher thinks you're quiet, he pushed you aside and had the nerve to make Koichi number one! That boy's just a son of a woodcutter who probably stole enough to have a little money. Sonny, you just stay here. Granny's going to school to tell them off.'

Kosaku started to cry, but Granny Onui was beyond hearing. She stalked down the stairs and out the door.

Kosaku sat by the north window until it dawned on him that crying would not change matters. Then he stood up, went downstairs, left the storehouse and headed for the Upper House. Then he found that Granny Onui had not gone to the school but had come here instead. He saw her seated at the entrance of the Upper House, yelling something, while Sakiko, who herself had apparently just returned, was dealing with her. Sakiko was still wearing her maroon hakama.

Although Granny Onui's voice was raised, Kosaku's impression as he came into the earthen-floored entrance was that she was on the defensive and losing the battle.

Then he heard Sakiko. 'Since you've been entrusted to care for our dear Ko-cha, please make sure that his grades don't go down. You never check on his studies, do you? No child will do well if he doesn't study. Have you ever helped him with his studies? You haven't, have you?' The tone was harshly accusatory.

'My boy can do well even if he doesn't study.'

'That's impossible. And furthermore, please don't keep calling him "my boy, my boy".'

'He *is* my boy and that's why I call him my boy. You good-for-nothing!'

'Fine, so I'm good for nothing. Whatever happens, please don't let Ko-cha's grades go down. This is one thing I would like to make clear to you.'

Here was a fine reversal of things. Granny Onui had come to complain to Sakiko about Kosaku's grades, but somehow she herself was being blamed.

'That's enough,' she said at last. 'I won't listen to such nonsense.' Her face was pale.

Kosaku ran outside and round to the back door. He peered into the kitchen and saw Grandmother Tane standing alone, looking distraught. From time to time she turned towards the entrance where Sakiko and Granny Onui were quarrelling, pricked up her ears to listen, then mumbled over and over, 'Oh, Saki, you're in the wrong. Oh, Sakiko, why don't you be quiet?' But there was no possibility that her words would reach Sakiko.

'Grandmother!' Kosaku called.

Acting as if she had just noticed Kosaku, Grandmother Tane said, 'Come here, sonny. Come here, and I'll give you something good.'

Despite her words, she offered him nothing. She was too agitated. Grandmother Tane, who was as kind and gentle as Buddha, always held the view that if she could take the blame for whatever unpleasant thing happened and bring matters to a harmonious conclusion, she would do so. Now she wore an anguished expression as if some tragedy had occurred. For Kosaku it was sad, almost too sad. Not only were the two people he loved most, Sakiko and Granny Onui, fighting about him, but his gentle grandmother of the Upper House was distressed on his account.

He dashed from the Upper House in distraction. Where should he go? He decided to go to Heibuchi on the Nagano, a tributary of the Kano River. During the summer he could always find some children from his hamlet at one of the several spots where the village children went to swim. Along the ravine where the Kano flowed, there were large pools called Otsukenofuchi and Obuchi, but this year, for some reason, the younger children were not going there, and instead congregated daily at Heibuchi. The girls likewise had changed their swimming holes this year, from the main river to Kinchakubuchi on the tributary.

When Kosaku arrived at Heibuchi he found some twenty children lying about on various boulders, Yukio, Kameo and Yoshie among them. They had all been in the water until their lips turned blue, and now they were warming their bodies on the sun-drenched boulders scattered along the streambed. When naked, every child in the village looked scrawny, an effect somehow heightened by the rather muddy tan they got from swimming in the river, so unlike the tan bestowed by sea water and salty air.

Kosaku quickly undressed, jumped into the stream, and splashed about in the shallows. The pool was deep enough that in places he could not touch bottom. Yukio and Yoshie jumped back in to join him, and the three of them were in and out many times, alternately chilling and baking as they pressed their bodies against the boulders. The children called this warming of their bodies on the boulders 'drying their shells'. And they actually did look like Kappa* water-sprites.

When the boys became bored they invaded the girls' swimming hole after making their way downstream to Kinchakubuchi by jumping from boulder to boulder. Where the distance between rocks was too great they went into the water. By this route it took them less than five minutes to reach Kinchakubuchi. They found the girls with towels wrapped round their heads, a fashion gesture by which the girls aimed to differentiate themselves from the boys.

'Okay now! Let's chase those stupid girls out of here!' Yukio shouted as he stood on a large boulder.

The boys then began randomly tossing pebbles into Kinchakubuchi, whereupon the female watersprites dashed up the river bank in a flurry. It was not that the girls were really afraid of the boys; they simply believed this was the way they should behave. When boisterous invaders appear, little girls should be helpless, and there was a part of them that seemed to enjoy the charade. Kosaku liked watching the girls run naked, holding their kimonos under their arms as they scurried up the narrow cliff path to the road above. Large white lilies bloomed along the path, and dragonflies flew about in swarms.

---

* Kappa are mythical creatures, half-man and half-turtle. They are said to live both on land and in the sea, and supposedly drag other animals into the water and suck their blood.

Kosaku and his friends usually played at Heibuchi until the sun had dipped below the horizon and they could no longer 'dry their shells'. Then they realized it was time to go home. On this day, it was only when he reached the highway in the pale twilight that Kosaku recalled what he had completely forgotten while swimming. Granny Onui and Sakiko had been fighting, and he wondered what had happened since then.

When he got home he found Granny Onui making rice curry under the pale pink blossoms of the crepe myrtle, which had been in bloom for some time. He smelled the curry as soon as he passed the garden of the main house.

On report-card days Granny Onui always made rice curry, which she considered her culinary forte. She always made two kinds, one heavily seasoned with curry and the other lightly seasoned. Kosaku enjoyed eating rice curry with Granny Onui.

'Sonny, eat some. It's hot, it's really hot. It's sure to make you cry,' Granny Onui would say.

Kosaku's was the lightly seasoned version but, thinking it to be the behaviour expected of him, he grimaced with each mouthful and said, 'Oh, it's hot!'

'Of course it is. Rice curry is supposed to be hot. Your great-grandfather loved it so hot that even I couldn't eat any,' Granny Onui would say.

Granny Onui's rice curry was delicious. It consisted of nothing more than diced carrots, radishes and potatoes with a small amount of tinned beef, all boiled in a mixture of flour and curry powder. But it had a flavour all its own. Sometimes they made the same dish at the Upper House, but it tasted totally different.

Once, Kosaku had eaten some rice curry that Sakiko had made at the Upper House and remarked, 'Granny's tastes much better.' Sakiko had been very displeased.

'This is real rice curry,' she told him. 'I learned to make this from a real cookery teacher. Granny Onui's is amateur stew. This tastes different, doesn't it?'

No matter how much Sakiko tried to convince him that hers had a better flavour, Kosaku clung to the conviction that only the rice curry he ate in the storehouse with Granny Onui was the real thing. Although he believed everything else Sakiko told him, he would not accept her judgement about rice curry. To him, the rice curry served at the Upper House was not really rice curry.

Kosaku ate with Granny Onui under the light of the lamp. Only when they ate rice curry or grated yam did Granny Onui believe that they should eat many bowls of rice.

'Now eat a lot,' she would say. 'When you're full, set down your chopsticks and lie back for a while. Then you can eat again.'

That evening as Granny Onui ate her curry, she was more vocal than usual in criticizing those of the Upper House. Sakiko in particular was described in foul terms: 'Osaki, that stupid girl', and 'that good-for-nothing Sakiko', and 'she goes to school all painted up', and 'the poor students certainly are unfortunate to have such a bitch teaching them'. Usually Kosaku defended Sakiko when Granny Onui spoke ill of her, but tonight he listened in silence. No matter how much Granny Onui disparaged Sakiko it was clear that this time Granny had totally lost the battle. Kosaku could very well imagine how it had happened.

After dinner Granny Onui sat with her sewing beside Kosaku, who had gone to bed early because he was tired from his swimming, and informed him about three new things. First, from next quarter he was to go to his teacher's place to be tutored for an hour a day.

'You're going to the university, so you have to study. Just try it out for a month, sonny. You'll be much cleverer than that good-for-nothing teacher Sakiko,' Granny Onui said.

The second thing was that his uncle, Principal Morinoshin Ishimori, was coming for him the next day and he would have to stay overnight at the Ishimori home in Kadonohara.

'Since they took the trouble to invite you, even if they are tightwads, they'll probably feed you something you like, sonny. And I'm sure they'll try to fill your head with rubbish, so I'll put plugs in your ears before you leave.'

At this news, Kosaku protested. 'I don't want to spend the night at Kadonohara,' he said. Uncle or no, the mere thought of staying overnight at the house of that intimidating principal was horrifying.

'You *have* to go. Even if it's that kind of family, Ko-cha, it's your father's family. Do them a favour and go,' Granny Onui said.

The last item was that in August Granny Onui and Kosaku were to visit Toyohashi, where his parents were stationed.

'I promised, so we'll have to go. We'll ride in a horse carriage, then we'll take a little train and then we'll ride in a big train and you will go with Granny to Toyohashi. And when we've stayed there two nights we'll come right home. If your mother says that we can't come home after two nights, this Granny won't hear of it.' And to emphasize her point, Granny Onui set aside her sewing for a moment and scowled ferociously.

The following afternoon at about three o'clock, Morinoshin Ishimori came to the storehouse. Kosaku was catching cicadas in the garden with Yukio and other friends when he saw his uncle advancing along the side of the main house.

'The principal has come!' Kosaku said.

'The principal?' Yukio, who was in the act of climbing the peach tree, stopped and turned pale. 'Shush,' he whispered. Kosaku moved away from the tree and approached Morinoshin Ishimori as if he were pulled in that direction like a frog mesmerized by a snake.

'Are you ready to go?' His uncle's voice was abrupt, his face stern as usual. He resembled Kosaku's father but was much more unsmiling, and perhaps because of his moustache he always looked angry.

'Yes, sir,' Kosaku replied meekly.

'Where's Granny?' As if those words had freed him, Kosaku immediately ran to the storehouse to inform Granny Onui of the visitor's arrival.

'Granny! Granny!' he called from below.

Granny Onui came out immediately and with a slightly strained expression stood in front of the storehouse talking to Morinoshin Ishimori. Granny Onui did the talking and the taciturn Ishimori stood silently with an ill-humoured look on his face. At length Granny Onui took Kosaku

43

upstairs and changed him into his best clothes.

'It's just for one night. You can endure it,' Granny Onui said. 'Sonny, you're a man. There's no reason why you can't endure it. It's not like you're going to a demon's house. I'm sure they won't eat you up.'

'I don't want to go!' Kosaku really did not want to go. He had never felt enthusiastic about it, and Granny Onui's words now fanned his reluctance.

'Even if you don't want to, you have to go. There is such a thing as duty in this world, you know.'

Granny Onui wrapped several pieces of crystal candy in some paper, thrust the package into his kimono bosom, then gave him instructions not to eat them all that day and to save some for his morning wake-up treat. Then she folded up a large furoshiki kerchief in case they gave him gifts, and she inserted this together with a towel between his sash and kimono.

'They might give you some corn, and if it's mochi corn you can accept. If not, tell them that we don't want any.' Granny Onui said.

Granny Onui had long refused to recognize as corn anything other than 'mochi corn', which had a glutinous quality. Only mochi corn was fit for human consumption; all other varieties she viewed as horse fodder. Kosaku left the storehouse and joined his uncle waiting outside. Just then he remembered that Yukio was still in the peach tree and he looked up. Yukio was hanging on to the largest branch, making himself as small as possible. Only his back was visible through the thick green leaves.

Kosaku left the storehouse with the principal and Granny Onui and as they went round the side of the main house, he shouted in a sing-song voice, 'Yuki-cha, I'll see you later.'

There was no response from Yukio.

By the gate of the main house Granny Onui said to Ishimori in a slightly formal tone, 'Well, please take good care of him.'

'Umm,' Ishimori grunted and nodded. 'Well then, Kosaku, let's go.'

Then he briefly bade goodbye to Granny Onui with his

44

eyes, and began to walk briskly ahead. Kosaku had no choice but to follow. Just outside the gate was a hill, and on the other side, at the bottom of the incline, was a place where carriages arrived and departed. Halfway up the hill Kosaku looked back. Granny Onui stood in front of the gate watching them and when she saw him turn she immediately started towards him, as though he had beckoned.

Kosaku thought she really need not come. But Granny Onui bent forward and quickened her pace, waving her arms about and half running.

'What is it, sonny?' she asked, panting.

'Granny, it's nothing,' he replied. Her expression showed she did not believe him.

'Granny will miss you, so you come home early tomorrow. It's enough that you stay one night for them. There's no need for you to hang around at Kadonohara. You just hurry up and come home.'

When Kosaku looked towards Ishimori, he saw his uncle's spare, erect form moving steadily far ahead of him. Leaving Granny Onui, he ran to catch up.

About fifty yards beyond the carriage stop was Sunoko Bridge, which served as a boundary with Ichiyama hamlet. Whenever they crossed this bridge the children were acutely aware that they had set foot in another village. They sensed the presence of many enemies and could not let down their guard whenever they were there. That day, however, Kosaku's feelings were totally different. As long as he was following the principal there was no need to fear attack; still he felt himself under surveillance from many directions.

His uncle proceeded along the Shimoda Highway, which ran through the centre of Ichiyama, with his gaunt body erect and his surly face with its clipped moustache turned straight ahead. It was the same at school; his uncle never turned to look at anything when he walked. Now Kosaku followed a few yards behind, occasionally trotting to close the distance between them. His uncle walked fast. As he neither looked back nor spoke, there was no break in the rhythm of his pace. He walked in the same manner and at the same pace on his daily, morning and evening, journey from

45

Kadonohara to Yugashima and back, a distance of almost two and a half miles each way.

Whenever they came to a settlement Kosaku grew tense. Strangely enough, though, not a single child appeared. Normally, the children were extremely quick to pick up the scent of an outsider from another hamlet and when one appeared they immediately gathered and jeered or threw rocks, but that day he might have been passing through a childless land.

Even so, Kosaku felt many pairs of curious eyes watching from the sides of houses, from behind the leaves of the pasania trees lining the streets, and from behind the paddy-field embankments. He knew that if he looked back after passing through these places, he would see several boys and girls. But he did not look back. He was too embarrassed to confront such a concentrated visual attack.

After Ichiyama, there was the Sagasawa Bridge and on the other side of the bridge, Kadonohara. Kadonohara was totally alien territory to Kosaku. Although it was part of the Kami-kano village, the children of this hamlet attended school in the neighbouring village of Nakakano because of zoning laws. Therefore Kosaku knew no child in this hamlet.

As they crossed Sagasawa Bridge, Ishimori stopped briefly for the first time and peered down at the water below. 'Your father almost drowned under this bridge a long time ago,' he said.

Kosaku looked down at the stream flowing under the bridge where his father had almost drowned. The Kano River was a little wider here than at Yugashima; there was more water and it was a deeper blue.

'He was just about your age. He jumped in even though he couldn't swim. He was a reckless boy.'

Without another word Ishimori then resumed his brisk pace. Kosaku had no way of reading his uncle's feelings from his face, which showed nothing other than its usual surliness. Had his uncle spoken in anger, or had he meant to tell a funny story? In any case, this was the only time his uncle was to speak to him during their long walk of nearly two and a half miles.

His uncle's house was located near the centre of the hamlet and a small mountain rose behind it. Still following his uncle, Kosaku turned off the highway on to a road that ran through paddyfields and dwindled to a path leading directly to the house. Kosaku had come to this place once before, but he did not remember it well. The house was surrounded by a low stone wall topped by close-planted camellia bushes. The house stood on higher ground than the path, and on the left side was a storehouse. In front of the main house was a spacious yard. As Kosaku reached the centre of this yard, his aunt emerged from the house.

'Oh my, I'm so glad you came, Ko-cha,' his aunt said.

She was a very small woman of about forty who, like his uncle, had an ill-tempered air that seemed to belie her greeting. Kosaku had met her on his previous visit and retained a somewhat negative impression. On this occasion, after welcoming Kosaku she immediately followed with, 'It must be awfully constricting for you to be here. It's a wonder a spoiled child like you would want to come and stay the night at our house.'

After this comment she made a face like the mask of a she-devil and laughed, showing blackened teeth.* Then she gestured with her right hand towards Kosaku's shoulder, almost as if to push him aside. Kosaku was startled and vaguely apprehensive.

'Ko-cha, you just play here. To will return from his errand very soon,' his uncle said, then he abruptly left the boy with his aunt and entered the house.

'Ko-cha, you play around there until To comes,' the aunt echoed, and she too went into the house.

Fine, I'll play, thought Kosaku. But at what, and all by myself? He spent some time looking round the big, unfamiliar yard and finally went towards the storehouse. Nothing particularly interesting round there. Nothing round the back of the house either, so he returned again to the front yard,

---

* From ancient times it was the custom for upper-class women to blacken their teeth, and all married women dyed their teeth during the Edo period (1603–1867).

then went out on the path in front of the house and stood there. What a boring place.

Presently his aunt reappeared from the main house and said, 'Ko-cha, don't get into mischief, and please be a good boy. Because you've come to visit, Ko-cha, Auntie has become very busy. If I sent you home without feeding you something special after you've come all the way to Kadonohara, Granny Onui would never forgive me, so I'm working hard to make some rice-cake dumplings for you.'

She displayed her dyed teeth again and laughed. Even if he wanted to, he couldn't get into mischief, Kosaku thought to himself. And although it was nice of his aunt to make rice-cake dumplings for him, she needn't make such a big show of it. His aunt went off somewhere but returned soon and stood at the gate. There she gestured again towards his shoulder as though she wished to push him aside.

'Wait with a good appetite, Ko-cha,' she said. 'The rice-cake dumplings at Kadonohara are the best ever. You won't be able to eat those at Yugashima once you've eaten mine.'

Then she bustled back to the main house. Kosaku was angry at her disparagement of the rice-cake dumplings of Yugashima. He wanted to tell her that the Yugashima rice-cake dumplings were delicious, too. Instead, he stood at the gate and gazed out at the paddyfields stretching away at his feet. After some time his uncle emerged from the house on his way somewhere. He paused briefly, eyed Kosaku critically from head to toe, and said, 'Don't just stand around. Go and play something.'

With that his uncle passed through the gate and struck out across the fields. Kosaku did not know whether he had been scolded or simply given an order. He watched as his uncle walked down the road through the paddyfields, his form gradually receding in the distance until he disappeared entirely behind a farmhouse. Then, suddenly, Kosaku was overwhelmed with a desire to go home. He wanted to be back at the storehouse having dinner with Granny Onui.

As he contemplated this desire, he caught sight of his cousin Tohei. Tohei was Kosaku's age. His name had been abbreviated to To by both parents. Now he came towards

Kosaku carrying a large watermelon in both arms. At the gate, Tohei paused and raised his eyes briefly to glare at Kosaku. The next moment he turned coldly and walked past Kosaku and into the house. It occurred to Kosaku that the watermelon had been purchased for his sake, too.

Shortly afterwards, he heard his aunt's voice: 'To, go and play with Ko-cha.'

'I don't want to,' was the reply.

'He's taken the trouble to come all this way, so please go and play with him.'

'What a nuisance!'

'You're talking nonsense.'

As Kosaku listened, his desire to go home returned, this time much stronger than before. Abruptly, he left the gateway and stepped on to the path. Soon he was walking through the paddyfields towards the highway. By the time he set foot on the highway, his resolve to go home was firm and immovable. He turned his feet towards Yugashima and soon broke into a run. 'Granny! Granny!' he called out as he ran. He reached Sagasawa Bridge out of breath and stopped for a short rest. The white summer dusk was closing in.

He resumed his journey, running and stopping, running and stopping, until he reached the long road that ran through the centre of Ichiyama, where he slowed to a frantic walk. Now the sun had gone down and it was night.

'Granny!' he continued to gasp as if it were a magic incantation. The road seemed so terribly long, as if it would continue on and on and never end. And on this road Kosaku walked in a frenzy, thinking of nothing.

Just as he reached Sunoko Bridge and thought he had finally returned to Yugashima, he heard a call from behind: 'Kosaku!'

It was unmistakably his uncle's voice. Kosaku immediately broke into a run. It would be terrible to be caught now, he thought. His uncle called a second and a third time, but the boy paid no attention. He ran on to the carriage stop and from there up the hilly old highway that led to his home, all in one sprint. He had a stitch in his side, but he could not let that stop him.

Reaching the storehouse, he pulled open the heavy door and wailed as loudly as he could, 'Granny! Granny!'

'Is that you, Ko-cha?' she cried out in astonishment. 'What happened? My goodness, what in the world!' The beloved voice went straight to his heart.

Just then, Morinoshin Ishimori arrived. Granny Onui stepped outside with a bewildered look. Kosaku stood in the darkness of the lower floor of the storehouse waiting with bated breath. He heard his uncle and Granny Onui speak in low tones and now and then made out Granny Onui's voice saying, 'My goodness,' or 'Well, that was a lot of trouble for you,' or 'Children are such trouble, aren't they?'

At length he heard his uncle's departing footsteps, then all was quiet. Granny Onui returned to the storehouse shortly.

'Ko-cha, they gave us lots of rice-cake dumplings. Even if he is the principal and your uncle, he's no match for you, Ko-cha. You got him to chase you all the way from Kadono-hara carrying these.' She laughed softly.

Contrary to his expectations, Granny Onui looked pleased. He went upstairs, and there he and Granny Onui ate the dumplings that his uncle had brought.

Granny Onui laid out Kosaku's bedding and tucked him in. Then she said, 'Well, now, I must go to the Upper House with some rice-cake dumplings and tell them all about you, Ko-cha.' She turned out the lamp and went downstairs.

Kosaku was left alone in the storehouse, but he was used to this. Here in the storehouse he never felt lonely even when he happened to be alone. Whenever Granny Onui was out at night the mice came out from somewhere and ran round his pillow. It was the same this night.

'When Granny's not here, the mice will look after you,' Granny Onui had often said, and he truly believed it: the mice came to visit him. Therefore he never feared them nor felt repulsed by their presence. Moreover, whenever Granny Onui left Kosaku alone at night she placed some sweets on a piece of paper a short distance from his pillow in the belief that this would ensure that the mice would not harm him. And indeed the mice had never scratched or bitten him. Thus, even on their most rambunctious visits, when they ran about on his pillow and scampered over his bedding, Kosaku could fall asleep without misgivings.

On this night, he had trouble falling asleep, probably because he was still keyed up after his flight from Kadonohara. Images flickered in front of him: his uncle's face; his aunt's demon mask with its blackened teeth; Tohei's surly, resentful glare.

The next day when Kosaku went to the Upper House his Grandmother Tane, with the sad expression she always wore in the wake of some childish misdeed, frowned and said reproachfully, 'Ko-cha, so you ran away and came home. After he took the trouble to take you home to stay overnight. Your aunt and uncle of Kadonohara were very distressed.'

His grandfather also chimed in. 'You shouldn't have come home without telling them. You're impossible!' His tone was clearly scolding.

Only Sakiko spoke a little differently. When she saw Kosaku she said, 'You certainly did it, didn't you, Ko-cha!' She pretended to glare, then burst out laughing.

That day for the first time in a long while Sakiko took Kosaku and Mitsu to the hot springs in Nishibira. At the Nishibira bath house they found Motoi Nakagawa, the fifth-form teacher, bathing alone. Nakagawa was a twenty-eight-year-old substitute teacher who was held in great esteem by the villagers and the students alike because he had graduated from a university in Tokyo. A doctor's son from the neighbouring village of Nakakano, he was unemployed and marking time after graduation when, two years ago, the village office had asked him to come to Yugashima and fill in as a substitute teacher at the elementary school.

Kosaku liked Mr Nakagawa. He was the only teacher Kosaku could approach in the playground without feeling self-conscious. The young teacher often called him 'Ko-cha' in unteacher-like fashion, and sometimes he even picked him up with both hands and raised him high overhead. He did this not only with Kosaku, but with other students as well. Therefore whenever the students saw this young teacher, they surrounded him at once.

51

'Mr Nakagawa is here!' Kosaku said now.

'Oh, my! Mr Nakagawa!' Sakiko acted as if she had just noticed his presence. Then with an apologetic shyness she asked, 'Would you mind leaving? I'm going in now.'

'Of course,' he replied at once. 'I'll go to the river and swim. You can bathe in the meantime.' Then he looked at Kosaku and said, 'Ko-cha, let's leave the ladies here and go for a swim.'

Motoi Nakagawa got out of the bath wearing only a pair of shorts. Kosaku was naked. Together they went to the river and jumped from boulder to boulder, making their way towards the children's swimming spot at Obuchi, about fifty yards downstream. Obuchi was crowded with children who shouted a noisy welcome from their perches on the boulders or from the water when they saw Mr Nakagawa.

Putting his hands together, Nakagawa executed a perfect dive into the pool from a large boulder, then disappeared into the depths. When he surfaced he swam with strong, precise overhand strokes as the children watched from the rocks. Kosaku also watched, filled with reverence for the teacher's beautiful movements.

After alternately swimming and drying himself with the children for about half an hour, Nakagawa said to Kosaku, 'Let's go back, Ko-cha.'

Kosaku and Nakagawa found Sakiko and Mitsu, finished with their bathing and already dressed, awaiting their return. Kosaku thought Sakiko looked beautiful, freshly made up after her bath. The four set off for home, with Mitsu and Kosaku walking together while Sakiko and Nakagawa strolled leisurely side by side and chatted.

When they reached Shimoda Highway, Sakiko suggested that they take the footpath through the paddyfield and visit the shrine on their way home. Kosaku would have preferred going directly home rather than taking a detour through the shadeless paddyfield in the heat of day; nevertheless, as Nakagawa immediately agreed with Sakiko, he had no choice but to follow them.

When they reached their destination, Sakiko and Naka-gawa entered the shrine compound and Mitsu and Kosaku followed them into the woods surrounding the shrine. As the villagers never came here except during festivals, the ground was knee-deep in summer weeds, and the whole shaded area was shrill with the calls of cicadas.

Sakiko and Nakagawa sat together on the veranda surrounding the run-down shrine building and dangled their feet as they talked. Kosaku and Mitsu searched for cicadas in the trees and threw pebbles at them. From time to time Kosaku looked at the two adults to see if they might be ready to leave yet, but always he found them in the same position, talking animatedly. After several glances in their direction, he began to feel a sense of jealousy. Sakiko was so absorbed in her conversation with Nakagawa that she seemed to have forgotten about him and Mitsu, and Nakagawa seemed willing to do whatever Sakiko asked of him.

And then a wasp stung Mitsu. She started shrieking, and with that commotion the two teachers finally broke off their conversation and ran towards the children. Mitsu pressed her forehead with both hands, but it swelled up before their eyes.

'This was no ordinary wasp. It was a poisonous one,' Nakagawa declared. And holding the child, Nakagawa pressed his mouth against the swelling on her forehead and sucked out the venom. As he did so, Sakiko hovered near him in a manner strangely attentive.

3

Several days after Kosaku fled from his uncle's house in Kadonohara it was decided that he and Granny Onui would visit his parents in Toyohashi. The news of their forthcoming trip was all over the hamlet, probably because Granny Onui told everyone, and many of the villagers had words of advice and caution to offer.

Some said: 'Ko-cha, you have to ride on the train for a long time. Don't forget your way home and please come back.' Others said: 'It's better that you don't return and that you go to school in Toyohashi instead. You should stay with your daddy and mummy and not be exploited by Granny Onui.'

But Kosaku was unconcerned about any such remarks. For in his mind, he had already decided that the trip to Toyohashi was going to be a happy event, and he heard all the villagers' words as good wishes on his behalf.

At the time when Kosaku was taken in by Granny Onui, his father had been assigned to the regiment in Shizuoka; only later was he transferred to Toyohashi, where the 15th Division was stationed. Although Kosaku had no recollection of Shizuoka, he felt a special warmth towards the town because he knew he had once lived there. Toyohashi, by contrast, was totally unknown to him. Somehow it seemed it must be a much larger city than Shizuoka, because it was in a different prefecture, because it was much further away than Shizuoka, and because it was a base for a whole division.

The day before they left, Granny Onui appeared to be unusually busy. They went to the bath in Nishibira, but this time she did not go in and out of the bath several times or sit patiently waiting on the edge of the tub for someone to come along so she could chat. Instead, she grabbed Kosaku with great energy and determination, and soaped his body thoroughly down to his smallest toes, ruthlessly scrubbing away at grime, and rubbing his heels so hard with a pumice stone he thought his skin would come off. When she finished washing him she bent her thin body and washed her hair. Then, holding a small mirror in her left hand and a straight razor in her right, she peered into the mirror and deftly shaved around the nape of her neck. As she did so, she kept muttering alternately, 'I'm so busy, I'm so busy,' and 'It's not easy travelling to Toyohashi.'

That night Kosaku was put to bed early. He was so excited that he had difficulty falling asleep. Even after he nodded off he awoke many times. Each time he wakened he sat up in bed thinking it was time to get up. And each time he sat up, Granny Onui stopped her sewing and peered above her glasses to reassure him. 'Ko-cha, don't worry. Go to sleep.'

When he had sat up for the umpteenth time, Granny Onui said incredulously, 'What? You can't sleep, dear? Well then, I'll do some magic on you.' At that she went to the cupboard, took out a pickled plum, removed the seed, and pasted the plum on Kosaku's forehead. Then she said, 'There. You can sleep with this. Now close your eyes.' He wasn't sure it was the magic working, but he soon relaxed and presently fell into a sound sleep.

When he woke the next morning, Granny Onui was standing by his pillow getting dressed in her good kimono.

'Granny, did you sleep?' Kosaku asked from his bed.

'Of course I slept. If I didn't sleep how could I go to Toyohashi? Anyhow, when we get there I probably won't be able to sleep because their bedding is so heavy. Even Granny can't bear that.'

Her words were sarcastic, but her tone was elated. She too was obviously happy to be going to Toyohashi. It had been some years since she had last left the mountain village in Izu.

As Kosaku was washing his face, Grandmother Tane from the Upper House arrived. She seldom came inside the store-house, but on that morning she even came upstairs and helped prepare breakfast. She also dressed Kosaku in his best kimono.

They were to leave on the ten o'clock carriage. Around nine o'clock the neighbours gathered at the storehouse. In addition to his grandmother, Kosaku's grandfather and Sakiko and Mitsu came from the Upper House. Almost everyone brought furoshiki kerchiefs or paper bundles with gifts for Granny Onui to take to the family in Toyohashi. The contents were in all cases either azuki beans, dried shitake mushrooms or wasabi horseradish. Since she could not carry so many gifts, Granny Onui packed some in her baggage and placed the rest in the cupboard.

A large group of neighbourhood children also assembled. They circled Kosaku, standing at a distance and regarding him with an uncustomary detachment born of envy and curiosity.

'Choo-choo, on the other side of the tunnel, oh-my, you'll be all black,' Yukio sang to an improvised tune, and the others, apparently drawn in, piped up with their own random tunes, 'Oh-my, all black, oh-my, all black.' The 'choo-choo' was the sound of the train blowing steam, and the 'all black' meant his face would be black from the engine smoke. At about 9.30 the whole gathering, headed by Granny Onui and Kosaku, streamed down the hill towards the carriage stop. The carriage was already there, with Roku-san, the old driver, standing by with the reins and waiting to sound his usual trumpet blast five minutes before departure.

When the children arrived at the carriage stop they surrounded Roku-san and silently watched his face in the hope that he might let one of them blow the trumpet. Once in a while Roku-san would generously offer the trumpet to one of the boys and say, 'Why don't you blow this?' But that happened only when he was in an extremely good mood. More commonly he was unfriendly and scolding. 'Out of my way, out of my way,' he would say, and push the children aside. Then, jumping quickly on to the carriage platform, he would pick up the trumpet that was hanging by a string from the carriage top and bring it to his mouth. At such times the children were by turns disappointed and resigned, and usually they contented themselves with running along together a little way beside the moving carriage.

That morning, there were only two other passengers, both village men travelling to a neighbouring town. Since the carriage was built for six people it was roomy with only four, and the neighbourhood women who came to see them off kept repeating, 'Aren't we lucky? Aren't we lucky?' as if it were their own good fortune. When there were six passengers they were packed so tightly in the small compartment that no one could move.

That day Kosaku thought Granny Onui looked particularly splendid and refined. No one in the city would outshine her, he felt.

'In the old days I went like this three or four times a year to Tokyo to see the plays. I brought money and scattered it around, and my, what a good feeling that was!' Granny Onui bragged as they waited for the carriage to depart.

No doubt that was true, but it did not sit well with the listeners. Two or three women looked away at once and one put her tongue out. Only Grandmother from the Upper House acknowledged Granny Onui's remarks with a benevolent 'Oh yes' and 'Of course, of course'.

Roku-san's trumpet blared out resoundingly. Kosaku scrambled on to the carriage first. Yukio and Tamekichi followed him on, then poked him and quickly got down from the driver's seat. Yukio repeated the performance a few times until Roku-san rebuked him and he scratched his head in embarrassment.

When the trumpet sounded for the second time, the three adults entered the carriage.

Sakiko spoke to Kosaku from outside the window. 'Kocha, isn't it wonderful that you're going to ride on the train? Now, don't forget to do your homework even if you're having a good time. Remember, you have to be number one in the second quarter.'

Granny Onui's expression tightened slightly at this

remark, but because of the occasion she pretended not to hear and said nothing defensive.

'Well then, everybody,' she said as she pulled Kosaku up by his shoulder pleats and made him stand beside her. Simultaneously, the carriage jerked into motion and the two staggered. Granny Onui flailed her arms wildly and was about to fall when one of the male passengers caught her.

Kosaku heard the shouts of the children merge with the sound of the turning wheels. The adults all waved and the children ran with the carriage. Yukio paced the runners, staying right behind the carriage and gritting his teeth all the way to the edge of Sunoko Bridge before abandoning the race. Kosaku saw the figures of the adults receding. Roku-san, who had continuously blown his trumpet and whipped his horses for thirty or so yards up to Sunoko Bridge, now put down the trumpet and slackened the reins. Beyond the bridge the road curved in a wide arc and from there until they entered the heavily wooded hamlet of Ichiyama the passengers could still see the small forms of their well-wishers.

Kosaku felt his own face contort just as he had seen Yukio's a short while before. For some unfathomable reason he thought he might start shouting. He was continually jostled in the carriage, yet he kept his eyes fixed on the people who had come to see him off. He saw some of his playmates glance back as they headed home. He could no longer distinguish the faces of his grandmother, Sakiko, Mitsu and Yukio. His last glimpse was of two or three hands waving, and then the whole tableau disappeared from view. The carriage was already rolling along the gentle incline of Shimoda Highway, which cut through the middle of Ichiyama.

As Kosaku was seated immediately behind the driver, he could see directly ahead the powerful surge of the horses' haunches and the simultaneous swing of their gold-tinged tails. From time to time Roku-san raised his whip, which cracked against the horses' rumps and quickly rebounded in a wide curling arc which resembled a morning-glory tendril.

'Isn't this easy, Ko-cha! We don't have to walk. All we have to do is let the horse carry us along.'

Although Granny Onui said this, Kosaku thought she did

58

not look all that comfortable. She had placed a triangularly folded kerchief on her kimono collar and was clinging with both hands to the overhead straps.

They passed through Ichiyama in what seemed an instant, then crossed Sagasawa Bridge, where his Uncle Ishimori had informed him his father had once nearly drowned. Just as they entered Kadonohara and came in sight of the hedge and store-house of the Ishimori home in the distance at the foot of the mountain, a woman stepped into the middle of the road and spread out her arms. The carriage stopped. The woman came round the side of the carriage and called out, 'Ko-cha! Ko-cha!'

It was his aunt with her blackened teeth. She opened her mouth wide like the Noh-woman demon mask and laughed. 'Ko-cha, thank you for all your trouble the other day!' she crowed. 'You must have been busy, Ko-cha, but Auntie was busy, too. When you get to Toyohashi, drink a lot of your mother's milk.' Then she turned towards Granny Onui and said, 'I didn't have anything much to give them, but I brought this. They live in the city and are used to luxuries, so they might not eat this. If not, Ko-cha can throw it out with the rubbish.' The last statement was directed at Kosaku.

The carriage began to move again. Granny Onui placed the paper bundle on her hand and raised and lowered it a few times as if she were weighing it.

'Buckwheat flour, two pounds,' she said. 'Ko-cha, remember this, please. I have to put it on my list later.'

'Buckwheat flour? Let's see.' The male passenger who had broken Granny Onui's fall a short while before extended his hand. And he, too, raised and lowered the package. 'It's barley flour, that's what this is. It's about a pound and a half of barley flour. I don't think there's two pounds here,' he said.

Kosaku didn't care whether it was buckwheat flour or barley flour, but he felt irritated by this man saying the gift weighed only a pound and a half after his aunt had taken the trouble to give it to them and Granny Onui had guessed its weight at about two pounds.

After Kadonohara, the carriage crossed a small bridge near some bamboo groves and entered Tsukigase. Kosaku had two sets of relatives here, and both families lived in homes along the road. One family brewed and sold sake; the other were farmers. The farming family was one into which Kosaku's father's elder sister had married. Here also he found an aunt waiting, and she too ran out into the street. She was tall for a woman.

'Kosaku, when you see your mother and father, please give them my best regards,' she said as she stuck her head into the carriage. Then she turned towards Granny Onui and, bowing her head slightly, said, 'Thank you for all your trouble.'

Kosaku was annoyed that this aunt called him by his plain name. He had met her only two or three times and wondered why she presumed to act in such a familiar way. When the carriage started to move she deliberately went round by the driver's seat and handed him something wrapped in white paper. 'Kosaku, this is for you,' she said.

Kosaku handed the gift to Granny Onui. 'It's probably ten sen,'* she said.

At this point the other male passenger interrupted, 'It's probably only five sen.'

Granny Onui thereupon unfolded the paper and held up a ten-sen piece. 'Ko-cha, please remember for me. I have to put this on the list later.' She put the coin in her purse.

After the carriage left Tsukigase it rolled along beside the Kano River for some time, then entered Aohane village. This village boasted both an elementary school and a post office, which to Kosaku's mind gave it a certain cultural superiority. In addition, it had a bicycle repair shop and a meat shop, neither of which was to be found in Yugashima. Kosaku was still slightly disturbed by these comparisons as the carriage slowly passed through Aohane. Just outside the village the driver stood up and bore down on the horses with his whip. After that the carriage went on unchecked, at full speed, to the next carriage stop in Deguchi.

Here Roku-san stepped down from the driver's seat for the first time and gave water to his horses. And here an

---

* One-tenth of one yen

elderly woman brought teacups and a teapot on a tray, and a separate tray of cheap sweets. The passengers drank their tea and ate some sweets, and when Roku-san returned to his perch Granny Onui and the men each placed two or three copper coins on the tray.

After this stop they passed many villages unfamiliar to Kosaku. The Kano River, which appeared and disappeared on the left-hand side of the road, was about twice as wide here as in Yugashima and had dry river beds on both sides. Kosaku preferred the river as it was near Yugashima, with large boulders strewn about: that, he thought, was truly how the Kano River should look. Just before they reached the last stop, at Ohito, the carriage crossed a high bridge called Ohito Bridge. This bridge was famous because many suicides had jumped there. Now, as the passengers peered down from the carriage, the pool of water under the bridge appeared dark green, murky and stagnant, altogether haunted.

When they entered Ohito, Kosaku found it totally foreign territory. Here was a bustling road, which continued on for much longer than the new road in Yugashima, and he saw children with faces much more citified than those in Yugashima, and wearing much nicer clothes, standing at the side of the road. Here also was a cinema, and shops with banners in front.

Finally the carriage stopped at its destination: Ohito station. From there a small railway ran to Mishima at the base of the Izu Peninsula.

The four passengers stepped out of the carriage, entered the cramped waiting room and, looking much relieved, took places on a bench. No one spoke for some time. After four hours of jostling in the carriage, no one had any energy for conversation.

Granny Onui finally broke the silence. 'Do you want to eat your lunch, sonny?' She had taken off her wooden clogs and was lying on a bench. She spoke to Kosaku as if she had just remembered he was there.

'Uh-uh.' Kosaku shook his head.

'Well, then, we'll eat after we get on the train. Our stomachs should be settled down by then. I heard that

61

people get sick on Roku-san's carriage, and I really did get sick. It's terrible to ride with such a clumsy driver. We'll ride on the train next, so we'll be comfortable from now on.' Apparently Granny Onui had actually suffered travel sickness in the carriage, for her face had been very pale. The two men, similarly afflicted, were now lying on their backs on the benches. With two hours yet to wait before the train left, they could afford time to rest.

Kosaku was not at all tired. His lack of hunger was due not to fatigue but to excitement – excitement at being in Ohito, a village with a real railway station. From the entrance of the waiting room he gazed wide-eyed at the many shops that lined the streets on the other side of the open space in front of the station. Then he went to the wooden gate at the side of the waiting room and stared untiringly at the two sets of rails, which seemed to run endlessly through the paddyfields.

When the small train finally started off, Kosaku experienced what one might call the hyper-awareness of the traveller. He took in the mournful sound of the train whistle, the sight of the station platform and the station workers, the wooden gate and the Ohito children who peered through it, the faces of his fellow passengers, and he felt a strange sense of sadness.

'Are you hungry?' Granny Onui stood up and produced from one of her bundles a selection of home-made sushi, morsels wrapped in seaweed. They were neatly aligned on a large wood shaving. She picked up one from the edge and offered the rest to Kosaku. 'Have some.'

He shook his head. No one else was eating, and he didn't want to be the only one.

'Ko-cha, what's wrong? You only ate breakfast, and you haven't had a thing since.' She felt his forehead, then: 'Oh, this is terrible! I should have known something was wrong. You have a fever!'

Without giving him a chance to protest, she thereupon forced him to stretch out on the seat, using her lap as a pillow, so that he could no longer see the scenery outside. But as he lay there Kosaku gradually grew sleepy and dozed. Now and then he opened his eyes to learn where he was.

This was usually when the train had stopped and the coach shook violently. The next moment he would hear the conductor calling out a station name and the clanging of the doors as they opened and closed.

Before he knew it, it was dark outside and he became aware of a great thirst. 'Granny, I want some water,' he finally said when he could no longer bear it.

'Water!?' Granny Onui looked distressed. 'Just wait a bit. I'll get some for you,' she replied.

When the train stopped at the next station, she stuck her head out the window and loudly summoned a railway worker, then talked at length with him. As Kosaku lay on the seat he could see that many of the passengers were looking towards him. After a while someone brought a tea kettle full of water into the coach. As soon as she received this, Granny Onui said, 'Now, dear, the water has come,' and she persuaded him to sit up. As he sat she tilted the kettle and told him to drink from the spout.

In time he fell asleep again. His continual state of excitement since morning had totally robbed him of appetite and made his forehead fiery hot. Kosaku was drained.

When next he woke, he was in a strange room and Granny Onui was sleeping beside him. He wondered where in the world this might be. Looking around at the unfamiliar ceiling and sliding doors, he thought perhaps he had arrived in Toyohashi. Granny Onui woke up as soon as Kosaku sat up. 'Ko-cha, are you hungry?'

Kosaku quickly replied that he was. Actually, he was famished. Granny Onui felt his forehead and, finding his fever gone, was greatly relieved. She then took out the same sushi that she had offered on the train.

Kosaku ate the sushi sitting on his bed late at night.

'Where are we?'

'We're in Numazu.'

'This is not Toyohashi?'

Granny Onui laughed. 'After paying such a price as to make your eyes pop out, Ko-cha, it wouldn't be worth it for us to arrive this soon in Toyohashi,' she said.

When Kosaku had eaten his fill, he got out of bed and

walked to the window. It was a western-style window that opened and closed vertically. He lifted the white curtain and looked out into the night. Through the glass he saw a deserted clearing in front of a train station. He heard the hiss of a steam engine somewhere. As he continued staring at the large building on the other side of the clearing, it occurred to him that Numazu must be a big place – a proper city with a lot of people. And the reason he saw no children must be that it was so late they were all asleep in their homes.

'Ko-cha, Granny won't know what to do with you if you get your days and nights mixed up,' Granny Onui complained, so Kosaku went to bed.

After he lay down Granny Onui felt his forehead again and exclaimed, 'Oh my, you have a fever again!'

Kosaku dozed fitfully for the rest of that night and heard the sound of the steam engine many times. And he told himself, I am in Numazu, a town where many people live, and I am staying in an inn in front of the station, where trains come and go all day and all night.

The next morning Kosaku woke at eight o'clock to find Granny Onui sitting primly beside his bed enjoying a smoke from her long tobacco pipe. The smoke issued from her mouth and nostrils. She patted his bedding and told him to stay in bed until it was time for the train to arrive, but when he heard the tobacco holder rap against the ash receptacle the second time, he could no longer bear to lie still.

As soon as he left his bed he went to the window and looked out. He saw many people walking in the square in front of the station. There were adults and there were children. Some carried handbags, while others carried babies on their backs. Some pushed baby carriages; others rode bicycles. Almost ten jinricksha were neatly lined up on one side of the square.

Kosaku continued to stand by the window and gaze at the busy scene. Granny Onui urged him a few times to go downstairs and wash, but he was too engrossed to hear. After a while, she brought a basin of warm water and a cup

64

of cool water to the room. Kosaku rinsed his mouth from the cup and spat out the water on to the roof below. Then he scooped water from the basin with one hand and dabbed his face a few times.

When a young maid brought breakfast to their table, Kosaku gulped. He found it alarming to see fried eggs, dried fish and dried seaweed offered all at once. Steaming miso soup in beautiful lacquer bowls was also served. He did not know where to start and felt confused. He was impressed at the way Granny Onui showed no awe at this feast and ate as if this were ordinary fare. Kosaku ate slowly, taking a long time. When he put out his rice bowl for the fourth time, Granny Onui said, 'I know it's good, but I think you had better stop now.'

'But Granny, I still have some fried eggs left,' he protested.

'Well then, just eat that without rice. You didn't eat a thing yesterday, and today you're stuffing yourself.' She spoke as though she were talking to herself.

After Kosaku finished his breakfast he lay on his back for a while. Even without that fourth bowl of rice, he was painfully full. Granny Onui, who sat beside him, expressed anger that not one of the relatives in Numazu had come to call, even though she had written them in advance.

When Kosaku's pain from overeating subsided, he stepped outside the inn and stood by the entrance. Buildings solidly lined both sides of the street. Now and then the town children walked by. They looked even more clean-cut than the children of Ohito, and they all wore wooden clogs or straw sandals. Kosaku himself was wearing his best wooden clogs on this trip, but he was not used to them; he had already developed blisters from the straps and his toes hurt. Straw sandals were much lighter and easier to wear. Kosaku wondered if city children wore every day all the clothes he considered his best things.

Whenever a child passed by, Kosaku averted his eyes, afraid to look directly or have it known he was watching. He felt he was no match for these children in any way – not in his looks, in his kimono, in the way he walked, or in

65

anything else. To Kosaku the city children's speech sounded clear and pleasant and incredibly bright.

At length, feeling utterly outclassed, Kosaku retreated into the inn and returned to his room. There he found Granny Onui talking with a strange woman. She was a slender person of thirty-five or thirty-six years, and even Kosaku could see that her clothes were of exquisite quality. When she turned and saw Kosaku she said, 'So this is Ko-cha.' Her voice was subdued and melodious.

'Umm,' Kosaku responded sullenly.

Then Granny Onui said, 'Ko-cha, this is Auntie from the Kamiki house.'

The woman next unwrapped a large paulownia box of sweets from a purple silk-crepe furoshiki kerchief and offered it to Granny Onui, saying, 'Please give them my best regards.'

'Yes, thank you. This is so very kind of you. You have taken so much trouble.' Granny Onui seemed to have lost a bit of her usual spirit, possibly because she was overwhelmed by this person who was mistress of the Kamiki house.

After the visitor left, Granny Onui, who had been subdued during the visit, said, 'Even if they're very rich, they'll go bankrupt spending like that.' Then she said seriously, 'Ko-cha, when you grow up, don't get a bride like that.'

'A bride? Was that auntie a bride?' Kosaku asked.

'She's older now, but once she was a bride. If she wears such extravagant clothes at her age, nothing good can come of it.'

Just after Granny Onui uttered this criticism, a middle-aged couple arrived. Kosaku did not recognize these visitors at all, but it appeared they were distantly related to Granny Onui. The woman called Kosaku 'Ko-cha', but the man called him 'sonny-Ko'. This was the first time Kosaku had been addressed in that way, and he felt a bit embarrassed.

When the couple brought out a box of sweets from their bundle, Granny Onui gave in return the packet she had received at Kadonohara intended for the family in Toyohashi. Then, wrapping some money in a separate piece of paper, she thrust it towards the pair. At first they both firmly refused to accept it, but in the end the man picked it up and raised it reverently over his head, then stashed it in his kimono bosom.

About an hour later, when Granny Onui and Kosaku left the inn to go to the station, the couple accompanied them to the station platform. From the time he entered the station Kosaku was excited because he knew he was going to ride on a *real* train at last. He made no reply when Granny Onui or the couple spoke to him. Kosaku had no idea what they said.

Soon a monstrous train, incomparably larger than the one they had boarded at Ohito, slid into the station with a thunderous rumble. Granny Onui clutched Kosaku's hand tightly and told him he mustn't let go under any circumstances. The couple would hand them their baggage through the window. Kosaku was worried that the baggage would not fit through the window. Indeed, he was so distracted by this concern that he slipped and fell on the train steps, even though Granny Onui was still holding his hand.

When they had settled down in the train, Granny Onui stared at Kosaku's feet and asked, 'Ko-cha, what happened to your clogs?'

Kosaku looked down at his feet and saw that they were bare.

Granny Onui abruptly stuck her head out the window and shouted loudly, 'The clogs! Ko-cha's clogs!'

Kosaku was ashamed at the commotion Granny Onui created in front of strangers. In the brief glance he cast around him, he saw many who looked like city folks, and all the passengers were watching curiously. Soon the couple passed Kosaku's clogs through the window with the rest of the luggage. They said they had found one on the platform, the other on the train step.

Granny Onui did not even thank them. Instead, as soon as she received the clogs she said, 'Wasn't that wonderful, Ko-cha! Here,' and she bent over and placed them by his feet. She then removed her own clogs, sat on the seat with her feet tucked under her, and looking relieved loosened her kimono collar and began fanning herself. Finally she spoke again to the couple standing on the platform. 'Don't fight now. Everything is patience, patience.'

67

The woman said, 'Of course, that's right.' She rolled her eyes at the man. 'Please listen well, dear. Everything is patience, patience.' The man scratched his head bashfully and stuck out his tongue, then quickly poked the woman in the hip. 'Oh!' the woman yelped. She acted shocked, then slapped playfully at the man. He quickly stepped aside. Such behaviour between a grown man and woman struck Kosaku as startling and strangely disturbing.

As the train moved away from the platform and their distance from the couple increased, Granny Onui said to Kosaku, 'Those stupid fools!'

Even so, she waved her handkerchief from the window. She waved for a long while, then she pulled in her hand and, folding that handkerchief in a triangle, placed it round her kimono collar.

'Well, Ko-cha, there is nothing more we must do. We don't have to walk another step and the train will take us to Toyohashi. Isn't it wonderful? This is heaven.' Granny Onui looked genuinely relieved.

Kosaku, imitating her pose, sat on the seat with his feet tucked under him. It wasn't very comfortable, but he thought it must be the proper thing to do. The two seats facing them were empty, so they took up the space by putting their luggage there rather than on the overhead rack.

'When you think about it, it was a big job to come this far, wasn't it, Ko-cha?' As there was no one else nearby, Granny Onui kept talking to Kosaku.

He agreed with her. They had left Yugashima only the morning before, but to Kosaku it felt as if many days had passed since he had parted from his grandparents and Sakiko of the Upper House, and from Yukio, Yoshie and Kameo.

Absorbed in these thoughts, he was astonished to discover Mt. Fuji looming in front of his eyes. It definitely was Mt. Fuji, but a much, much larger Mt. Fuji than the one he saw every day from Yugashima.

'Ah! Mt. Fuji is here, too!' he shouted.

Then he heard laughter. Four young women seated on the other side of the aisle were all looking at him and chuckling. Embarrassed, he quickly turned away and looked out the window. He wondered why they found his words so amusing. Were they laughing at his country accent? If it wasn't that, Kosaku could not understand at all why they were laughing at him.

Granny Onui meanwhile was in continual motion, fanning herself, smoking, brushing off soot that entered from the window. From time to time she also used her towel to brush soot from Kosaku's kimono. Kosaku remained motionless and looked out the window at the scenery flying past him. It was all unfamiliar and he was not in the least bored.

Each time the train stopped, Granny Onui took out her little notebook and pencil and ordered Kosaku to write down the name of the station. Kosaku obediently copied down the names from the signs: Hara, Suzukawa, and so on. She also had him write down the names of the largest rivers. Back home in Yugashima he had been told every night that before they reached Toyohashi they would cross four large rivers – the Fuji River, the Abe, the Oi and the Tenryu – and Kosaku was looking forward to seeing for himself just how large these rivers actually were.

The first one they crossed was the Fuji. It was wide all right, but mostly it was made up of dry beds with little water flowing through. This river is nothing great, Kosaku thought. He saw some children in the water and sniffed contemptuously. He and his friends who swam at the Heibuchi and Otsukenofuchi swimming holes were far braver swimmers.

'This Fuji is a shallow river,' he said scornfully.

Granny Onui was indignant. 'What are you talking about? It is not shallow,' she said, defending the river.

'It's much deeper at Heibuchi,' Kosaku argued.

'Don't be silly. There's no comparison. The Kano is not even a river compared to the Fuji River. Just keep watching, we'll come to the Oi River very soon,' Granny Onui said.

The Oi River did not appear for a long time. The train took plenty of rest at each station and even then did not resume its unhurried journey until everyone was sure that not a single person had been left behind.

At Shizuoka, station hawkers went back and forth on the platform selling items packed in boxes. Granny Onui bought some lunch and tea. Kosaku felt a return of his nostalgia for Shizuoka. He had no memory of the town or of the home he had lived in, but just the knowledge that he had lived here for a year and a half gave him warm feelings towards the place. He felt the hawkers at the station and the railway workers were not strangers.

Kosaku was told to write 'Shizuoka' in the notebook, and below it 'Abekawa rice cakes'. Abekawa rice cakes were a famous local product and he wrote as he was told. But Granny Onui did not buy any rice cakes. 'We can look forward to that on our way home,' she explained.

Just as the train left Shizuoka and Kosaku was about to open his lunch box, Granny Onui cried out, 'It's Abe River! It's Abe River!'

The train made a thunderous sound as it crossed a steel bridge, and Kosaku looked out. To him the Abe River also seemed smaller than the Kano.

'Well, isn't it big?' Granny Onui asked. 'Now write it down before you forget,' she urged. Kosaku opened the notebook and next to 'Shizuoka' wrote 'Abe River'.

After she had finished eating her lunch, Granny Onui covered half of her face with her towel and said, 'Granny will take a little nap.' Kosaku wasn't sure why she covered half her face with a towel, but he thought probably it was because she wanted to keep the soot out of her mouth.

After Granny Onui fell asleep Kosaku continued to record the station names as they came up. At length he became drowsy, but he felt he had to stay awake to write down the names. By then there was nothing new to see outside. The same kinds of paddyfields and hills with similar intervals between them came towards him then flew past, and that was all. None of the new stopping places were as large as Shizuoka and they too all looked alike.

At Kakegawa a middle-aged, heavy-set woman intruded into the seats that just the two of them had occupied until then. She picked up their bundles and set them on the luggage rack above, and placed her own luggage beside theirs. Because the woman had moved their luggage without permission, Kosaku felt immediately suspicious. She might possibly be a pickpocket. With Granny Onui sound asleep, he felt he had to keep an eye on this woman in Granny's place.

After the woman was seated she smiled at him and offered him a paper-wrapped rice cracker. 'Here, sonny, let me give you this.' Kosaku accepted it silently but thought it safer not to eat it since she was such a suspicious character. It could be poisoned. Why else would a total stranger offer him such a thing?

'Eat it, sonny. It's all right to eat it,' she urged.

Kosaku thought to himself, I'm not about to fall into her trap. As he would not talk to her, she stopped talking to him and looked out, then at length closed her eyes. No sooner had her eyes closed than her jaw slackened, her mouth dropped open, and she fell into a deep sleep. Sweat stood out on her forehead and poured from the creases of her fat neck. As Kosaku watched her, he also grew drowsy, and before he knew it he too was asleep.

'Sonny, it's Tenryu River! Tenryu River!' Granny Onui's voice woke him.

The train was about to cross the steel bridge over the river when he clutched at the window frame and looked out. Again he saw a river bed many times the width of the Kano but the blue water flowing near one bank was just a trickle, thin as an obi sash. Certainly this river was not nearly so large and deep as the Kano River where he and his friends swam, Kosaku thought.

He yawned and looked at Granny Onui. She had spread out a paper wrapper on her lap and was eating a rice cracker from it. He looked around but could not find the one he had been given a while before.

My, what a calamity! he thought. When he looked at the seat in front, he saw that the woman who had got on at Kakegawa was eating the same type of rice cracker as Granny Onui. They had become friendly, and they were laughingly absorbed in a conversation. Kosaku cast a casual glance upwards at the luggage rack. Their bundles were still intact where the woman had placed them. But Kosaku was still suspicious.

'Granny, are they the crackers that I got?' Kosaku asked pointedly.

'That's right, sonny. Here, you have some, too.'

Kosaku pushed away the wafer she offered and shook his head. He wanted to tell Granny Onui that the rice cracker might be poisoned, but because the strange woman was looking right at him he kept silent. Instead he faced the window and started chanting in a sing-song voice, 'It's-better-that-you-don't-eat it. It's-better-that-you-don't-eat-it.'

When they stopped at the next station, Kosaku opened the notebook to jot down the name. He wasn't sure how many stations they had passed during his sleep, but he planned to leave a little space before making this notation. When he picked up the pencil he saw writing in the note-book different from his. The station names were written in Granny Onui's hand where he had left off. After the train crossed Lake Hamana, the woman said, 'Sonny, it's not far now.'

Apparently Granny Onui had told her their destination. Granny Onui continued to talk to the woman as she crunched on the rice crackers. The woman lowered her bag from the luggage rack and pulled out a small box.

'Here, I'll give you this,' she said, offering the box to Kosaku.

The box was about the size of a pack of cigarettes, and on the front a heart-shaped hole had been cut out and covered with cellophane so that the contents were visible. The box was filled with small sweets, red, green and other colours.

'Those are jellybeans. Try them. They're good,' the woman said.

This was the first time that Kosaku had ever seen the sweets called jellybeans. Even so, he wondered why this woman had given them to him. He handed the box to Granny Onui but immediately took it back because he thought Granny Onui might eat some of these as well. The rice crackers apparently hadn't poisoned her, but he couldn't be sure about these things.

At the next small station, shortly after she gave him the jellybeans, the woman got off the train. She politely said goodbye to Granny Onui and patted Kosaku's head, then picked up her suitcase and left.

Kosaku brushed his hand over his head where the woman had touched him and told Granny Onui, 'She might be a bad person.'

'What are you saying? She gave you lots of nice things. She's a good person,' Granny Onui said and she took the box of jellybeans from Kosaku's hand and stared at it awhile.

'Ko-cha, do you want to eat some?'

'Uh-uh.'

Granny Onui put the box in a small handbag and Kosaku wrote down the name of the station where the suspicious woman got off. It was called Washizu. By this time Kosaku was becoming bored with his train trip. He got up from his seat and walked along the aisle or went to sit in empty seats on the other side. But whenever the train stopped he rushed to stick his head out the window and find the station name so he could copy it in the notebook.

Two or three stops after the woman left, Kosaku heard the station worker call, 'Toyohashi! Toyohashi!' The station sign-board was right outside Kosaku's window. No mistake: it read 'Toyohashi'.

'Granny, isn't this Toyohashi?' Kosaku asked.

'Let me see.' Granny Onui looked out the window, then yelped. 'It is! Goodness! It is Toyohashi!'

After this she began calling, 'Ko-cha, Ko-cha,' in a staccato way and bustling about. Two passengers seated nearby stood up and came to lower their luggage and help Granny Onui find her clogs.

When Granny Onui and Kosaku stepped down to the platform after having created a great commotion, two women approached them. It dawned on Kosaku that one of these women was his mother, and as soon as he recognized her he tried to hide behind Granny Onui. Then he looked around to see whether there might be another place where he could make himself disappear completely.

Kosaku watched the woman he had identified as his mother and waited with bated breath. He was not sure whether she was an enemy or an ally, but he knew she was a special woman to him. In what way she was special was not clear, but she was so special that he could perceive at a glance that she was his mother.

'Welcome,' she was saying. 'You must be very tired.'

'Not at all.'

'It must have been very hard on you, coming out of the country after so many years.'

'It was no trouble at all.'

Kosaku's mother was smiling, but Granny Onui was already showing by her facial expression and the brevity of her words the agitation and wariness she felt at stepping into enemy territory.

'Where's Ko-cha?' At that question from his mother, Kosaku mingled with a group of departing passengers passing by just then and took off in the same direction they were moving. He wanted only to hide somewhere his mother could not see him. He felt too embarrassed to talk to her or expose himself to her. If possible, he wanted to observe this special woman called Mother from a place where no one could see him.

'Ko-cha!' When he heard a voice that was unquestionably Granny Onui's ring out in a no-nonsense tone, Kosaku threaded his way past several people in front of him and walked briskly still further away. He slipped out through the ticket gate in the middle of a group of people. Ahead he saw a large square, much larger than the one in front of Numazu station. The group who surged out with him from the ticket gate scattered randomly in different directions when they came out to the clearing. The sun had set. The banners of several sweet-ice* stalls lining a corner of the square fluttered nervously in the wind. Unexpectedly, Kosaku felt overwhelmed by a sense of isolation greater than he had ever known.

Having left the station alone, he naturally became anxious. He looked back towards the ticket gate where the flow of passengers continued unabated. In time he saw Granny Onui come through the gate, looking in all directions.

'Ko-cha! Ko-cha!' Granny Onui stopped a short distance from the gate and suddenly called his name in a strange

---

* Ice with sweet syrup poured on it

sing-song tone that he had never heard before: 'Ko-cha! Ko-cha!'

Kosaku felt that many people were looking at him and again he tried to hide. The next moment his mother, Nanae, appeared right beside Granny Onui, and Kosaku saw that she too was concerned and was looking in all directions.

'Kosaku! Kosaku!' his mother called.

Compared to Granny Onui, his mother's voice sounded much younger and more resonant. Kosaku began walking towards his mother as though drawn by an irresistible force.

When Granny Onui at last spotted Kosaku, she exclaimed, 'Oh, Ko-cha!' and her body relaxed with relief. 'You shouldn't make us worry so, Ko-cha. If you do, your mother will be angry with you.'

Indeed Kosaku thought his mother's face looked very frightening at that moment.

'Kosaku, you mustn't walk around alone here anywhere you please. This isn't like the country in Izu,' his mother said. Her tone sounded very sharp to Kosaku.

'Umm,' Kosaku replied.

'Say "yes",' his mother corrected.

'Umm.' When Kosaku realized he had responded in the same way again, he grabbed Granny Onui's sleeve in a fluster.

When his mother went to call some jinricksha, all his pleasure evaporated and he felt a strong urge to return to Yugashima. He felt he had come to a terrible place.

'Granny, let's go back to Yugashima.' He shook her sleeve back and forth.

'What are you talking about? After all the trouble we've taken to come and visit your very own parents?' Granny Onui replied.

His mother returned with two jinricksha. Kosaku got in one with Granny Onui, and his mother rode in a separate jinricksha with the luggage. The maid who had come with his mother was to walk home. Kosaku, braced between Granny Onui's legs, gazed with mixed feelings of anxiety and curiosity at the passing houses lining both sides of the street in the city dusk.

'Isn't this easy, sonny?' Kosaku heard Granny Onui's

voice from above.

'Umm.'

He stood with Granny Onui's legs as his support, and although he wasn't exactly comfortable, the fact that he could go through the street without moving his legs was something that one might call 'easy'.

After they had travelled through city streets for about fifteen minutes they turned off into a quiet lane and the jinricksha men set down their steering poles in front of a latticed two-storey residence which faced the street. Kosaku was dizzy when he got off.

When the lattice door opened, Sayoko, his sister three years younger, peered out and as soon as she saw Kosaku made a mad dash inside. She went so fast she tripped and fell over the threshold. And she screamed and cried loudly. A strange woman appeared from inside and picked up Sayoko. She smiled at him and the others and simultaneously tried very hard to comfort Sayoko. Kosaku learned later that the strange woman was a next-door neighbour.

Even Kosaku could tell that the kimono Sayoko wore was not everyday wear. It was floral-patterned and had a tie-dyed sash with a large bow. Kosaku realized that Sayoko had donned her best clothes to welcome them.

As they were drinking tea before unpacking, Kosaku's father, Shosaku, came home wearing his military uniform. Kosaku, imitating Sayoko, went to the entrance and bowed in welcome. Shosaku sat on the entrance platform with his back turned to them and slowly removed his shoes. Then he entered the room, patted Kosaku's head, and passed on into another room. Kosaku didn't know how to interpret his father's behaviour.

'Daddy hit me,' Kosaku told Granny Onui, who sat fanning herself near the veranda in the sitting room.

Overhearing this remark, his mother said, 'Ko-cha, that's stupid. Why would your daddy hit you?' At that moment his mother's eyes appeared accusing and harsh.

'Mummy glared at me,' Kosaku reported to Granny Onui.

As Kosaku watched, his mother really did glare at him. 'You certainly have become a strange child. Why do you tell all kinds of tales to Granny, when you've just arrived and we haven't even had dinner? I have no reason to glare at you.'

Seeing his mother thus angered, Kosaku clung to Granny Onui.

Then Granny Onui set down her fan, turned towards Nanae and said, 'What kind of parent gets so angry at what a child says? It only makes matters worse.'

At this his mother came over and sat in front of Granny Onui. 'Granny,' she said, 'I'd like to make this clear. Kosaku is my child. I will raise him as I see fit. If, when I leave him in your care, he turns into a strange child, then I'll have to think that over.'

Granny Onui, a little flustered, said, 'There's no reason why he should become a strange child. Ko-cha was born a very bright child.'

'He's already turned into a strange child. Telling tales is a despicable thing.' His mother was emphatic.

'Yes, I know. I'll explain this carefully to Ko-cha. Ko-cha, apologize to your mummy. The best thing to do in this house is to apologize. It's best to know when you can't win,' Granny Onui said.

'What a terrible thing to say!'

As Nanae spoke, Kosaku's father came down the veranda and asked 'What's going on so early in the visit?' And, as if to indicate he would not be involved in women's disputes, he turned towards Nanae and said, 'Hurry up and get dinner on the table.'

When at length dinner was served in the centre of the eight-mat family room, the five family members – Shosaku, Nanae, Granny Onui, Kosaku and Sayoko – arrayed themselves around the circular table. Kosaku had not spoken a word to Sayoko yet. From time to time Sayoko glanced up at him, but whenever their eyes met she looked away and noisily ate her food. Kosaku imitated her and ate just as noisily.

'Stop eating like that!' their mother warned.

'I'm just copying Sayo-cha,' Kosaku replied.

'Sayo-cha wouldn't do such a thing! You have bad manners,' his mother rebuked.

77

Kosaku thought this very unfair. 'Sayo-cha really did it,' he countered.

Granny Onui interrupted, 'Now be quiet, Ko-cha. There is nothing we can do about it. In this house when you put rice into your mouth you must gulp it down without chewing.' Then she took a small amount of rice from her bowl, put it in her mouth and feigned swallowing it.

Nanae turned away. Kosaku found the atmosphere most unpleasant during this first meal in his parents' home. Shosaku ignored the whole exchange, kept his eyes on the newspaper on his lap, and from time to time picked up his chopsticks as if he had just remembered why he was there. Shosaku acted from the very beginning as if he could not hear Granny Onui and Nanae.

After dinner, Shosaku took Kosaku outside. Sayoko followed. At every home along the street a gas lamp shone beside the entry gate. The bluish-white light was novel to Kosaku; it made him feel he had come to storyland.

'Elder Brother.' When Sayoko thus addressed Kosaku for the first time he felt confused. But actually he was Sayoko's older brother, and there was nothing so strange about what she said. Across from their house was a storage area for a china shop where such items as earthenware pipes, large hibachi braziers, hot-water bottles and various other earthenware products could be seen through gaps in a dilapidated black fence.

It soon became obvious that Sayoko was overjoyed at Kosaku's visit, and after she became more used to him she followed him like a shadow, calling 'Elder Brother, Elder Brother', over and over. And whenever she lagged behind from looking around, she ran to catch up and invariably fell down. Kosaku took on the role of picking up Sayoko whenever she fell. At such times his father simply stood there without making any attempt to help and signalled with his chin, 'Kosaku, go and pick her up.'

It wasn't only those instances that made Kosaku feel even more distant from his father than from his mother. Shosaku seemed to be just like Uncle Morinoshin Ishimori of Kadonohara. When father and son were supposedly taking a walk together, Shosaku walked briskly ahead and seldom looked back. To keep up, Kosaku had to run from time to time, and furthermore each time he ran Sayoko did too, and he had to pick her up. At first Kosaku always brushed the dust off Sayoko's kimono but towards the end he only picked her up. Kosaku did not enjoy this walk at all.

At eight o'clock Kosaku was put to bed in a back room with Sayoko. He wanted to sleep with Granny Onui, but his mother directed everything. Granny Onui was to sleep alone in the living room. Sayoko fell asleep as soon as she went to bed, but Kosaku lay awake a long time. Compared to the storehouse in Yugashima the ceiling here was much higher and the room much larger. From where his bedding rested, the tatami mats seemed to spread out like the sea.

Beginning the next day, on his mother's orders, Kosaku had to do his school work for two hours every morning. He got up at 6 a.m., had breakfast at seven, and after seeing his father off at 7.30, sat down to study. After he was released from his studies at 9.30, he swept the yard round his home, then went shopping with the maid and carried the shopping bag.

In the afternoon, his mother told him, he could play freely, but he discovered there was no way he could really play even if he wanted to. He didn't have a single friend, and there was no river, no mountain, no paddyfield.

'Play with Sayoko,' his mother said.

But it wasn't any fun to play with Sayoko. When he was with Sayoko he had to be on the alert all the time. If she played near his desk she acted as though she might pick up something and throw it. If she went on the veranda she looked as though she might fall off. And if he took his eyes off her for one moment she would climb the stairs and slip and fall after two or three steps.

During the daytime Granny Onui stayed in the maid's room and did not come out other than for meals. There she spent her time smoking tobacco and doing a little sewing. Nanae and Granny Onui tried to avoid each other.

79

Whenever they saw each other they got into some sort of dispute. Now and then Kosaku ventured into the maid's room. Then Granny Onui would tell him that it was eight more days or seven more days, informing him that their departure date was drawing closer.

'Ko-cha, it must be hard on you being a babysitter and being worked to death, but it's just a little bit longer. Be patient, dear.' Or she might say, 'Everything is medicine. When you get angry or frustrated, remember that this is all discipline.'

Kosaku also looked forward to their departure day. He wanted to be swimming with Yukio and his other friends at Heibuchi or catching dragonflies in the shrine precincts. But he refrained from saying he wanted to go home because somehow he knew it would hurt his mother's feelings.

One night Kosaku lay in bed listening as his mother and Granny Onui argued loudly in the next room. After assailing Nanae in vulgar terms, Granny Onui declared she would take Kosaku back with her to Yugashima no matter what. Nanae was just as adamant in her refusal. 'I don't care what you say, it's been decided that Kosaku will stay here,' she kept repeating.

After much protesting and shouting in this vein, Granny Onui then turned subservient. 'I beg of you, please let Ko-cha come back with me. Do you plan to let me go home alone without Ko-cha? Do you intend to let me live alone in the storehouse in the country?'

But still Nanae would not listen.

'Well then,' Granny Onui proposed, 'let's ask Ko-cha how he feels. If Ko-cha says he'll stay here I'll give up gracefully. If Ko-cha says he wants to return to Yugashima, please let him do as he says. It's best to let him make the decision.'

Still, Nanae would not listen. Then Granny Onui stood up abruptly and again began to shout. After a while Shosaku came down from upstairs and mediated between the two women, telling them they should find out how Kosaku felt and base the decision completely on that. Nanae wasn't happy about it, but she finally agreed. Kosaku was relieved. He thought it would be terrible if Granny Onui were to go

80

home alone and leave him in a place like this.

The next morning during breakfast his father asked, 'Kosaku, do you want to return or do you want to stay here?'

'I'm going home with Granny,' Kosaku replied without hesitation.

Then with an I-told-you-so look, Granny Onui said, 'Kocha, there are some things you can say honestly and some you can't. However, whatever you say, you can't take it back.'

Nanae glared at Granny Onui and remained silent.

Shosaku said, 'Very well, it's settled. Granny will raise Kosaku. Country living should be all right for him while he's a child.'

The day before Kosaku and Granny Onui were to leave, Kosaku went with his mother, Sayoko, and the maid to shop in town after their evening meal. They stopped at a large confectioner's called Wakamatsu-en and there ate sweets in a tearoom. This was the first time Kosaku had eaten in such a magnificent place. The yellow gelatin dessert looked so beautiful he hesitated to insert his spoon. It was delicious and melted in his mouth. Kosaku regretted that he couldn't share this treat with his grandmother and Sakiko of the Upper House and Yukio and his other friends. He didn't think he could explain it to them in words.

Nanae visited many shops – clothing, stationery and sweet shops – to buy gifts for Granny Onui and Kosaku to take home. And the maid and Kosaku carried the purchases. For Kosaku, Nanae bought crayons in a beautiful box, and notebooks. He was very pleased that his mother had bought these gifts for him.

'Ko-cha, do you want to stay in Toyohashi?' Nanae asked teasingly as they walked along the bustling street.

'Uh-uh.' Kosaku was flustered by the question but shook his head strongly.

'Granny can go home alone tomorrow and Ko-cha, you could stay just for the summer holidays and go back later,' Nanae said again.

'Uh-uh – I want to go home with Granny,' Kosaku said desperately. He reflected that it would be awful if he were to be left here alone without Granny Onui. Then, thinking it would also be terrible if his mother did not understand him, he repeated, 'I'm going home with Granny. Ko-cha is going home with Granny.'

Nanae, apparently irritated at this insistence, said, 'I understand. You are such a nuisance!'

Up to this point in the shopping tour, Kosaku had been feeling a certain warmth towards his mother, who was showing a gentle manner, unlike her usual self. Now he again felt distanced from her and thought, She is a mean, cold person after all.

When his mother entered a kimono shop Kosaku, feeling somewhat rebellious, did not go in with her. Instead he stood outside for a while until he noticed a goldfish shop across the street. There, a group of children in summer kimonos squatted and peered into a goldfish bucket or scooped up the fish with small nets. He joined them and sat for some time gazing at the goldfish.

'Scoop some up,' the shop owner, a man in his fifties, encouraged. At first Kosaku did not think the man was speaking to him, but when the owner repeated his offer he realized he was being addressed. 'Go ahead, sonny! Try to scoop some. I'll let you have the first one for free. It's all right for you to scoop it.' Kosaku did as he was told, picked up a small net and dipped it into the water bucket. A goldfish flipped about in the net.

When Kosaku tried to catch another, the shopkeeper said, 'No more. You can't have any more.'

Kosaku was disappointed, but returned the net.

Then he watched other children scoop up one free fish just as he had. A fair-complexioned young girl with pretty, regular features, the likes of which he had not seen in Yugashima, raised her high-pitched voice as she chased a large goldfish. A highly strung young boy, again unlike any boy in Yugashima, frowned and chased after a small, spotted fish. Kosaku wondered why it was that city children looked so intelligent and spoke so clearly.

He had no idea how much time he had spent in front of the goldfish shop before he suddenly remembered his

mother and stood up, seized by a premonition that something terrible was about to happen. He immediately crossed
to the kimono shop. Just as he had feared, he did not see his
mother or Sayoko or the maid inside. He took a right turn,
running from the shop, then stopped and ran in the opposite
direction. After quite a distance he came to an intersection
where he frantically took a left turn. From about that point
things went from bad to worse. Kosaku became totally
distraught. He wondered what in the world would happen
to him. He took random turns on unknown roads. He ran
helter-skelter until he was exhausted. Then he walked slowly.

'Granny! Granny!' he muttered over and over.

In time Kosaku heard the unmistakable chuff of a steam
engine nearby, and paused to look around him. It was a very
desolate spot with not a soul in sight. He had no idea how he
had come to this dark, lonely place. Moving on, he found
himself walking beside a wooden fence on a road that
seemed endless. Several times he was sorely tempted to turn
back and walk the other way, but he felt a little less fearful
going forward.

He quickened his pace, half crying as he ran. He no longer
heard the steam engine but now the sound of frogs croaking
filled the air. Without realizing how he had got there,
Kosaku was in the middle of a dark paddyfield. He slowed
down again, walking and sobbing softly, plodding forward
with a dim notion that he must continue until the road came
to an end. All the while, the croaking of the frogs filled the
ricefield.

Then, abruptly, he stopped both crying and walking. In
the far distance ahead, he saw small, dim bobbing lights,
and he was paralysed with fear. It was as if cold water had
been dashed over his whole body. He considered turning
back but was afraid. He was still more fearful of going
forward. He stood cowering as he watched. He knew the
lights must be lanterns, but who might be carrying them? As
the lanterns bobbed closer he stood rooted to the spot,
certain that he was really going to be eaten up alive. How
sad Granny and Sakiko would be!

Suddenly he found his voice. 'Granny!' he shouted at the

top of his lungs. 'Granny! Granny!'

The lanterns moved more quickly towards him and he caught the sound of voices.

'Wah!' Kosaku screeched. It was the cry of one about to die. 'Aii, I'm going to be caught. I'm going to be eaten.' His feet remained as though glued to the ground. 'I'm going to be eaten! I'm going to be eaten!'

'I wonder what this child is doing here,' someone remarked and thrust the lantern towards him.

The light shone on the paddyfield path, on the grasses that grew on the path, on a part of the ricefields on either side of him, and on his bare feet. Kosaku had lost his clogs somewhere. The lantern bearers were a group of two men and three women. They surrounded Kosaku and talked noisily among themselves. Kosaku stood rigidly, obsessed with the conviction, I'm going to be eaten! I'm going to be eaten! He had lost his voice, and his heart was now filled with all the sadness of a child born to unhappiness, a sadness that permeated his whole being.

'Whose child are you?' one woman asked. Kosaku only sobbed.

'Where are you going?' a man asked.

'Granny! Granny!' Kosaku wailed.

'I wonder if he's been tricked by a fox,'* another voice piped up.

'Granny! Granny!'

'Where do you live?'

'Granny! Granny!'

'What in the world happened?'

'Granny! Granny!' No matter what he was asked, Kosaku kept repeating, 'Granny! Granny!'

'Look here!' With a loud shout a man abruptly picked Kosaku up by the nape of the neck and shook him violently, then set him down. Finally, still holding him by the nape, the man slapped Kosaku twice.

---

* This refers to a Japanese superstition that a fox can enter and possess a person's body in a manner similar to the Western idea of possession by the Devil.

'Wah!' Kosaku was desperate. He felt certain the time had come when his hair would be pulled out, his arms torn off, his body taken apart in pieces and eaten. He must not let that happen. He must survive and return to Granny Onui. With all the strength he could muster, he began flailing his arms and legs and shrieking.

The man slapped Kosaku's cheek a third time, then said, 'How's that! That should get rid of the fox.' Peering into Kosaku's face, he asked, 'Where did you come from?'

Peering back, Kosaku was startled to see that the man's face resembled that of the schoolteacher, Motoi Nakagawa. He almost believed it was Mr Nakagawa, but he discovered that was wrong. Even so, the momentary impression that the man was Mr Nakagawa was enough to restore some of his composure.

Seeing that Kosaku had quieted down, the man repeated his question more gently. 'Where did you come from?'

'Yugashima.' Kosaku spoke for the first time.

'Yugashima?' Apparently the man had not heard of Yugashima. 'Did you come here alone?' he asked.

'I came with Granny.'

'Where did your granny go?'

'Toyohashi.'

'What part of Toyohashi?'

'Mummy's place.'

'Where's Mummy's place?'

'Toyohashi.'

The men and women then conferred loudly among themselves, and one of them said, 'I don't know whether he's lost or tricked by a fox, but in any case we'd better take him to the police box.'

One of the women said, 'Come along, sonny. Let's walk,' and she took Kosaku's hand. Surrounded by the grown-ups, Kosaku started walking. He gradually settled down as he walked.

'Sonny, how come you're here?' the woman asked.

Kosaku himself had no idea why he had come to the middle of a paddyfield and he could not respond.

Just then, with a loud cry of 'Wah!', the woman hit Kosaku's back with all her strength. Kosaku was about to fall

85

forward, but she caught him with her other arm. 'The fox has certainly left him this time.' She spoke to the others, not to Kosaku.

As Kosaku was not sure when someone might hit him again, he now walked more warily on the path lit by the lanterns. The group speculated animatedly about whether one would walk such a distance when tricked by a fox. And indeed the path in the paddyfields seemed endless. Even Kosaku was surprised to learn he had walked so far.

By the time they reached a settlement where shops lined the street, Kosaku was exhausted and his legs were numb. He thought that once he entered town he must escape. These men and women kept referring to a 'police box', and Kosaku felt certain that if they were to take him to a police box he would never see Granny Onui or his mother again. And he would probably never return to Yugashima. And it would be terrible if that happened.

No, he must escape somehow. When the group surrounded a passer-by to ask directions to the police box, Kosaku slithered off into an alley, then immediately took a right turn. This time he was on a narrow road that went on endlessly. He ran frantically in the direction his feet were pointed, driven only by fear and the certainty that should he be caught by the police it would be a catastrophe.

The road became wider and there were now no shops, only residences. The gas lamps had been turned off here, and few people walked the dark street. Just about this time Kosaku began to cry softly again. He sobbed and he sniffled, and his legs moved at a mechanical pace. He walked on past many things. He passed a place with a wooden gate, and on the other side naked men washed two horses. He passed a shrine. In a building that looked like the administrative office of the shrine, he saw twenty or thirty men having a party, and the scene was like a frame on a slide film.

He went up a gentle slope and down the other side. As he walked, a few passers-by spoke to him but he ignored them, thinking they would either kidnap him or take him to the police box.

In time, even his crying became mechanical: three sobs,

one sniffle; three sobs, one sniffle, in perfect rhythm with his pace. And in his mind he continued to call, Granny! Granny! Granny!

He wasn't sure how far he had walked or how much time had passed when he collided head-on with someone coming towards him.

'Aren't you Ko-cha?' a woman asked. Kosaku was startled to hear a familiar voice. Then she asked again, 'Aren't you Ko-cha from Yugashima?'

'Granny!' Kosaku cried.

'It *is* Ko-cha.' The next moment warm palms pressed his cheeks. The hands abruptly grasped his shoulders. 'Ko-cha! Oh, Ko-cha!' the woman moaned. The next moment she was shouting, 'Mother! Father! I found Ko-cha!' Her tone sounded a bit like that of a rooster crowing in the early dawn.

He then heard footsteps running towards him. It was Toki, the maid. She fell on her knees in front of Kosaku and murmured, 'Young master.' Then she raised her voice and cried.

Kosaku felt that Toki always treated Sayoko well and was horrible to him, and in general he didn't like her much. Now, however, he almost felt affection for her. She kept hugging him, repeating, 'Stupid young master! Stupid young master!' as she rubbed her cheeks against his.

Then Granny Onui was there and Kosaku started walking again, this time with Granny Onui on one side and Toki on the other, holding his hands. The house was but a short distance away. As soon as Toki saw Kosaku home, she left. She went to find Kosaku's mother and father, who were still out searching.

After they entered the house Granny Onui sat Kosaku on the summer guest cushion and placed a box of sweets in front of him.

'Eat some. Eat some,' she said, using the local accent.

Sayoko, who had been sleeping alone in the next room, appeared just then. Apparently she had been forced to go to bed early because Kosaku was lost. Now she quietly sat beside him and gazed wide-eyed.

'Sayo-cha, you can't have any sweets,' Granny Onui announced. 'Unless you get lost, you don't get any. That's the way it is.' Meanwhile she kept plying Kosaku with the sweets.

As they were thus occupied, his mother and Toki returned. When Nanae entered the room and saw Kosaku her body sagged with relief. 'Ah, I'm so glad!' she sighed. Then her questions began. 'Ko-cha, where in the world did you go? And how did you manage to find your way home all by yourself?' Her tone was tinged with admiration and wonder.

'This is what a bright child is all about,' put in Granny Onui. 'No matter where he's left behind, he comes right home. Isn't that right, Ko-cha?'

'It's cruel for you to say I left him behind. But let's say no more about it tonight. Regardless of what happened, I'm very relieved. I'm so glad. I'm glad he was found.'

His mother brought sliced watermelon from the kitchen and, pushing aside the box of sweets, set down the melon.

Then his father arrived accompanied by a policeman. Apparently these two had learned that Kosaku was back only as they entered the house, and their voices rang loudly from the entrance. 'Oh my, oh my,' and 'Really? Is it true?' Kosaku was afraid the policeman would scold him, and he cringed and sat motionless. At length the policeman left, and Nanae and Granny Onui, who had gone out to the entrance with Shosaku, returned to the room.

'Well, Kosaku, I'm glad you found your way back. Where and how did you walk? Tell me,' Shosaku asked seriously.

But Kosaku did not know how to respond. He didn't know where to begin, and furthermore he was not sure how much of what had happened was a dream and how much was reality. He talked in fragments about walking through the paddyfields and about seeing the horses. Before he had related half of what he remembered, he was forced to go to bed.

But once in bed, Kosaku did not fall asleep until quite late. In the next room he heard Shosaku, Nanae and Granny Onui talking animatedly about his disappearance. Because he had returned safely and because Granny Onui and Kosaku were going back to Izu the next day, there was a harmonious feeling among them. He heard Granny Onui's laughter and he also heard his mother's laughter. Finally, after listening to that, he felt somehow relieved and before he knew it he fell into a deep sleep.

The next morning Kosaku went to the entrance to see his father off to work and to say goodbye.

'Next time will you come during the New-Year holidays?' Shosaku asked.

Before Kosaku could reply, Granny Onui spoke for him. 'Our next visit will be next summer. Right, Ko-cha?'

Kosaku felt bad for his father and said softly, 'It's all right to come during the New-Year holidays.'

'Is that true?' Shosaku emphasized, then laughed. 'You mind Granny well and study hard.' Then he left.

About an hour later Kosaku and Granny Onui left with Nanae to go to the station. Granny Onui had awakened early and packed their luggage so it would be ready. Their baggage had increased tremendously since their arrival. There were quite a few presents for Kosaku, such as the crayons and notebooks his mother had purchased for him, but the major portion consisted of gifts for their neighbours in Yugashima.

A few days before their departure date Granny Onui had gone on an indiscriminate buying spree.

'This is a little expensive, but it can't be helped,' she had said as she bought undergarment kimono collars for Grandmother Tane and Great-Grandmother Shina of the Upper House. And, 'I don't have to buy a gift for that brat Mitsu, but, oh well, I'll get her something.' She eventually bought some glass-bead games for Mitsu. She also chose gifts for the hardware-shop people, for their next-door neighbour at Sadoya, for the doctor in the main house, and for various other families with whom she was on some sort of speaking terms. Naturally Kosaku's parents were also sending gifts, but Granny Onui wanted to distribute her own gifts to all the villagers she knew.

Kosaku was worried that no gift had been selected for Sakiko of the Upper House. Perhaps she had been forgotten. But he hesitated before asking Granny Onui. Another problem he felt more keenly was what to give his playmates, Yukio, Yoshie, Kameo and the others. Since there was no reason for Granny Onui to buy for them, Kosaku thought he might have to give his friends some of the crayons and pencils he had received.

When he remembered how the group of children had chased his carriage when he left Yugashima, and especially how Yukio had gritted his teeth and run all the way to the edge of Sunoko Bridge, Kosaku felt his chest constrict. He missed all his fighting mates and guessed how eagerly they all must be awaiting his return. Since they had seen him off so grandly and he had come all the way to Toyohashi, he felt he must somehow bring back something really special for them. Preoccupied with these thoughts just before departure, he suddenly felt discouraged. Surely the gifts he had received would not be enough?

When the jinricksha came to the house, Kosaku and Granny Onui rode in one vehicle, just as on arrival, and his mother rode in the other.

As Granny Onui was about to step up on the jinricksha, Sayoko suddenly ran out of the house and clung to Granny Onui's legs. 'Oh, Granny, I don't want you to go home!' she sobbed.

'Oh my!' Granny Onui crooned. For the first time since she had come to this house, she spoke to Sayoko in a loving tone.

Nanae, who sat in the front jinricksha, turned and said, 'Children are very sweet, aren't they, Granny? No matter how badly they're treated, they become attached to you.'

Granny Onui pretended not to hear.

Kosaku thought he should say goodbye to his sister. 'Sayo-cha!' he called. She had reverted to the same bashful behaviour she had shown when Kosaku arrived, and she now only looked up at him shyly and would not come near. Seeing her thus brought out Kosaku's brotherly love. He wished he had been kinder to her during his stay.

When the jinricksha started off Kosaku, supported between Granny Onui's legs, twisted round and waved at the maid Toki and at Sayoko, who stood by the house entrance.

He remained in this position until the two forms grew very small and he could no longer look back.

Directing his gaze ahead, Kosaku saw his mother being jostled in her jinricksha just as he and Granny Onui were in theirs. His mother had opened her parasol, and from Kosaku's vantage point he could see only her head and shoulders. She looked young and beautiful. He thought that in all of Izu there probably was not a single woman as splendid as his mother at that moment. He kept his eyes on her.

When the distance between the two jinricksha closed, Kosaku called out, 'Mummy!' His mother turned briefly and raised her right hand. Her serene face shaded by the pale-blue parasol looked even more beautiful than before.

'I'll come again at New Year!' Kosaku said, not knowing what else to say after he had gained her attention. Then close above his head, Granny Onui's voice said emphatically, 'We don't have to come. We'll eat our New-Year rice cakes in Yugashima, Ko-cha. Since you've been raised in Yugashima, city rice cakes won't taste good to you.'

When they reached the station, the jinricksha men lowered their bundles one at a time and piled them up in a corner of the waiting room.

Nanae said, 'There are seven pieces. One handbag, two suitcases and four furoshiki-kerchief bundles. Ko-cha, you remember this well, else you'll have trouble if Granny should forget.' And she warned Kosaku to check their number without fail each time they transferred conveyances.

'Umm,' Kosaku responded absent-mindedly. He was watching with amazement as the station attendant swept up all the bundles at once and carried them towards the train. He looked quite old to Kosaku, but he carried the many heavy bundles over both shoulders with ease.

Soon after they stepped on to the platform the eastbound train slid in.

'Ko-cha, be careful not to lose your clogs,' Granny Onui cautioned as she ascended the steps.

But this was Kosaku's second train ride and he felt like a veteran. He had no concern this time that he might lose his clogs. Furthermore, although his stay in Toyohashi had been

91

brief, he now could boast that he had lived in a big city and he felt he had taken on some of the air of a city person. A city boy did not rush on to a train or exclaim in a loud voice.

When they got on the train the attendant had already lined up their luggage on the overhead rack. Granny Onui handed the man the copper coin she had just received from Nanae. He thanked her and left the carriage. Kosaku felt that they had suddenly become wealthy. Ordinary people carried their own luggage, after all. Indeed, he felt all those in the carriage were looking at them now with admiration. Yes, no question about it. The way the passengers watched them now definitely was different from the curious stares they had drawn before when they boarded the train in Numazu.

When the whistle for departure sounded, Nanae, who stood near the train window, pushed her face into the car and said, 'Well then, Ko-cha, give my best regards to the folks in the Upper House. Take care of yourself. You too, Granny.'

She had added Granny Onui as an afterthought. Even so, Granny Onui responded graciously. 'Thank you for your hospitality. Thank you very much.' And she bowed many, many times.

Understandably, Kosaku felt sad at leaving his mother. When the train started off, he leaned out the window and waved. He decided he'd wave until he could no longer see his mother.

'Ko-cha, that's dangerous!' Granny Onui tried to pull him in. But Kosaku was reassured by her grasp and continued to lean out the window.

'Ko-cha, that's enough. Is there no end to it?' Finally Granny Onui pulled him forcibly back on to the seat.

After he settled down in his seat, Kosaku suddenly felt hungry. 'I'm hungry!' he said.

Granny Onui looked startled. 'What about breakfast? Didn't you eat?' she asked.

'I ate, but I'm hungry!'

'Of course. In Toyohashi we didn't get anything good to eat.'

Toyohashi receded in the distance. Kosaku became Granny Onui's child again, and Granny Onui became his sole protector.

4

It was twilight and a chill autumnal wind was blowing on the day Kosaku and Granny Onui returned to the village. They had stayed the night before at Numazu, left Numazu early in the morning, travelled on the small train to Ohito, where they visited Granny Onui's distant relative and ate lunch, and then boarded the carriage to come back to their beloved Yugashima.

Once in the carriage, Kosaku was continually aggravated by the slowness of the journey. Surely the carriage had moved much faster when he rode in it before? By the time the horses took a rest stop at Deguchi village, he was in a foul mood. When Granny Onui and the other women passengers spoke to him, he pouted, turned away and sulked.

From time to time Granny Onui spoke to him with concern. 'What's the matter, Ko-cha? After all, we're on our way home.' But most of the time she had other things on her mind. She bragged continuously to the other passengers about the stay in Toyohashi. 'It's very luxurious, you know. When we reached the station, a jinricksha took us all the way home. Without taking a single step, we arrived right in front of the house. And then there's this thing called a gas light, a contraption that lights the front of the gate and, you know, the gasman comes to light it. Because it belongs to the family, most people would think the family would have to light it. But that's not the case at all; they take the trouble to come and light it for the family. And of course, you know, it's not free. Each month they have to pay a lot of money. Poor people couldn't make it in the city.'

Granny Onui chattered on and on about the things she had seen and heard in Toyohashi. She talked about the Wakamatsu-en confectioner's, which sent a salesman with a box of samples to take orders for sweets every morning. She talked about the Takashigahara army-training field and the Toyokara Inari Temple which Nanae had taken her to see. Her revelations continued one after another and were apparently endless.

At last one woman got a word in. 'Is Toyohashi larger than Mishima?' she asked.

At this Granny Onui responded with the energy of one in a tantrum, and with a facial expression that said country bumpkins are a truly impossible lot. 'Is there an army division in Mishima?' she demanded. 'Even Shizuoka only has a regiment. Now, isn't that so? Toyohashi has an army division. An army division is a matter of many regiments gathered together. If you think of just that one thing, you must know that Toyohashi would cry if you tried to compare it to Mishima. Isn't that so, Ko-cha?' As Granny Onui rattled on in this manner, Kosaku couldn't help but agree.

After the carriage passed Aohane, its progress was slowed still more by an incline that quickly forced the horses to a walk. Kosaku watched with frustration as the animals laboured on, their tails swinging back and forth. He felt he might do better to leave the carriage and run the rest of the way home.

When they came into Kadonohara, they could see the storehouse wall of the Ishimori house, small and white at the foot of the mountains. Kosaku crouched low until they passed beyond Kadonohara. Why he did this, he did not fully understand. He only knew that his uncle the principal and his aunt with the black teeth might come out of the Ishimori house and speak to him, and if that should happen he could not bear the embarrassment.

After they left Kadonohara and entered Ichiyama, Kosaku stood up and said, 'Granny, we'll be getting off soon.'

94

'I know that, sonny. Sit down or you'll hurt yourself.' No sooner had she spoken than Kosaku staggered and fell into the lap of the person seated in front of him.

'See, I told you so,' said Granny Onui; and so saying, she too stood up and fell. 'These are mean-tempered horses,' she remarked.

'They are not mean-tempered,' the driver retorted without diverting his eyes from the road.

'In Toyohashi there's not a single horse like these,' Granny Onui spat back.

'Even in Toyohashi they have carriages, don't they? There must be a lot worse horses there,' the driver said.

'I didn't see any.'

'I don't believe you.'

'In a city with an army division you'd never see skinny horses like these. You should feed them a lot better.'

'What!' The driver, Roku-san, turned with a flushed face and glared at Granny Onui, then cracked the whip on his horses. The horses began to run. The whip bore down relentlessly and they ran faster. In a twinkling they shot up the gentle incline of Ichiyama and drew a wide curve beside the farmhouse with the water wheel.

Then Kosaku saw it, saw what he had waited and waited to see. The Nagano River, Yugashima village, the greenery around the homes and the encircling trees, the white highway, and the ridges of Mt. Amagi.

'Yaiih!' Kosaku shouted and stood up.

Granny Onui said something, but Kosaku did not hear. The carriage rolled over Sunoko Bridge and up the final hill to the carriage stop. Two or three bundles fell off the seat. Roku-san blew the trumpet very, very loudly. Simultaneously, the wind blew in. It was a cold, clean autumn wind unlike any wind even imaginable in Toyohashi.

When they arrived at the stop, Kosaku was the first to leave the carriage. A knot of village children, all preschoolers, stood near the roots of the cherry tree and stared in his direction. No one else was in sight. Then Kosaku saw some adults on the hilly road of the old highway, alerted to the carriage's arrival by Roku-san's trumpet. Several neigh-

95

bourhood women came down the hill in a mad dash as if on their way to a fire. Kosaku himself wanted to run. The other way. Home.

But Granny Onui said, 'Ko-cha, please wait.' And he waited. Granny Onui had Roku-san lower her luggage to the ground, then she too stood beside the bundles and waited.

Soon Grandmother from the Upper House arrived, panting, and said, 'Oh my, oh my, welcome home. Such a long distance. Oh my. . . .' She spoke as if they had returned from foreign lands.

Possibly because they had not seen each other for a while, the neighbours who came to meet them also exchanged extremely polite greetings with Granny Onui. 'How good that you are in good health,' or, 'I pray that you favour us with your goodwill again.' They said these things as though they were meeting for the first time. After that, without exception, they stared at the luggage by Granny Onui's feet.

Granny Onui responded in a somewhat lofty manner, as if the trip to Toyohashi had raised her rank. 'It's good to hear that you are all well. Have there been any changes in the village?'

'The blacksmith's wife had twins,' one neighbour reported.

'Oh, my! I'm shocked.' Granny Onui feigned an exaggeratedly astonished expression, such as she had never shown in Toyohashi, and added, 'Such a stupid wife. That bitch once said spiteful things to me! Divine retribution is a frightening thing.'

'Then the sake brewer's dog bit Take-san, the errand boy at the village office,' another reported.

'Oh, my goodness!' Granny Onui said. Now she assumed a more judicial expression. 'If you keep a good-for-nothing dog, you cause trouble for others. They must have learned their lesson at the sake brewer's place.'

Just then first-former Heiichi, from the sweet shop, pushed his way past the adults and said, 'The persimmon tree fell over – from its roots.' The boy had slipped in unnoticed among the adults.

'The persimmon tree? Whose persimmon tree?'

'The persimmon tree at Ko-cha's place.'

'Oh, my goodness!' Granny Onui listened attentively. 'The one by the stream or on the other side?'

'The one by the stream.'

'If it's the one by the stream, then it's the sweet persimmon. Why did it fall over?'

'I don't know.'

'If that tree toppled, it's terrible. It's Ko-cha's favourite persimmon. Say, you – did you climb it and make it topple over?'

'I don't know anything about it.' Heiichi pulled back.

'Well, in any case you must go home and rest now,' said Grandmother of the Upper House as she picked up a piece of luggage. Imitating her, the others reached for the rest of the bundles, some quarrelling over a bundle as if it had become a point of honour to bear away a piece of the luggage. Those left without baggage to carry latched on to Granny Onui's parasol and her handbag. Thus the group of about ten people proceeded towards the storehouse.

Heiichi ran ahead, stopping now and then to look skyward and shout, 'Ko-cha is home! Ko-cha is home!' in a voice loud enough to inform the entire village.

Kosaku was angry with Heiichi for this. As it was, he had strangely mixed feelings at finding himself home after such a long time. His heart glowed with every familiar sight, yet at the same time he felt self-conscious about it all. The villagers' faces, the homes on the hillside, the stream, the weeds that grew along the stream as if to cover it, the stones – Kosaku felt love for all of them, but he could not express his feelings.

At Heiichi's shouts, the children appeared out of nowhere. But they did not draw near Kosaku. They were all his playmates, but they gathered at a distance as if on guard. Kosaku, for his part, did not approach his friends. Instead he stayed with the adults and entered the storehouse. When he was inside he heard a chorus of voices chanting, 'Ko-cha, let's play. Ko-cha, let's play.' He recognized several voices in that chorus. Just listening, he could tell exactly who was outside.

When Kosaku had changed his clothes his grandmother of

the Upper House gave him sweets, and after eating them and drinking tea he ran outside. The children shrieked and scattered in all directions and Kosaku returned to the storehouse. The second time he went out the children were gone. The white summer twilight had fallen, and apparently they had all gone home for dinner. Kosaku decided to go to the Upper House. He wanted to see Sakiko to tell her about Toyohashi, but there were so many things to say. He wondered where in the world he should start.

He climbed the stone steps of the Upper House without hesitation, but for some reason found it difficult to enter the house. The only one there whom he'd seen so far was Grandmother, and he had a sinking sensation at the thought that the others might all speak to him at once. Thus he did not enter. Instead he climbed the arbor vitae tree beside the entrance. From there he could hear his grandmother and Sakiko talking inside the house. He could also hear his grandfather's voice. He heard them say 'Granny Onui' and 'Ko-cha'. Apparently his grandmother was telling them about the travellers' return.

At length the front door opened suddenly and Sakiko stepped out. She softly hummed a tune as she went down the stone steps. Then she turned abruptly and said, 'Who's that up there?' Kosaku said nothing.

'Who in the world are you? Come down, now. Imagine climbing up the tree in the dark like this!' Then she repeated, 'Come down,' this time in her firm teacher's voice.

Kosaku began to come down the tree, and Sakiko looked startled. 'Is that you, Ko-cha?' she said more loudly. 'Ko-cha?'

'Umm.'

'What are you doing?'

Kosaku reached the ground and looked up at Sakiko for the first time in a long while. The twilight was deepening, but he could see her fair-complexioned face clearly. In that instant he wondered whether this was really Sakiko. She did not appear greatly altered, but there was something different about this Sakiko from the Sakiko he had known before going to Toyohashi.

'Why were you climbing the tree without even going into the house?'

Kosaku could find no reply.

'Now go into the house and tell everyone about Toyohashi. I'm going out for a little while, but Ko-cha, you go inside.'

'Ko-cha wants to go with you,' he said.

'No, you can't. Go in and say hello to your grandfather.'

'Ko-cha's going with you,' he insisted.

'No, you may not.' She spoke as though pushing him away.

'Where are you going?'

'It doesn't matter, does it?' Her voice now held an icy edge that Kosaku had never heard before.

Instinctively, he looked up at her. Then, as if she had become aware of her tone, Sakiko said, 'Oh, Ko-cha, you are such a coward.' Simultaneously, she pressed her palms against his cheeks and enveloped his face in her hands. 'Go inside. I'll be right back.' This time her voice was gentle.

'Umm,' he grunted. Then he pushed away her hands. 'I don't like the smell of face powder,' he said.

'Don't be silly. It's perfume.'

With that, she left him abruptly and tripped down the stairs; as soon as she was out in the dark road she turned right and walked briskly away.

That night Kosaku bathed and ate dinner at the Upper House. He was told that Granny Onui was exhausted from her trip and had gone to bed, and he played until late at the Upper House. Around ten o'clock his grandmother walked him back to the storehouse. Sakiko, who had left in the early evening, still had not returned.

Back in the storehouse, he saw that Granny Onui really was in bed. A dinner tray sent from the Upper House sat untouched beside her pillow. Kosaku breathed in the storehouse smell, and after his grandmother had placed his bedding beside Granny Onui's he went to bed. He had slept alone in Toyohashi and now he felt a little cramped sleeping beside Granny Onui again.

When the second term began in September, Kosaku went every night to be tutored by a new teacher named Enomoto, a graduate of a teacher-training college, who had just been hired by the Yugashima-district elementary school. Enomoto had board and lodging at Taniai-ryo Inn, the largest of the three hot-spring inns in the village; hence, every night after dinner, Kosaku went back to Taniai-ryo. According to Granny Onui, of all the teachers at Yugashima Elementary School – including Principal Morinoshin Ishimori – only Mr Enomoto, the new arrival, had formal teaching credentials. He had earned his degree from the college in Shizuoka, the prefectural capital, and that made him a very distinguished person indeed.

'You can rely on what this teacher tells you, Ko-cha. After all, he is a graduate of the training college. For all the airs your uncle from Kadonohara puts on because he's principal, he's no match for this new fellow. Your uncle never graduated from any college – just took a teacher's equivalency test.* Five out of every ten things he'll teach you will be wrong. And the same goes for Motoi Nakagawa. He talks about graduating from a Tokyo university, but how do we know what he was really doing at that university? Anyway, Ko-cha, remember that *your* teacher graduated from a teacher-training college – and not in the second department,† either. He graduated from the *real* college. This is the first time a teacher I approve of has come here!'

Granny Onui was most enthusiastic. Word soon spread throughout the village that Kosaku was being tutored every night by Mr Enomoto. Granny Onui told everyone she met that Kosaku would be going to university in the future, and therefore it was high time she started him on the way to becoming a proper scholar.

---

* A system devised in old Japan to deal with teacher shortages
† The first department of teacher-training college required two years of middle school after six years of elementary school for entrance, and students took a five-year course. Those in the second department entered the college after completing four or five years of high school, but their course was for only two years.

Mr Enomoto proved to be an extremely serious, ill-humoured teacher. Kosaku had to sit in front of him for two hours every night replying to questions, transcribing kanji characters, and writing compositions. However, Kosaku did not dislike his studies, because he felt that in being taught by a teacher who had graduated from teachers' college, he was becoming a superior child quite unlike the child he had been before. Nor did his classmates or the other village children seem to harbour ill feelings towards Kosaku for being tutored by Mr Enomoto. Rather they appeared to accept the notion that since Kosaku was going to college, this was simply something he had to do.

'Ko-cha, when are you going to the university?' From time to time some child would ask this question in a respectful tone. But Kosaku had no answer. He knew it would be some time far in the future. He still had years to go before completing elementary school, then he must go to middle school, then to a school at a higher level yet. Only after that would he go to the university.

When a child pressed persistently, Kosaku replied, 'It will be a long while yet.' And in fact it *would* be a long while.

What distressed Kosaku after the second quarter began was the rumour that spread among the village adults and then the schoolchildren, that Sakiko of the Upper House and Motoi Nakagawa were lovers.

'Something's-going-on-between-Sakiko-and-Motoi. Something's-going-on-between-Sakiko-and-Motoi.' It seemed whenever children met to play, they intoned those words like a jeering chant. Indeed, it was the fad among the children that autumn. When they went to gather earth-hornet* nests, when they played hide-and-seek, when they slid down the hill called Kanzabu on the other side of the river, they congregated in clusters and kept repeating it as if it were a folk song: 'There's-something-going-on-between-Sakiko-and-Motoi.'

Kosaku felt pained when he heard those chanting voices.

---

* A type of hornet that builds its hive in the earth. The baby hornets are considered delicacies and are eaten.

He felt that both he and Sakiko were hurt by the words.

Sometimes young men of the village asked Kosaku, 'Is it true that the young lady of the Upper House goes to visit Mr Nakagawa every night?' And among the young men this question was invariably attended by some vulgar innuendo. Kosaku also heard neighbourhood women gossiping about Sakiko and Motoi Nakagawa, but the women always lowered their voices if they saw Kosaku. He felt a violent antipathy towards these women. Even those he had liked until then, he now disliked.

Inevitably the rumours reached the Upper House and Granny Tane was deeply troubled. When she heard the children chanting, this grandmother who had never criticized anyone since the day she was born, who it seemed could only look inexpressibly sad and furrow her brow when deeply troubled, came out of the house to reprimand the tormentors.

'Now, now, stop that, you children,' she said as she approached the group. The children let out a loud cry and scattered, and the grandmother never caught them.

As a result of such demonstrations, the atmosphere at the Upper House became gloomy. Grandfather Bunta and Grandmother Tane were often observed in sombre discussion, and if Kosaku approached them at such times his grandmother said, 'Ko-cha, be a good boy and go away.' But he knew they were talking about Sakiko.

Meanwhile, the target of all this attention calmly continued to teach at the school. To be sure, Sakiko avoided being with Motoi Nakagawa at school, but after classes were over and it was time to go home, the two usually walked out the school gate together. And almost every day Nakagawa visited Sakiko in her upstairs room at the Upper House, where he drank the tea she served him and sometimes had dinner. At about eight o'clock he would go home to the detached cottage he rented at the sake brewer's house. (Grandfather Bunta had come from that house and therefore the family at the Upper House was closely related to the sake brewer's family.) And when Nakagawa left, Sakiko would walk with him to his lodgings, a distance of two blocks or so.

Once Kosaku met the two of them in front of the Upper House as he was coming home from a session with Mr Enomoto, and Sakiko said, 'Ko-cha, let's walk Mr Nakagawa home.'

Since it was night and he thought he would not be seen by the villagers, Kosaku decided he would go.

'Ko-cha, are you one of those who sing "Something's-going-on-between-Sakiko-and-Motoi"?' Sakiko asked, laughing.

'Uh-uh. 'Course not,' Kosaku replied.

Then Sakiko said, 'Well there really *is* something going on, so why shouldn't they say it? Right, Ko-cha? And this Mr Nakagawa – even though he's a man, he's getting nervous. Isn't that funny? If it were you, Ko-cha, it wouldn't bother you, would it?' She addressed Kosaku, but it was obvious her remarks were aimed at Nakagawa.

Nakagawa did not respond. Instead, he looked up into the sky and said, 'The stars are high tonight, aren't they?' Kosaku also looked up. The stars in truth looked far away.

When they reached Nakagawa's cottage, Sakiko told Kosaku and Nakagawa to wait outside. She then entered and turned on a light, made some rustling noises, and finally came back outside. 'I've laid out your bedding for you,' she said to Nakagawa. Kosaku noted an unusual buoyancy in all her words and actions.

After they left Nakagawa, Sakiko invited Kosaku to walk with her a short way further. Kosaku had seldom walked at night with Sakiko and recognized this as a special treat. He obediently fell into step behind her. The way she chose led to Nagano village. Kosaku was familiar with this road; not a single house would be seen until they reached Nagano. In summer, whenever he went to swim at Heibuchi, he flapped along the road in his straw sandals in the early-afternoon sunshine. However, he had not often walked here after dark.

'I don't play with you these days at all, do I, Ko-cha?' Sakiko said. 'Are you studying? This time you have to be number one.'

'Umm,' Kosaku nodded.

'You know, Mr Nakagawa is still studying even though he's already a teacher.'

'Umm.'

'You like him, don't you, Ko-cha?'

'Like what?'

'Mr Nakagawa.'

'Oh, you mean Mr Nakagawa. I don't like him,' Kosaku replied.

'You're lying. Ko-cha, you told me before that you liked him.'

'I don't like him.'

'Why are you being so petulant? You're not as sweet nowadays as you used to be. Tell me you like him. If you say you like him, I'll buy you a present. I'll be going to Numazu with Mr Nakagawa soon. We have two days' holiday at the end of this month, you know. That's when we'll go. Now say it. Do you like him? Mr Nakagawa?'

'I don't like him,' Kosaku replied.

But it was not true. What Kosaku didn't like was the way Sakiko brought Motoi Nakagawa into every conversation and kept talking about him.

'All right, then, you're being hateful, Ko-cha.'

She looked as if she might slap him, and Kosaku turned quickly and ran back in the direction they had just come.

He looked back after about fifty yards and saw her walking on alone. Her movements were serene and leisurely.

'Elder Sister!' he called to her, his voice slightly sing-song. After a few seconds she responded with a briefly raised right hand, then languidly turned round. Kosaku squatted on his heels and waited. She walked back very slowly, so that it was some time before the distance between them grew less.

At one point as she drew nearer, Kosaku suddenly had the impression that it was Nanae coming towards him, for Sakiko's walk appeared identical to that of his mother. This should not have seemed so strange, perhaps, since the two women were sisters, but even so, Kosaku was astonished.

'Look at you, crouching down like that. You're a man, aren't you? Stand up!' Sakiko said. Kosaku thought that even in the way she scolded him she was like his mother.

104

In November the shrine musicians came to the village. They were villagers from a hamlet about twenty-four miles distant, and for generations the shrine musicians who toured the Izu Peninsula had all come from this same hamlet. Usually six or seven toured with the group: there were two young men who wore the lion's head and danced, two comedians who danced and acted, and the rest were charged with playing the drum, flute and shamisen.* One or two women were always included among the performers.

The shrine musicians took many days to make their rounds in the village. They stopped at every house and played for a long time wherever they were paid a lot of money. Each day when school was over the children scurried off to follow the shrine musicians on their village rounds.

The children were restless in class when the musicians were in town. At the tootle of the flute or the tattoo of the drums, their souls were transported to the village streets. The musicians offered much the same performance at each house, but the children were not bored no matter how many times they watched. Now and then, the lion's head opened its mouth wide and charged at the children. Each time their fright was real, and they created a great stir trying to escape or falling down and crying.

Granny Onui tipped generously for these entertainments. In fact, the grandparents of the Upper House were astonished at the sums she gave. And for that reason the lion made a special trip to the second storey of the storehouse, trembled all over a few times, shook its head continuously, gnawed at the post by the stairs, then descended into the front yard and in general performed two or three times longer than at other homes. A man wearing a hyottoko† mask and a woman wearing a homely okame‡ exchanged insults and hit each other over the head with fans. Kosaku

---

* A three-stringed instrument played with a plectrum
† A comic male mask with puckered lips through which the performer puffs streamers meant to represent flames
‡ A fat-cheeked woman's mask

was pleased to see that more neighbours and children assembled in front of his own storehouse than anywhere else.

After the shrine musicians left, the children felt a great sense of anticlimax, as though an energizing demon had suddenly left their bodies. But before long they found a new pleasure: the autumn athletics meet.

The elementary-school athletics meet was to be held this year on a Sunday in mid-November. When talk of the meet began, the children were possessed by a perfect fever of anticipation. Even after school was out they stayed and played in the school grounds – not because they had to practise for the events or in any other way prepare for the meet, but simply because they were loath to leave the spot where the contests were to take place. What if something should happen here while they were playing elsewhere? That would be terrible. A cedar arch had to be made for the athletics meet. A flag had to be raised in the school grounds and seating had to be built. No one knew when these projects would begin, but the children felt it would be a calamity to miss a thing.

The first firm information about the athletics meet took the form of an announcement that the Nakakano sweet shop had accepted an order to make bean-cake buns to be distributed to all the students on the day of the meet.

'My family's going to make the manju buns,' second–former Kishichiro of the sweet-shop family blurted. 'The teacher came yesterday.'

That news spread among the children immediately, and for a while Kishichiro was regarded with unaccustomed respect. Several children began gathering in front of the Nakakano sweet shop each day, peering in to see if the manju buns were being made yet.

Then three days before the athletics meet, all kinds of exciting things started happening at once. The whole family at the sweet shop started making the manju buns. At school, many teachers went out to the yard, where a flurry of activity ensued. Motoi Nakagawa was in charge of making the cedar arch, for which Kosaku and his friends helped him cut branches at Mt. Ura. Mr Enomoto, Kosaku's tutor, took

106

charge of stretching banners round the yard, and Sakiko assisted him.

The cedar-arch project was the most popular among the students and many gathered round Nakagawa. When he ordered them to perform some task they cheerfully complied. Now and then Nakagawa and Sakiko stood together and talked, but now there was no jeering from the children. They were much too absorbed in the athletics meet to care that the young teachers had 'something going on'.

Kosaku could not sleep the night before the meet. It was just like the night before he left for Toyohashi; anticipation had put him in an unusual state of mind. He got up many times to go to the lavatory. It was a big task, going to the lavatory. He had to feel his way downstairs in the total darkness, push open the heavy storehouse door, go out into the yard, and make his way to the trunk of the plum tree. There was an outhouse to one side of the storehouse, but at night Kosaku always went to the plum tree. The third time he got up he sneezed, and Granny Onui rose and followed him with a neck scarf. On the way back from the plum tree she wrapped him in the scarf.

As soon as he got back into bed, Kosaku felt the urge to go outside again.

Granny Onui by now was exasperated. 'Well, then,' she said, 'I'll do some magic on you.' She sat up on her bedding and muttered a chant, then said, 'All right, Ko-cha, you're cured. Now you won't have to piddle any more. Now you won't have to go for some time – for two or three days.'

Two or three days. That was a little unsettling. In fact, it became a great worry for Kosaku. 'I'm going to check and see if I can't go any more,' he said.

'Don't. When you really have to go, Granny will break the spell.'

'What if you can't break it?'

'Of course I can.'

This conversation was repeated many times until Granny Onui dozed off, then Kosaku too fell asleep.

The next day Granny Onui and Kosaku overslept and were awakened by the children's voices calling, 'Ko-cha,

107

Ko-cha!' When Kosaku rubbed his eyes and remembered that this was the day of the athletics meet, he was out of bed and into his kimono in a flash. As he dashed down the stairs Granny Onui said something about breakfast, but Kosaku was not interested in breakfast. He scooped some water from the stream, dabbed his face and wiped it with his kimono sleeve, and without further ado went straight to the paddyfield to join his friends. Today the group went directly to school without dallying.

The school had undergone a complete transformation. The children felt as if they were guests somewhere as they passed under the cedar arch with its sign that read 'Autumn Athletics Meet'. Surely no other school in all of Japan could be so splendid? Beyond the arch they saw flags of many nations, all made by the children in the upper forms, strung vertically and horizontally about the grounds. The earth was swept clean, and in one corner of the yard were two seats, one made especially for the principal and the other for the village mayor. These men were to give out the prizes.

Kosaku and his friends thought it would not be right to run around before the meet began, so they grouped together quietly in one corner of the playground. Students from other hamlets also arrived earlier than usual and, in rapid succession, came through the arch.

But nothing happened for a long time. The meet was scheduled to start at nine o'clock, a full hour later than regular classes, and the wait seemed endless. Unlike the students, the teachers took their time arriving. Sakiko appeared in her usual clothes, but the male teachers all wore white sweatshirts and white caps with visors. Each time another teacher came through the arch the students let out a loud cry.

At nine o'clock Principal Ishimori took his place on the podium to perform the morning assembly. At that moment there was an explosion of rockets set off by the young men. The children remained standing to attention in the playground, moving only their heads to steal a look at the clear autumn sky where the smoke from the fireworks drew black lines that paled and then dissolved.

The sound of the fireworks brought a rush of villagers to the school. When the principal's talk ended the organ sounded from one corner of the playground and the students began walking to their designated places in time to the music. Sakiko played the organ. She wore a purple hakama skirt and moved her body rhythmically. Watching her, Kosaku thought how beautiful she looked.

Motoi Nakagawa was in charge of the programme. He used a megaphone to call the names of the participants, and Kosaku thought his voice must be resounding through the entire village. Sakiko had told him that Mr Nakagawa's voice was the best for this task, and now it seemed she was right. What's more, Nakagawa looked splendid and manly holding the megaphone and wearing those white trousers.

The athletics meet was divided into two parts, one in the morning and one in the afternoon. In Part One, Kosaku performed exercises and took part in the cap-taking contest. He was the first to lose his cap and he was glad that only a few villagers had arrived by then and his weakness was not observed by many. The members of the Upper House had not yet come, nor had Granny Onui.

By the time Part One was over, the family seats and the observers' seats were filled. Many students came with their teachers from the elementary school in the neighbouring village of Tsukigase. In addition, many parents from distant hamlets, holding the hands of toddlers dressed in their best kimonos, came through the arch and filled the yard.

Granny Onui joined his grandmother and other family members of the Upper House on one side of the families' seating area. Now and then Kosaku left his seat and went towards Granny Onui, only to turn back. He never went right up to her. For some reason he felt embarrassed to talk to Granny Onui, to his grandmother, or to Daizo on that day.

During the period after the first part ended and before the second part began, the students ate lunch. In the family section, too, the spectators sat on straw mats and spread out their lunches. Kosaku was eating seaweed-wrapped sushi when he saw Granny Onui out on the athletics field and

109

heading in his direction. She was bringing him something, no doubt. But when she was about midway across the field one of the teachers called out to her through the megaphone.

'Granny, you mustn't walk there!' The voice rang out all over the playground and was followed by a burst of laughter. Kosaku saw Granny Onui stop, look round, then continue walking towards him, her back slightly bent.

Again the amplified voice: 'Please don't walk across the athletics field. Go round the back of the family seating area.'

Granny Onui stopped once more, but this time she cupped her hand to her mouth and shouted something. Her words did not carry. Brazenly, she started walking again and kept on until she had crossed the sports field and reached the students' section. There she asked, 'Is Ko-cha here? Is Ko-cha here?'

Kosaku was mortified. He wished for a hole to crawl in. Seeing no escape, however, he straddled the rope and ran towards her.

'Ko-cha, here are some eggs for you,' she said.

'I don't want any eggs.'

'Of course you want some eggs.'

'Hurry up and go back! You know they get cross if you go into the sports area.'

'Don't worry. It doesn't matter. I pay my taxes.'

Granny Onui cut across the athletics field again, and returned to her seat. No voice stopped her this time, but Kosaku cringed all the while she was on the field. Such disgrace for a few boiled eggs. Boiled eggs were the last thing on his mind.

When Part Two began the young men's band struck up a drum roll. The atmosphere suddenly became light-hearted and, buoyed by a naval march, the contests resumed in a festive mood. Students, family members and young men from the village ran races. There was a special tug-of-war for the mothers. Kosaku entered many kinds of competition, but he never won a prize. Just once, he thought, he would like to have Granny Onui, his grandmother and other members of his family see him handed a prize by Principal Ishimori.

Shortly after three o'clock the popular long-distance race began. This race was judged at two age levels: third form and under, and fourth form and above. All students were expected to participate. Kosaku had absolutely no confidence that he might win. Whenever he started running he got a stitch in his side and ended up crouching by the side of the road.

On this day Kosaku met Sakiko near the toilets just before the race for the younger children was about to start.

'I'll give you this,' she said. 'Drink this. You can run well.' She placed three kaoru antacid pills on the palm of his hand and Kosaku took them.

As he was stripping down to his undershirt in preparation for the race, Granny Onui came to him and said, 'Ko-cha, if you get a side-ache, you stop running.' Then, 'There's no reason for you to run until you get a fever.'

Actually, whenever Kosaku overexerted himself he later ran a fever. The fever would be gone the next day, but it had happened many times.

For those in the third form and below the so-called long-distance race was not in fact any great distance. The participants left the school, passed the street by the Upper House and entered the Heibuchi road; but without turning off to Heibuchi they ran straight to Nagano village, and there circled an old pasania tree before heading back to the school.

When about fifty students were arrayed at the starting line, Motoi Nakagawa, who was to blow the whistle to signal the start of the race, approached Kosaku and spoke to him alone. 'Ko-cha, you come in number one. You run until you drop dead.'

Kosaku thought this was asking the impossible. His side was hurting already, and the race hadn't even started.

Yukio stood beside Kosaku with a towel round his head for a sweatband. His eyes were bright and his face tense. 'Rats!' he said. 'I have to pee again.' Yukio had made several trips to the bathroom in the last half-hour.

'Yot-chan, let's you and I run together, okay?' Kosaku spoke to Yoshie, who always seemed to come in last in every competition.

111

'Umm.' Yoshie nodded, then added, 'I have a toothache. I'm going home and have them fill my tooth with medicine. Let's go together.' So he planned to stop and have medicine put in his tooth during the race. Kosaku said nothing.

'On your marks, get set. . . .' Nakagawa's call seemed to penetrate every nerve in Kosaku's body. He was deeply stirred. He felt himself about to depart on an expedition to a distant land that lay beyond uncharted mountains and rivers. He must climb many mountains and cross many rivers, and the way would be strewn with hardships. All right then, he determined. I'll go. I'll go and endure all kinds of suffering. He raised his eyes towards the seats filled with people. The starting whistle blew and the students broke from the starting line in a stampede.

Kosaku followed Yukio, looking neither right nor left. He didn't know when he passed the family seating, ran through the arch, came out on to the road. His side was beginning to hurt dreadfully. As the runners neared the Upper House in a group, Kosaku saw his Grandfather Bunta by the roadside and ran towards him. 'My tummy hurts,' he complained.

'Your stomach hurts? A stomach-ache gets better if you run,' Bunta said with no softening of his usual expression. Having gained no sympathy from that quarter, Kosaku started running again. The distance between him and Yukio had increased, but Kosaku caught up quickly. They passed the sake brewer's house where Yoshie lived, but Kosaku could not see Yoshie anywhere nearby, probably because he was running last as usual.

At about this point some students stopped running and crouched by the roadside or started back towards the school. Kosaku and Yukio continued running. They passed the road leading to Heibuchi and started up the slope towards Nagano village.

Kosaku no longer felt the pain in his side. The kaoru medicine Sakiko had given him must be working. At that thought his legs seemed lighter and he felt he could run for ever. Meanwhile Yukio, without benefit of the kaoru, was beginning to flag.

'Ko-cha, I'm giving up. Let's give up,' he panted.

He would have stopped many times, but always Kosaku ran on silently and Yukio too kept running. At the edge of Nagano, however, Yukio abruptly crouched down in the middle of the road and Kosaku left him behind and ran on.

The drop-outs now increased rapidly in number. Many students stood at the roadside, third-years as well as second-years, and shouted encouragement as Kosaku ran by. Kosaku overtook first one runner then another. Each time he thought how well Sakiko's medicine was working. When he came near the turn-about point at the pasania tree, he met students already on their way back. The lead runner was a small second-former called Yoshihei, from Shinden. When he met Kosaku he stopped briefly and asked, 'How many pencils for first prize in the long-distance run?' He did not seem the least bit tired.

'I don't know.' Kosaku could barely gasp out an answer.

The second runner who came towards him was also a second-year, again from Shinden village, whose name Kosaku did not know. He too showed no signs of fatigue. As he brushed by Kosaku he said with a serious expression, 'Hello.'

The third runner was his classmate Kanematsu, and when Kanematsu saw Kosaku he suddenly stopped and said, 'I'm going back again. I dropped five sen somewhere between here and the pasania tree. When I checked a while ago right here, the money was in my obi sash. Will you help me find it?'

'Umm.' Although Kosaku nodded agreement he felt he could not spare the time. He marvelled that Kanematsu would give up the honour of being number three in the race in order to find a five-sen piece. Kanematsu began running back to the turn-about point with Kosaku. Kanematsu wore a kimono; apparently he had tied the money to his obi sash.

Kosaku saw Kanematsu looking at the ground as he ran. They soon met a group of several children running towards them, all panting painfully and wearing desperate expressions.

Kanematsu asked, 'Did any of you pick up a five-sen piece?' Nobody answered.

Shortly after that Kanematsu and Kosaku reached the pasania tree. The school janitor was standing beside the tree.

'You got here very early, Ko-cha. You're number eleven,' the man said. Then, seeing Kanematsu, he cried out in astonishment, 'Oh my, you again?'

'I lost my five sen,' Kanematsu said.

'Five sen! Stupid!'

The man suddenly turned serious and looked around his feet, then he and Kanematsu started to search the area. Kosaku meanwhile went round the pasania tree and started on the return run. The news that he was number eleven gave him renewed energy and he quickened his pace. Now he met many runners, all behind him in the race. In fact only some of them were still running; others openly walked.

At the Heibuchi road junction Kosaku passed three students seated on a log by the roadside. They looked exhausted. All three were visibly gasping for breath. Kosaku continued without resting. The kaoru medicine must still be working. In front of the sake brewery he overtook two more. They had lost all will to compete and were walking slowly.

Kosaku ran on past the road by the Upper House and then out on to the highway. Now the school gate loomed before him, now he was through the arch and Mitsu of the Upper House was jumping out from the sidelines yelling, 'Ko-cha! Ko-cha!'

A cheer like the sound of raging surf enveloped him. It seemed that all the spectators in the playground stood up at once, all straining their voices to urge him on. The band played, the flags fluttered, and the wind lifted the dust in whirlpools.

Kosaku reached the finish line and knew at that moment that the effects of the kaoru had ended. His vision blurred, he staggered, and everything about him seemed suddenly to recede far into the distance. He was barely aware of Sakiko catching him in her arms, laying him on his side on the ground, and removing his shirt.

'Ko-cha, you're number five. Now get hold of yourself.'

He watched Sakiko's face intently as she said this, and as his mind gradually cleared he understood that he was actually a winner in the long-distance race. It was impossible, yet it was true.

'Am I dreaming? Is this a dream?' he asked.

'Stop acting like a sleepwalker and get up.' Sakiko tugged at his hands and Kosaku stood.

Motoi Nakagawa came over and urged, 'Ko-cha, hurry and get your pencils.'

Kosaku went to Principal Ishimori to claim his prize. His uncle handed him the paper-wrapped award without a smile. Kosaku accepted reverently.

'Strange things do happen,' the principal said. 'It's probably going to rain. Write a letter to your father in Toyohashi and let him know you came in fifth. Don't make any mistakes in your writing.'

'Yes, sir,' Kosaku responded clearly, then withdrew.

When he returned to the storehouse that day, Granny Onui placed the precious pencils on the household altar and chanted fervently. Then she told Kosaku that they were making red rice* for him at the Upper House, and he must wait until it was ready even though he might be quite hungry.

'Everyone in the village must be astonished at how well you ran, sonny,' Granny Onui repeated many times as she poured and drank sake in celebration of his triumph.

The next day school was closed because everyone was tired after the athletics meet. Kosaku felt extremely proud of himself. Every villager he met on his way to the Upper House spoke to him.

Some complimented him straightforwardly: 'Well done, Ko-cha.'

Others were sarcastic: 'Strange things certainly do happen. Hope we don't have an earthquake.'

Everyone at the Upper House offered praise, but many agreed when his grandfather said, 'Just wait and see. Granny Onui will make a big fuss over this.'

Kosaku went to the Upper House many times that day.

---

* Red rice is made of azuki beans and glutinous rice. The azuki beans turn red as it is boiled. Red rice is used for celebrations and as a congratulatory gift.

Even Mitsu apparently discovered some respect for him; at any rate she wasn't quite as mean as usual.

In the afternoon Sakiko invited Kosaku to take a walk in the paddyfield. Normally he did not like to walk with Sakiko the teacher, but that day he didn't mind so much. The small fields were terraced like steps and descended from the side of the sake brewer's house to the ravine. Sakiko led the way down. Kosaku had no idea where they were going, but he followed silently. He did not care where they went; it was happiness enough to be with Sakiko.

The bottom paddyfield was strewn with strawstacks, and as they passed one of the stacks Motoi Nakagawa suddenly appeared.

Kosaku was startled, but Sakiko obviously was not. 'Did you wait long?' she said.

The three sat down, leaning against a stack. It was a spot just right for relaxation. The gentle November sun was low in the sky and the scene was wonderfully peaceful. When Motoi Nakagawa brought out some caramels, Sakiko pulled tangerines from her kimono sleeves. The tangerines were still small and green.

Kosaku left Nakagawa and Sakiko to pick red camellias by the cliff and to look at the birds that sang in the thicket. Although he played alone he was not bored. Sakiko and Motoi Nakagawa were chatting happily nearby. Kosaku was filled with contentment.

Once when Kosaku approached them, Sakiko called out, 'Ko-cha, come and sit here!'

'Uh-uh. I'll stand guard,' Kosaku replied.

Kosaku had nothing particular in mind when he said this, but it got a rise out of Sakiko.

'Oh, my!' she cried, and stood up abruptly.

Something told him she was about to chase him. He ran off, and just as he thought, she came after him. She caught him by his kimono sash as he was running up the second paddyfield. She was panting, and she held on to him until her breathing returned to normal. Then she said, 'So you were standing guard! I appreciate your doing that, but now please go home and get me some pickled scallions!'

116

'Pickled scallions?'

'That's right. I have such a craving for pickled scallions –
now dash home and get me some!'

Kosaku decided she was serious, so he complied. He went
to the Upper House and, without consulting anyone,
opened the kitchen cupboard, picked a few scallions from a
jar, and put them on a small plate. Then he returned to the
lowest paddyfield.

From that day Kosaku took on the role of Sakiko's bringer
of pickled scallions. When she called to him at school he
went home to get pickled scallions, and when they were on
their way to the communal bath together he took a detour
home to get pickled scallions. It was not just a few times that
this happened. But always Kosaku loyally carried out his
strange task.

Around the beginning of December the village gossips
began saying Sakiko was pregnant. In a normal year, after
the elementary-school athletics meet was over, the shrine
musicians had come and gone, and the village festival had
ended, a long, boring time began in the mountain villages of
Izu until the arrival of the New-Year festivities. That year,
however, the rumours about Sakiko kept all the adults in the
village abuzz. At the mention of the name Sakiko, the eyes of
the village women glittered and they pursed their lips, put
their heads together, and lowered their voices. Groups of
wives and young women could be seen all over the village.
Sakiko was their only topic of conversation as they washed
their radishes in the stream and as they walked at night to
the communal baths in the ravine.

The men handled it a bit differently. They harshly and
specifically denounced Motoi Nakagawa and left Sakiko out
of it. The young men declared in agitation that Nakagawa
should be forced to stop teaching, if not banished from the
village. Only the elders, men and women over the age of
fifty, mentioned no names. Instead they said such things as
'It is a difficult situation,' or 'There must be some way to
resolve this harmoniously,' as they knit their brows and
conferred sagaciously. Kindred phrases seemed to become a
form of greeting among them. On the road they looked deep

117

into each other's eyes while the cold north wind blew, nodded, and said, 'Of course, of course,' or shook their heads and murmured, 'Not at all, not at all,' as they folded their arms or filled their tobacco holders.

In short, for all the adults in the village – young and old, men and women – talk of Sakiko and Motoi Nakagawa filled the tedious hours until the New Year.

The children also gossiped, but somehow they put little energy into it. Two months before, when they had chanted 'Something's-going-on-between-Sakiko-and-Nakagawa', they had more or less understood what they were saying, but the excitement over the rumoured pregnancy was confusing. There was always some village woman with a big belly – what was so remarkable about that in Sakiko's case? And in any event they could not think of an appropriate chant like 'Something's-going-on . . .' to fit the situation. Thus when they did gossip about Sakiko, they usually borrowed their parents' words.

Yukio said, 'They don't know what to do at the Upper House.'

Kameo said, 'Oh my, oh my! It has become such a burden. The bitch is pregnant.'

Sometimes, however, the children relieved the sobriety of these remarks by shouting randomly and jumping about.

Sakiko stopped teaching at the beginning of December and confined herself to her room in the Upper House. She seldom came downstairs; therefore Kosaku saw little of her. He continued to go to the Upper House every day to play, and he often gazed at the stairway from a distance. But he avoided going near, as if something frightening lurked on the second storey.

Only Grandmother Tane went upstairs from time to time, always with an unhappy, dark look that remained when she came down again. If Kosaku approached her at such a time she would say, 'Go away! Be a good boy.' Then her sad face would contort and her hands would wave violently.

Grandfather Bunta became rather more difficult than usual, although Kosaku could not be sure Sakiko was the cause. Nowadays the old man remained glumly distracted.

118

He took to muttering to himself and rubbing the tip of his alcohol-reddened nose with the small folded towel he used in place of a handkerchief.

Even when Kosaku played with his friends he avoided going near any adults he saw talking together. He did not want to hear what they said about Sakiko.

The day before the winter holidays began, Principal Ishimori made a terse announcement at morning assembly that at the end of the current quarter Motoi Nakagawa would terminate his services in Yugashima and transfer to a school on the west coast of the peninsula. Motoi Nakagawa then ascended the podium and gave a farewell speech that was very much in character. He smiled throughout and said that there were many tangerine trees in the village where he was being posted. He told the children he would like them to come and visit. He would guide them to the tangerine groves and let them eat so many tangerines they would turn yellow. That was the content of his speech.

As he stepped down from the podium a murmur like a soft wind stirred through the student body. It was not a sound of talk or laughter. It was more like a collective involuntary sigh, and it rippled across the morning assembly area from one end to the other. Kosaku knew that every pupil standing to attention felt saddened. And no wonder. They all knew that Motoi Nakagawa was different from other teachers, and somehow their ally.

Kosaku shared the general sadness, but he also felt a certain relief. It occurred to him that with Motoi Nakagawa's departure Sakiko's position was certain to become easier. He did not understand how he had arrived at this insight, but he trusted it sincerely. If Nakagawa's departure meant an end to the villagers' verbal abuse of Sakiko, then it was for the best.

As Nakagawa descended from the podium Kosaku thought how noble he looked. Almost certainly he was making this sacrifice for Sakiko. This was true sacrifice – to leave of his own volition in order to save Sakiko. He would probably never come to this village again. Kosaku felt that he himself was the only person in the world who truly understood

119

Motoi Nakagawa. At that thought and the sweet sadness it occasioned, Kosaku's whole body trembled.

Later that day Kosaku learned from Granny Onui that Nakagawa and Sakiko were to be married early in the New Year.

'It's a complicated affair,' said Granny Onui. 'The usual procedure is for a woman to get married and then have a baby. But at the Upper House Sakiko has the child first and then they hurry up and get married. I haven't heard of many such cases.' Her words dripped with poison.

This was unexpected news for Kosaku, and it required some rethinking. It was one thing for Motoi Nakagawa to sacrifice himself for Sakiko and depart for a faraway place. It was another thing for Motoi Nakagawa to marry Sakiko and depart for a faraway place. If Sakiko married Nakagawa, she would go with him to his post on the west coast in the village with many tangerine groves. When Kosaku thought about that, everything seemed to go black. He felt foolish to have sympathized with Nakagawa. Not only was Nakagawa not a victim, he was a villain who was about to snatch Sakiko away.

It was impossible to imagine a life without Sakiko. True, Kosaku had not seen her for many days since she had stopped teaching, but it wasn't because she was not there. It was merely that she never left her room. But she was there – upstairs in the Upper House. And even though Kosaku couldn't actually see her he could go to the Upper House and play in a room below her room. Or he could look up at her room with its heavy, storehouse-style window when he played on the old highway in front of the Upper House.

With the arrival of the winter holiday the children grew restless and excited in anticipation of the New-Year festivities. They followed the young men into the woods as they gathered pine branches,* or swarmed around village women who washed the mortar and pestle to be used in pounding New-Year rice cakes. Kosaku also looked forward to the New Year, but his elation was moderated by a tinge of

---

* Pine branches are placed at the entrance of each home during the New-Year festivities to welcome the god who protects the rice and barley crops.

sadness. Soon after the festive season Sakiko would be married and leave the village.

In the event, however, Kosaku's fears proved groundless. After the New Year, Sakiko remained in her upstairs room as before, and he heard no more talk among the villagers about the wedding. The only change was that Nakagawa now came and went at the Upper House more openly. On New Year's Eve Nakagawa moved out of his lodgings at the sake brewer's and into the Upper House. There he behaved just as if he were a member of the family. He even partook of the traditional rice-cake soup* at the Upper House. After Nakagawa moved in, Sakiko began to come downstairs now and then. At such times Kosaku looked back and forth between her face and her swollen belly and wondered why her form was so altered since the time he last saw her.

One day Kosaku asked Granny Onui, 'When is Elder Sister Sakiko getting married?'

Granny Onui pursed her lips and replied, 'The wedding is over already.' Then, after a pause: 'They didn't even hold a reception, and they tell us the wedding is over. Granny has lived a very long time, but I've never heard of such a thing as this. Your grandmother at the Upper House must feel very small in public.'

Hearing that the wedding was over, Kosaku felt a sense of anticlimax. He had believed that Sakiko's marriage would bring great changes. There would be a big wedding and then Sakiko would be gone. Now he learned that the wedding was over and Sakiko was still here. He felt at once relieved and deflated.

The day before the third quarter began, Motoi Nakagawa piled his luggage on the carriage and left for his new post. Kosaku had warm feelings for him again because he left Sakiko behind. In fact Kosaku went to the carriage stop with his friends Yukio, Yoshie, Kameo and Shigeru to see Nakagawa off. Also at the carriage stop were Grandmother Tane, Daigo and Mitsu from the Upper House. Not a single adult

---

* On the first morning of the New Year, family members get together to eat a vegetable soup containing cakes made of pounded glutinous rice.

neighbour appeared, however. That night when Kosaku reported to Granny Onui that he had seen Motoi Nakagawa off at the carriage stop, she said, 'Granny and all the neighbours knew he was leaving, but we pretended not to know. They didn't have a reception after the wedding, so how in the world could we possibly address him as her husband!'

The omitted reception was not the only thing about Sakiko's wedding that Granny Onui found infuriating. It was her view that even for a 'sham of a wedding' involving family members only, Kosaku should have been invited.

'You are the proxy for your mother and father of Toyohashi, Ko-cha. It was wrong for them not to invite you.'

Whenever she touched on this subject Granny Onui became positively livid. Kosaku himself could not quite see what all the fuss was about. It seemed an exaggeration to say he should act as proxy for his parents when he was clearly too young to be invited to a wedding. He understood that as far as the Upper House was concerned, Bunta and Tane considered him only a grandchild, nothing more.

After Nakagawa left, the villagers no longer gossiped about Sakiko as much as before and when they did the former malevolence was gone. Sham wedding or no, the fact that Sakiko and Nakagawa had formalized their union made the villagers accept it and for the time being quieted their curiosity. But the children started chanting again. 'Sakiko-and-Nakagawa-katcha-katcha-katcha. They-got-married. Katcha-katcha-katcha.' When Kosaku heard their chant he felt foolish and hated the children who sang.

5

After the New Year the next event the children looked forward to was the 'horse speeding', which took place in April. On the other side of the small pass beyond Nagano was the village of Kamiomi, and on the near edge of that village was a small level area called Ikadaba. Here by long tradition amateur horse races were run every year at cherry-blossom time. No one called it horse racing: the popular term was 'horse speeding'. On horse-speeding day young men came from the ten surrounding villages to vie at racing their horses round the small Ikadaba course. The riders were village youths, and their mounts were workhorses. The pace of the competition was leisurely, with a field of three or four horses running round the course about once an hour, but a great number of spectators turned out for the event. They laid out straw mats to set up party areas, admired the cherry blossoms between races and, all in all, thoroughly enjoyed a day in the spring sunshine. Stalls were open to sell oden* and white-rice manju cakes. The food stalls were an established sideline for certain women of the villages, and almost every year the same women set up their shops. Beyond question it was a happy occasion for adults as well as for children.

In some ways, horse speeding held even greater appeal for

* A dish consisting of various types of fish cakes boiled together in soy sauce and kelp stock

123

the children than the Obon lantern festival or the New-Year holidays. It was the only topic of conversation among Kosaku and his friends after about the beginning of March. A young man called Kiyoshi, the second son of the village koya, or dyeing house, always took his horse to the races. At the end of March the children's gathering place was in front of the koya, and then when they played in the street they bounced and galloped and held invisible reins in imitation of mounted horsemen.

On the day of the horse speeding the children dressed in their good kimonos, with spending money wrapped in their obis, and went to school prepared to go directly to the racing field as soon as classes were over. Even the school made special allowances on that day: classes met for only two hours in the morning and everyone had the rest of the day off.

Kosaku and the other young boys of Yugashima gathered in one corner of the school grounds after classes were over and wasted no time in leaving. They ran to Nagano in one dash and, after passing through the village, ran again without pause to Kokushi Pass, leaving a cloud of dust behind them along the highway and scrambling in single file up a road on the slope of the mountain. They ran in a kind of desperation and with but a single thought: they must reach Ikadaba before the horse speeding was over.

Even so, when Kosaku and his friends reached the top of Kokushi Pass they paused to rest. The sides of the mountains near the pass were covered with miscanthus grass, which grew in some spots to heights of one or two feet. In other spots the ground was still blackened from the New-Year mountain fires, deliberately started so that fresh sprouts would grow. Where the miscanthus grew tall, it glittered silvery grey and from a distance looked like elephant skin. This was the area known to the villagers as kayaba, or 'miscanthus place'.

Kosaku and his friends now sank into the tall grass and struggled to catch their breath after the long run. This took some time. From where they lay they could see the mountains of Izu spread out before them, their peaks numerous beyond imagination, overlapping and receding range behind

124

range into the distant mist. And further still, the blue, snow-capped Mt. Fuji floated in the sky like a shining toy.

After he caught his breath, Yukio shouted, 'Come on, let's run!'

In response, ten children stood up at once. Some got up clutching their sides, but their faces showed that no side-ache would keep them from the horse speeding. They sprang out of the grass like locusts flying out of a paddyfield, and once on the highway again, they thundered down the slope towards Ikadaba.

About two hundred yards down the pass Kosaku heard a din of human voices, muffled yet forceful, like the noise of the surf. He was sure the horses had started off just then and the spectators' roar signified the beginning of a race. The stop at the pass had caused them to miss some great excitement, he thought, and he frantically increased his speed. The others apparently felt the same, for they all forgot their companions and plunged ahead pell mell, every man for himself.

At last the racing area came into view. In a small, level clearing on the plateau, where the hilly road ended its descent from the pass, they could see many people moving round the edges of the deserted racecourse, some drinking sake, others walking about from party to party. Three or four food stalls were in operation, standing amid cherry trees in full bloom.

Kosaku and his companions fell silent as they entered the area of shifting bodies. There was so much to see that they had no time for talk. Even so, they stayed together as they threaded their way through the crowd.

'Konnyaku!'* They had reached the front of an oden stall when Yukio called out in a brassy voice. He turned to his friends to test their enthusiasm. No response. The sight of konnyaku boiling in a steaming pot made their mouths water, but perhaps something even better awaited them at the next stall.

Yukio again looked at his friends. 'I'm going to buy some konnyaku,' he said, this time as if he were making a pro-

---

* A paste food made from a vegetable-root flour

nouncement. 'Missis, I'd like some konnyaku,' he said to the old woman who ran the shop.

'Yes, yes.' The woman produced a long skewer, pierced a single triangular morsel of konnyaku, and deftly deposited it in a bowl of miso. 'Yes, yes, here you are,' she said. 'Give me your money. You can't have it if you won't give me money.'

Yukio bent his head. 'Maybe I'll change my mind,' he said.

'What are you saying, little boy!' The old woman pouted.

'The konnyaku at the other stall is bigger,' Yukio said. He was right. At another, similar oden stall near the entrance to the racing area, the konnyaku was definitely larger.

The old woman glowered and said, 'You little bed-wetter! Whose family do you belong to?'

'The general store,' the other children chorused.

'The general store? You mean the general store in Yugashima? No wonder you're such a cheeky brat! When you go home, you tell your father this – when I bought a packet of nails in his shop recently, it was three short!'

Then she looked round at the other children and suddenly extended the skewer towards Kosaku. 'Here, sonny, I give you this. I give it to you for nothing.'

Kosaku was startled. He drew back a few steps. Then Yoshie of the sake brewer's family extended his hand, took the skewer from the old woman's grasp, and brought it to Kosaku.

'She said she'll *give* it to you! So take it!' Yoshie urged. Kosaku, still unsure, drew back again and the konnyaku Yoshie was holding came off the skewer and fell to the ground.

Kosaku and his friends proceeded from stall to stall. There were sellers of boiled squid and sellers of white-rice dumplings. In the end, Yukio bought boiled squid, and Yoshie and Kosaku bought dumplings. After one purchase, none of them could buy anything more. This fact established, they remembered their original reason for coming: the horses and the horse speeding.

Several horses were tethered at a place not far from the crowded party area. Kosaku and his friends went to inspect the animals, first gazing solemnly at their long faces and then walking around to compare the long tails. Most years at least ten horses would be here, but this year for some reason there were not so many. That did not dampen the festivities, however, for the people did not expect a full day of continuous racing. They were quite satisfied to have four or five cherry trees in bloom and something like a horse race going on in the background now and then.

Kosaku and Yukio grew excited and attentive when Kiyoshi, the second son of the koya, brought his horse to the post. He was to compete with the horse of Tatsu-san, a plasterer from Omi, and Kosaku and his friends decided to cheer Kiyoshi-san on from seats on the north side of the course, where the crowd was sparse.

The start, usually the most difficult part of a race, went well on this occasion. The two horses broke from the starting line at the same time and entered the stretch running together. Shortly thereafter, however, Tatsu-san's horse suddenly stopped, reared, and blindly paddled its front hoofs as if running towards the sky. Tatsu-san immediately fell off its back. There was a roar from the spectators, and many left their parties and ran to the spot where the rider had fallen. When they saw Tatsu-san stand up, apparently uninjured, they all streamed back to their seats looking more bored than relieved.

Kiyoshi of the koya meanwhile completed his circuit of the track alone and then, as if that were not enough, rode round once again. Kosaku thought Kiyoshi-san looked very splendid. Even the adults, who normally spoke ill of him and considered him dissipated and lazy, praised Kiyoshi on that day. One old man said, 'If he decided to become a real jockey, that Kiyoshi could be the number-one jockey in Japan.'

Kosaku and his friends went round from one adult party to another, hoping to overhear such remarks. When they grew bored with that, they concentrated on the next race, or rather on one of the jockeys who was to run in the next race. This jockey wore fashionable, tight-fitting corduroy pants, held a leather whip in his hand, and looked eager for action. But as they followed him he merely went round the parties, drank a little sake here and there, and showed no signs of heading towards the starting post.

Then a young girl who worked as a maid at the hot-springs inn accosted Kosaku and asked, 'Ko-cha, is it true that Sakiko-san is about to give birth to a baby?'

'A baby?' Kosaku was confused. 'I don't know.' He shook his head. Then he asked his questioner: 'Is Elder Sister Sakiko going to have a baby?'

'I heard she started labour pains early this morning. Ko-cha, don't you know about this?'

Kosaku felt his heart pounding. 'I hadn't heard about it,' he said. It occurred to him that what the girl said was probably true. And if it was, that was terrible. Just why it was so terrible he couldn't be sure, but he felt certain that it meant something terrible was about to happen on this earth. 'A baby!' he whispered to himself. Why, then, he must get to Sakiko as soon as possible.

'Elder Sister Sakiko is having a baby,' he said to Yukio.

'What's a baby?' Yukio asked. Then he answered his own question, 'Oh, you mean an infant.'

No sooner had Kosaku responded, 'Umm,' than Yukio said, 'All right, let's go and see!' Eyes sparkling, he turned to ask the others whether they would rather go and watch Sakiko have a baby or stay here and see the horse speeding. Although they had all looked forward to the horse speeding for some time, the children were by now thoroughly disgusted with it, since it seemed to involve a lot more adult singing and dancing than anything else. They got similarly disgusted every year, but they always forgot their disgust after a year and remembered only the exciting moments.

'It's more fun to watch a baby being born,' said Heiichi of the sweet shop. 'I saw it happen once. The baby is born into a box.'

'That's a lie. No one has a baby in a box. They use a bathtub,' another said.

'It's not a lie. They use a box. I saw it,' Heiichi persisted.

Just then a shout went up. Three horses had left the starting line and three jockeys were standing up in their stirrups holding their whips high and continuously lashing at their mounts.

'It's a big race,' said an adult nearby. Kosaku heard the

remark and was somehow unimpressed.

When that race ended the children left without regrets. On the way home Kosaku felt impatient at the thought of seeing Sakiko. If they did not hurry, the baby might be born before they arrived. He wanted to see how Sakiko bore her baby and how the baby's face looked. He had not the slightest interest in other village babies but where Elder Sister Sakiko was concerned the situation was entirely different.

The children now ran earnestly up the same road they had so frantically run down two hours before, and at the top of the pass they again buried their bodies in the miscanthus field. Earlier, though, the air had been still. Now the miscanthus was continually whipped by a wind so fierce it seemed the very sunlight might be scattered by its force.

The sun continued to shine, but the air was extremely cold.

After their rest the boys formed a line and resumed their trek. When the wind gusted as they ran down the slope, they hunched over and crouched low to keep from being blown away.

The white spring dusk was beginning to close in on the road as they entered their own hamlet of Kubota.

When Kosaku saw the squat sake brewery where Yoshie lived and the old pasania tree beside it, he felt they had finally come home. Yoshie and the others apparently felt the same.

'I'm going to stop off at my house,' each boy said.

The only exception was Yukio, who stood in front of the brewery and glared. 'I thought we were all going to see the baby being born,' he said. 'Isn't that right, Ko-cha?' He looked to Kosaku for agreement.

Kosaku of course wanted to observe the birth, but he wasn't at all sure the others would be allowed to observe as well.

'Is everybody going?' he asked.

'Naturally.' Yukio's expression said it was understood.

Kosaku added a hint of doubt: 'I wonder if they'll let us all watch.'

'We could send out scouts and find out what's going on,' Yukio said.

The term 'scouts' seemed to fill them all with fresh vitality and to bring new sparkle to their eyes.

'I'm going to be a scout.' Heiichi of the sweet shop was the first to volunteer.

'Well then, you go ahead – reconnoitre and see if it's born or not.'

Thus dispatched by Yukio, Heiichi took off like a bolting horse, then steadied himself and headed at a more sedate pace towards the Upper House.

Kosaku was beginning to feel irritated at the way Yukio was treating Sakiko's confinement – rather as if it were a game. 'I'm going over there to see for myself,' he said. He started to walk away.

'No, no, that won't do,' Yukio said. 'You'll be caught right away. She didn't want us to see, so she made a point of having the baby while we were at the horse speeding.'

When he heard that, Kosaku thought it was a real possibility.

'Just try telling them you want to see the baby,' Yukio persisted. 'Grandma and Grandpa will beat you. They're all on guard.'

Kosaku could not think of a solution to this problem, so he stopped walking. 'Then what should we do?' he asked.

'We'll all sneak up to the Upper House, and when nobody's looking we'll climb the trees. From there we can peek into the upstairs room.'

Kosaku wasn't so sure the plan was feasible, but since it appeared Yukio was now in charge he saw no choice but to follow orders. He was angry, though, that Yukio was ignoring the fact that he, Kosaku, deserved special recognition if they were going to watch Sakiko's baby being born.

Heiichi returned, out of breath. 'It's born,' he panted.

'Born?' Yukio echoed.

'Umm . . .'

'How do you know?'

'I heard it crying.'

'Is that true?'

'Of course it's true. I went to reconnoitre in front of the Upper House and I heard a baby crying. And that's why I rushed back.'

Heiichi's report was fully believable – there was nothing obviously questionable about it. But Kosaku could not help protesting. He felt he must protest. He felt that Sakiko simply could not have given birth to a baby so quickly without his knowledge.

'It's not born yet,' he declared.

Ignoring Kosaku, Yukio said, 'That's okay. Even if it's born it's probably still in the box. Let's go and see that. C'mon, Heiichi, follow me. I'll climb a tree, and then you come back and report to Kosaku. Understand, *you're* not to climb any tree.'

Yukio ran off with Heiichi on his heels. Kosaku could have joined them, but he was suddenly overwhelmed with anxiety. Until that very moment he had felt himself driven to go to Sakiko and watch her bear her baby, but now he was feeling something quite different. He sat down on a rock by the roadside. Nearby, the other boys were arguing about which one would get to see the baby next. 'I'm next,' said one. 'No, it's my turn,' said another.

Finally Heiichi returned.

'Yuki-cha climbed a tree,' he reported in a whisper.

At that, Kosaku stood up. 'You can all come later. We're going alone first,' he said, and motioned for Heiichi to accompany him. He felt insecure without Heiichi. They began walking towards the Upper House. Kosaku did not want to run, partly because Heiichi was out of breath from playing messenger so many times, but more importantly because he, Kosaku, felt that something frightening awaited them.

When they came to the road by the Upper House, Heiichi stopped and said, 'Listen, Ko-cha, you can hear it can't you?'

Kosaku also stopped and strained his ears to listen. The village lay silent in the dusk. Not only could he hear no infant's cry, he could hear nothing at all.

'See? You can hear it, can't you?'

'Of course I can't hear it.'

'Listen. You can hear it, can't you?' Heiichi spoke impatiently. Then he removed his straw sandals, placed them together on the ground and lay down with one ear pressed to the sandals. After a bit, he turned his head and used the other

131

ear for a while, presumably listening for subtle sounds travelling along the ground. Kosaku thought it highly unlikely
that one would hear an infant's cry from such a position.

'There's no way you can hear a baby crying from there,
stupid,' Kosaku said.

'You can hear better like this,' Heiichi replied. Then, 'Wait!
I can hear it, I can hear it. It's wailing.' He stood up, looking
very solemn.

At the top of the stone steps leading to the Upper House,
Kosaku paused by the entrance and peered in. There was no
sound from inside and no sign of anything amiss. Kosaku
went round to the side yard.

Suddenly a sharp 'Shh!' came from above. He looked up
and saw Yukio clinging to a high branch of the persimmon
tree.

'Climb up here,' Yukio said softly.

Kosaku complied. After taking off his straw sandals and
inserting them in his obi sash, he hugged the rough tree
trunk with his hands and legs and made his way gradually
upwards to Yukio's perch.

But even from this lofty vantage he could see nothing. The
upstairs window was completely closed.

'I can't see a thing,' he said. Outwardly he complained,
but inwardly he was relieved. 'C'mon, let's get down.'

As Kosaku turned to descend he saw two boys in the
persimmon tree next to his and three others starting to climb
the yew tree by the stone stairs. Apparently they had all
followed quietly not far behind him and arrived without his
knowledge.

'Gosh, I can't see a thing,' said a loud voice from the
neighbouring persimmon tree. It was Heiichi.

Just then a scolding voice thundered from the vicinity of
the back door. 'What are you up to, you stupid brats!' It was
Grandfather Bunta's voice. Several small bodies immediately
started scrambling in the trees, each trying to be the first to
get down.

Heiichi slipped on his way down the persimmon tree,
landed hard on his rump, and set up an ear-shattering wail.
Kosaku and Yukio both reached the ground at about the time

132

Heiichi's shrieks began.

'Run!' Yukio shouted. Simultaneously, Kosaku felt himself grasped by the nape of the neck.

'Stupid!' His grandfather's voice came down on him in a fury and he felt a stinging slap on each cheek. Kosaku stood motionless, waiting for further punishment.

'Stupid! How many times have we told you not to climb the trees!' As Bunta spoke he rubbed the tip of his red nose with his towel. Because of the habitual surliness of his expression his face did not look greatly different now that he was angry. Nevertheless, Kosaku cringed. This was the first time Grandfather had caught him by the nape of the neck.

'I only wanted to see the baby,' Kosaku said softly, his lip trembling.

'Baby?'

'Didn't Elder Sister Sakiko have a baby?'

Bunta's face was contorted as he replied, 'It's not born yet. She's not a cat, and it's not as simple as a cat having a litter. Stupid!' Bunta repeated 'Stupid!' several times. Then he rapped Kosaku's forehead with two fingers.

Late that night Kosaku was awakened by the sound of Granny Onui getting up and rustling about. 'Granny, what are you doing?' he asked from his bed.

She glanced at him and said, 'The baby's about to be born and I'm just off. You stay in bed, sonny.' She was absorbed in getting dressed and clearly had no time for him.

Kosaku got up. 'I'm going too.' If that baby was going to be born at last, he definitely wished to see it.

'It's just on its way. You couldn't see it yet even if you did go. Be a good boy and stay in bed quietly, and if two babies come out I'll bring one home for Ko-cha.'

As Granny Onui spoke, she tucked up her kimono sleeves with a sash and wrapped her head in a towel to contain her hair. Seeing her dressed like this, Kosaku thought she looked most efficient. He sensed that a serious situation was developing at the Upper House.

'I want to go too.'

Granny Onui's voice turned firm. 'Children should not come to the birthing place. Be a good boy and wait patiently.

133

I'll let you see the baby tomorrow morning.' Then she added, 'She talks big, but she can't bear her baby without Granny's help.' With that she turned out the lamp and went down the stairs.

Alone in the dark storehouse, Kosaku was not particularly afraid. Still, the darkness seemed somehow different now that he knew an infant was about to be born. Soon after Granny Onui left he heard a rooster crow in the distance. Must be near dawn. He got out of bed and opened the heavy storehouse window a crack. It was still dark outside. He had never longed for the coming of morning as he did that night. How would the new infant look? When would he see it? He couldn't stand this waiting.

When the real dawn arrived, Kosaku had fallen asleep again.

It was a week later that Kosaku saw Sakiko's son for the first time. In the meantime he had given a great deal of thought to the strange way in which a small human being called a baby suddenly appeared in this world, and to Saki- ko's mysterious role in the advent of such a creature.

On the day of the birth and the following day, he had gone to the Upper House many times and had heard the faint cries of the newcomer, but no one allowed him to see it. His grandmother, his grandfather and others all said, 'Go away.' Indeed, Kosaku felt that everyone at the Upper House had suddenly become nastier since the baby was born.

On the fifth day, as Kosaku passed in front of the Upper House, Grandmother Tane saw him and called out, 'Do you want to see the baby, Ko-cha?'

'Who wants to see that!' he replied. Not only was he somewhat piqued at the delayed invitation but more import- antly he was suddenly overwhelmed by shyness. Faced with the prospect of actually meeting the infant, he didn't feel quite ready.

'Don't say that, Ko-cha,' Granny Tane said laughingly. 'Please come and look at it.'

'I don't want to see it.' That was all he could find to say. His facial expression and his tone of voice were serious.

134

On the day the baby was given the name Toshiyuki, Kosaku went to the Upper House on an errand for Granny Onui and entered by way of the garden. As he crossed the veranda, he saw Sakiko in the sitting room. She was holding the baby.

'Ko-cha!' Sakiko called, and held out her bundle towards him. He approached and peered fearfully. It was an exceedingly small creature and didn't look much like a human child. It couldn't talk to him; in fact he wasn't sure whether it was dead or alive.

'What! Is this a baby?' he blurted, and quickly stepped back a few paces. It made his flesh creep to look for any length of time.

'This is your cousin, Ko-cha.'

'I don't like that.'

'Like it or not, he's your cousin,' Sakiko said. Then she quickly rose and went upstairs. At that moment Kosaku felt certain that this baby had deprived him of Sakiko's love once and for all. She would never treat him as affectionately as before. Well, then, he wouldn't be nice to the baby, either.

At dinner that night Kosaku said, 'It's a funny-looking baby.'

Granny Onui responded, 'Of course. How could it be a nice-looking baby? It's the brat that bitch Sakiko bore.'

Granny Onui had gone to the birthing convinced that she would be the one to take up the baby when the time came, but that role had been taken over by a young midwife from Nishibira. For this reason Granny still harboured ill will towards mother and baby alike.

The mysterious disappearance of Shokichi, a fifth-form boy from a farming family in Otaki, occurred about twenty days after the horse-speeding celebration. It helped to make April of that year an extremely busy month for Kosaku and his friends.

The news threw the whole village into a turmoil. It was not clear where Shokichi was last seen, but from what various people reported, it seemed that he came home from school, said he was going to gather firewood at Mt. Ura, left

135

home alone and did not return.

The day after Shokichi's disappearance one of the villagers whispered that he might have been 'hidden by the gods'.* At the elementary school, too, the students were in an uproar over the incident. Even in the playground they contrived to group together in order to avoid becoming victims themselves.

Kosaku had never actually spoken to Shokichi. The missing boy was large for his age, rather slow-witted, a poor student. And although he was not particularly mischievous, Kosaku had thought he detected a malign glitter in his beady eyes. More importantly, about half a year before and for no apparent reason, Shokichi had approached Kosaku near the school gate and hit him on both cheeks. It was natural that Kosaku did not have fond feelings for this older boy who had so suddenly struck him without warning and walked away without a word. Therefore Kosaku was not particularly disturbed at the idea that Shokichi had been 'hidden by the gods'. It seemed appropriate that the gods should punish a boy who would do such an outrageous thing.

After school that day the children gathered in the paddy-field where the mustard was starting to bloom and talked earnestly about the mysterious ways of the gods, wholly forgetful of the kites they had been flying there daily since New Year. Most of the village adults had been gone since morning, searching in the mountains for Shokichi, and to those left behind, the village seemed silent and lonely. To pass the waiting hours the children decided to go to the Sekido house and observe the activities of the woman the villagers called Okane. The Sekido house was situated on a piece of land facing Kosaku's back door, and the woman Okane-san often came to the stream running beside Kosaku's family's land to wash dishes or clothes. She never spoke to anyone. When she was young she was known to have

---

* In the past, 'hidden by the gods' was a common speculation adduced to explain a child's disappearance. Sometimes the disappearance was specifically attributed to the tengu, a mythical demon said to live deep in the woods. The tengu has a red face, an extremely long nose, and wings. It is supposedly a creature possessed of powers innumerable and invincible.

been hidden by the gods and found a week later in a grove of trees near Mt. Amagi Pass. She had been mute ever since. Shokichi's disappearance had suddenly reminded the children of her existence.

As usual Heiichi of the sweet shop took on the role of scout. He scurried along the path through the paddyfields and presently was lost to view behind the water-wheel shack. Then, just about the time he might be expected to have reached the Sekido house, he returned, panting.

'Okane-san . . . just went out . . . walking . . . towards Nagano . . . carrying a sickle.' This report got the children's attention.

'I wonder what she's going to do at Nagano.'

'She's probably not going to Nagano, but to the mountain behind Koshin-san.'*

'What's she going to do at the mountain?'

'She was holding a sickle?'

'She brought her sickle so she could whack off his head!'

They all gasped at the last child's words. It was agreed that there must be some connection between Shokichi's absence and Okane-san's visit, with sickle in hand, to the mountains behind Koshin cairn.

About fifteen children took off down the road leading to Nagano. Yukio, Yoshie, Kameo, Shigeru and Kosaku were among them and Kosaku was in the lead. They discovered it was just as they had imagined: they sighted Okane-san, clad in her work clothes, turning to the right on to the road just this side of the cairn. The children followed her in single file on the narrow pass up the sloping mountain, careful to stay far enough behind that she would not see them but not so far that they would lose sight of her. Since the mountain was in fact low enough to be more aptly called a hill, they reached the top in no time at all.

Okane-san did not once look back. At the top she paused and took a deep breath as if to stretch her back, then quickly started down the other side of the mountain. The children

---

* A cairn dedicated to Shomen Kongo, a deity who is said to protect people against illness

did likewise. One first-year started to say he wanted to go home, but Yukio would not allow it.

Below, at the foot of the mountain, they saw a level area surrounded on all sides by other mountains and containing many paddyfields in which a veritable carpet of purple lotus and yellow mustard plants bloomed. This was the first time Kosaku had come here, and he was surprised to find such a beautiful place hidden in the mountains. The children stopped on the slope to watch Okane-san. For a time she simply stood amid the beautiful flowers and did nothing. Eventually she chose a place where lotus blossoms bloomed, sat down, took a riceball from her furoshiki kerchief, and started to eat.

'What a bore. She's eating her lunch,' Shigeru said in a pained voice.

'Isn't she going to call Shokichi and cut off his head?' Yukio asked. Then he said, 'I want you all to hide here and watch. Understand? Don't come out until I give you the signal.'

The children did as they were told. They all sat down and kept their eyes on Okane-san's small form as she silently ate her lunch. Kosaku was convinced that something was about to happen, something momentous, with Okane-san as the central figure. He just knew it. His chest swelled with anticipation, and his gaze never wavered as Okane-san brought the riceball to her mouth, lowered it, and chewed for a long time. After a long wait she brought the riceball to her mouth again. Judging from the pace of her movements, it would be quite a while before she finished her lunch.

But in his child's mind, Kosaku was not at all bored. It seemed reasonable to be watching Okane-san sitting amid the lotus flowers and peacefully eating her lunch in the spring sunshine with the mountains and fields silent all around.

'Let's go home,' one boy said.

'No, no,' said Kameo.

Then Heiichi said, 'There's an earth hornet's nest here. I'm going to poke at it, all right?' No sooner had he said this than he screeched. 'Ouch!'

Kosaku looked towards Heiichi and forgot about Okane-san. Hornets were circling above Heiichi's head like a swarm

138

of gnats.

He ran frantically down the mountainside, hard on the heels of Yoshie and Yukio, who half stumbled in their haste. Many others should have been following, but Kosaku had no time to pay attention to such details. He was aware only of the continual high-pitched buzzing of hornets.

'Cover yourself with your haori!'* someone shouted.

Kosaku grasped the back hem of his haori and pulled it up over his head.

The children streamed into the paddyfields and ran helter-skelter round the paths until someone spotted the small pass on the west side that led out of the clearing. This turned out to be the only road out of the basin that did not involve going over a mountain.

Kosaku tripped and fell twice on the paddyfield path, but he immediately picked himself up and ran on. When he finally reached a large field from which he could see part of the familiar road to Nagano, he calmed down enough to look ahead and behind. He was astonished. Just in front of him, Okane-san was running as hard as he was. Yoshie was in front of Okane-san, and several children were far ahead of Yoshie. Still further in front was Yukio, running for dear life.

Yukio stood panting after he finally reached the highway. Surrounding him were younger boys, also panting. Heiichi was screaming at the top of his lungs and pressing his hands against his forehead. He was not the only one so distressed. Two first-years were screeching as if they were in contest with Heiichi.

'Come, let me see,' Okane-san said, and grabbed Heiichi's sleeve. Kosaku's eyes widened. So, he thought, she can talk after all. When Heiichi became aware that it was Okane-san who had grabbed him, he took on a despairing look and began flailing his arms and legs and wailing even louder than before.

Okane-san pulled the struggling Heiichi towards her and, holding him in her arms, brought her mouth to his forehead.

---

* A short kimono jacket worn over a longer kimono

'Help!' Heiichi screamed with all the voice he could muster.

Kosaku heard Heiichi's cry but stood stock still.

After Okane-san had sucked several times at the angry welts on Heiichi's forehead she released him and said, 'You'll be all right now.' Then she slapped his forehead.

The freed Heiichi staggered back a few steps and fell on the ground landing on his rump. At the same time, all the other children started running towards home, each one afraid that he would be next if they loitered.

Shokichi – the boy who had been 'hidden by the gods' – was found the third evening after he disappeared. A villager from Shinden, a little over two miles from Yugashima, had passed a cedar grove on his way home from work in the fields and spotted the boy dazedly sitting on a log. That day the rescue parties from surrounding villages had carried their search deep into Mt. Amagi, but the cedar grove where Shokichi was found was at the foot of Mt. Amagi and unexpectedly close to the village. Shokichi was too weakened by hunger to walk by himself, so the Shinden villager had carried him on his back. For the time being the boy was confined at a farmer's home nearby, where he was to spend the night before being taken home to Otaki.

Shokichi was found at about five in the afternoon and by nightfall the news had spread throughout the surrounding villages. Kosaku heard about it from Granny Onui that night, and he was greatly excited and had a hard time sleeping.

The next morning Kosaku woke earlier than usual. He left his bed at the time Granny Onui got up and, after washing his face in the stream, went round the side of the main house and out to the old highway. There he met Yukio, who had come with a towel to wash his face at the stream. Yukio was not usually an early riser either, but he was as excited as Kosaku at the news that Shokichi had been found.

'Shall we go and see Shokichi?' Yukio asked.

'Umm, let's go,' Kosaku replied.

Owing to the early hour, they both still had plenty of time before breakfast. Anyway, if they ran they could reach

Shokichi's home in Otaki in about fifteen minutes.

As Kosaku and Yukio ran through Shuku, along the highway, they saw that the front doors of many homes were still closed. On their way, first one, then two children joined them and by the time they reached Shokichi's home there were five of them. They fanned out and walked all the way round the house, but saw no family member at the front or back. Four of the children ventured into the dirt entrance at the front and emerged from the back. No one home, they reported. A little later some Otaki children appeared and told them Shokichi had stayed the night in Shinden and was about to be carried home.

'Shall we go to Shinden?' Yukio asked.

The others agreed. Their numbers had now increased by two or three, so that it was a group of seven or eight children who set out towards Shinden on the Shimoda Highway. They ran and they walked. On the way, Kosaku recalled the smell of the miso soup Granny Onui made every morning and suddenly felt hungry.

As soon as they reached Shinden they went directly to the small farmhouse where Shokichi had slept. A large number of villagers were gathered in front of the house, housewives and children mingling with many men. Imitating the men, Yukio and Kosaku crouched on the roadside and waited for Shokichi to put in an appearance. They waited and they waited, but there was no sign of Shokichi. From time to time one or other of the adults went inside, then came out and crouched by the roadside again. While this was going on, several women brought out fresh riceballs. Each of the adults received one and started eating, but none were offered to the children. Yukio and Kosaku spent an extremely boring and unprofitable time watching the grown-ups eating riceballs. After a while the adults began talking about going to the cedar grove where Shokichi had been found, in order to give thanks for his recovery, and then coming back here to take him home. Kosaku and Yukio were disgusted by this kind of talk, but when a group of about ten grown-ups started to walk off, the two boys joined them.

It was quite a distance to the cedar grove. Trying not to

miss a single word, Kosaku and Yukio continually watched the faces of the adults and compared them. They could not keep up unless they ran.

Just before they reached the grove one man noticed Kosaku and Yukio and said, 'What are you two doing here?'

'Whose brats are you?' another man stopped and asked.

'We're from Kubota,' Yukio replied.

'Kubota?' The man sounded amazed. 'What about school? You stupid kids.' Then he shouted, 'Go home!'

Daunted by the man's hostility, Yukio and Kosaku left the group of adults and went to the side of the road. It was then they became aware for the first time that they were the only two children around. Those who had accompanied them to Shinden had somehow evaporated.

For want of alternatives, they decided to return to the farmhouse in Shinden. There they found many more adults gathered than before, all cramming their mouths with fresh riceballs or drinking tea, and all talking noisily. Although the two boys continued to mingle with the crowd, thoughts of school intruded. Perhaps it was about time for school to start. Or perhaps school had started hours ago. Kosaku wanted to say something about this to Yukio, but he was afraid.

Apparently Yukio, too, was worried. 'Even if teacher scolds me,' he said, 'it's more fun to see Shokichi-san who was hidden by the gods. Isn't that right, Ko-cha?'

'Of course. This is much better,' Kosaku replied. He had no confidence that this way was indeed better, but he felt he had to say it was. He and Yukio played together every day, rain or shine, no matter what happened, but this was the first time they had seconded each other's ideas in this way.

'He'll come out soon. Let's watch,' Yukio said.

'If we don't watch, we'll lose out,' Kosaku said. Then he added, 'It will be fun pretty soon. When Shokichi-san comes out, everybody will shout and run off.'

To this Yukio responded, 'They'll run away without their riceballs. And when they do, I'll eat them.'

When Yukio talked about riceballs, Kosaku's mouth watered. He was terribly hungry.

As time wore on, Kosaku felt a growing desperation. If he

142

turned up at school now, he would be in great trouble. He had never been late for school before. And it was not only school that worried him. Granny Onui would be frantic wondering where he'd gone. Yet he continued to sit on the ground with his arms folded round his knees. And Yukio remained in the same posture, his body shaking slightly but continuously. Neither one made any move to get up. For some reason it seemed too much trouble. They went on watching the adults eating their riceballs as if this were a most edifying sight.

From time to time, Yukio said such things as, 'That man ate three.'

Eventually the group of adults who had gone to the cedar groves to pray returned, and the crowd in front of the farmhouse suddenly increased.

'What are you two doing here?' one woman asked. 'What are you doing out of school?'

Because of their earlier experience with prying adults, Kosaku and Yukio reacted immediately. They stood up together.

'Let's go home,' said Kosaku, broaching the topic for the first time.

'Umm, let's go home,' Yukio replied.

They left the farmhouse and went out on to the highway. Indeed, they ran to the highway. But when they reached it they started walking leisurely. The sun was high above. They were hungry. And somehow the thought of school made their legs feel like lead. After a while they stopped talking and walked side by side in silence. When they had but one more earthen bridge* to cross before reaching Otaki, Yukio suddenly stopped short. 'Ooops,' he said, 'isn't that the principal coming this way?'

Kosaku panicked. The man rushing towards them indeed resembled his uncle, Principal Ishimori. That way of walking, with the body bent forward, was identical to his uncle. Kosaku and Yukio stood paralysed until the small form

* A bridge constructed of logs and covered with soil

approaching them seemed to grow a size larger.

'It *is* the principal!' said Yukio. He turned to Kosaku. 'What should we do?'

Kosaku had no idea what they should do. The road was a single track with a cliff on one side, a mountain on the other, and no hiding place in sight. If they continued walking they would inevitably come face to face with Principal Ishimori.

'What shall we do, Ko-cha? What shall we do?' Yukio was blubbering now, and his face was stiff with desperation. Kosaku saw but one option. They must turn back. He executed an abrupt about-face.

'Let's run,' he hissed.

'All right,' Yukio replied, and sprinted away.

Kosaku also ran. Soon he was gasping for breath and felt as though he had a knife in his side, but he continued to run. He told himself he couldn't stop no matter how much it hurt. Nevertheless, after a few hundred yards Yukio stopped and crouched down on the side of the road, and Kosaku did the same. After a short while they could see that the distance between them and Principal Ishimori was decreasing alarmingly. They stood up together and began running again, then, after a short distance, sat down again and rested by the roadside. Four or five stops later, Kosaku began feeling distinctly queasy.

'Yuki-cha, I don't feel so good,' he said.

Yukio, who until then had been almost too dispirited to talk, suddenly regained his animation. He pulled himself together and looked around like one resolved to confront fearlessly whatever hardships might befall.

He pointed a finger. 'Shall we hide there?'

He had spotted a cedar grove – not the same cedar grove as that where Shokichi had been found, of course, but a dense cedar grove. It was a fair distance ahead, on the cliff side of the road.

Kosaku was crouched down, but he immediately stood up. He must get to that grove. He must make himself walk that far. After about a hundred yards of walking and stumbling in Yukio's wake, he again hunched over on the roadside. The nausea overwhelmed him and he retched

144

repeatedly, a series of dry heaves. He forced himself to stand and walk again. He must catch up with Yukio. Ahead, he saw Yukio leaving the road. Yukio went rapidly into the cedars without looking back.

Finally, after incredible effort, Kosaku reached the first trees.

'Ko-cha!' Yukio called from somewhere within the grove. As soon as Kosaku entered the stand of trees that grew on a gentle slope leading down to a blue river, he was enveloped by cool air and felt the dampness of the ground through his straw sandals.

He grabbed on to a tree for support, then went on to the next tree by practically throwing himself at it, too weak to propel himself in any other way. After moving in this manner through many cedar trees, he slithered down and sat on the ground.

He felt faint. At times the surrounding cedar trunks appeared to be stretching straight to the heavens, at times they seemed to intertwine, at times they lost all distinguishable form. Kosaku closed his eyes. He felt more comfortable when he closed his eyes.

'Ko-cha!' He heard Yukio calling, but he couldn't answer.

'Ko-cha!' This time he heard the voice more clearly and opened his eyes to see Yukio's face looking down on him from somewhere near his head.

At this sight Kosaku felt much better, but when he raised his head he was dizzy.

'I don't feel well,' he complained. Yukio did not respond immediately, but simply continued to stare. Then Kosaku saw his face scrunch up. It looked as if he were about to yell. Then it seemed he was trying to hold back tears. Finally, Kosaku heard rustling sounds and Yukio disappeared. But he soon returned.

'The principal has gone by,' Yukio said. 'He's probably gone to get Shokichi-san.'

Kosaku thought that was most likely true. He sat up. He did not feel as sick as before. But he still did not feel up to walking. He was afraid if he tried to walk he would grow faint again. Yukio disappeared again and Kosaku felt insecure.

145

He tried to call out. 'Yuki-cha! Yuki-cha!' Even he could tell how weak his voice sounded.

After a while Yukio returned and said, in a lowered voice as if to hush him, 'Shokichi-san will pass by soon. Until they take Shokichi let's stay here, okay?' Then he left again.

Thereafter Yukio returned from time to time with reports about the situation on the road. 'The people of Otaki and the old man from the village office just passed by.' Or, 'Shokichi's older sister just brought the furoshiki kerchief.' Or, 'My mum just went by.'

He made many trips and gave many reports. Meanwhile, apart from the cold, Kosaku felt no particular discomfort as long as he lay stretched out listening to Yukio's sporadic reports. Indeed he would have been quite comfortable but for the fact that his kimono was thoroughly damp and he was becoming unbearably cold.

After his umpteenth trip Yukio said, 'A lot of people have come to get Shokichi-san. The carpenter, Yoshi-san, is carrying him on his back. They are resting on the roadside now. Come and see.'

But Kosaku had neither the strength nor the desire to see. He preferred to lie quietly.

Yukio's reports became more detailed. For instance, 'Hide-san, the head of the fire department, is carrying him on his back now,' or, 'Shokichi-san went to pee.' After each such report Yukio again left immediately. Finally he came back to say that Principal Ishimori had gone home. This time he added, 'Let's go home too.'

Kosaku sat up gamely, only to collapse on his back. It was still easier lying down, after all.

Yukio stood looking down at Kosaku for a long time, then suddenly started wailing loudly. To Kosaku, this came as a totally unexpected development. Yukio hardly ever cried out, even when they fought and tears rolled down his cheeks. Kosaku looked up in wonder. He could not understand why Yukio was crying so hard. He could not understand why Yukio was crying at all.

After Yukio was apparently cried out, he left without a word. And this time he did not come back in a hurry.

Eventually it dawned on Kosaku that Yukio was not coming back at all. Abruptly he stood up. It would be terrible to be left alone in such a place. He was dizzy when he stood. He began to walk randomly among the cedar trees.

He no longer felt nauseous, but his knees kept buckling. He threw himself from trunk to trunk on rubbery legs, just as when he had first entered the grove. He went on and on, but he did not reach the highway. Every now and then he clung to a tree and rested. At some point he began to cry, not so much out of sadness but simply because it seemed natural to cry in time to his lurching movements. He walked, then rested; walked, then rested. No matter which way he looked he saw only cedar trees. He had lost all sense of direction.

He had no notion of how much time passed. He grew exhausted with crying and fell silent. Soon night would fall. At that thought he was overcome by fear.

Then, unexpectedly, he heard many voices calling, 'Ko-cha, Ko-cha!' The voices sounded far away. He stood in the middle of the cedar grove, blankly listening. Gradually the voices grew louder. 'Ko-cha! Ko-cha!'

He remained silent. He wanted to answer, but words caught in his throat. Soon the voices faded away again. From then on, Kosaku began walking aimlessly among the trees. He could no longer think. He was no longer frightened or sad.

A great stretch of time passed before he again heard the voices. 'Ko-cha!' By now he was sitting by the trunk of a tree.

'Ko-cha!'

'Ko-cha!'

Kosaku sniffled, and sobbed softly. Then he heard a loud shout close by, 'Ko-cha!' and immediately after it, a resounding cry. 'He's here!' Soon there was the sound of many feet hurrying over the cool forest carpet. Kosaku listened in a half-dream state.

'Ko-cha!' This time as he heard his name, someone pulled him to his feet. He watched with unfocused eyes while several people surrounded him, chattering noisily. Then he felt himself being picked up and placed on someone's back.

His sense of unreality persisted for some time. They were taking him somewhere, and on the way someone force-fed

147

him sugar water. The sweet liquid revived him a bit, and for a long while he was aware of rocking rhythmically on somebody's back.

After what seemed a great distance, he tasted sugar water a second time. Now he drank all the sweetness from the small cup and spoke for the first time. 'I want more.' After a second cup of sugar water he kept his eyes open and noticed that the person carrying him was a young man of Kubota. They were about to enter Shuku from Otaki. Kosaku also noted that in addition to many adults, countless children followed, scampering to left and right. Yukio was one of the children. And walking beside Yukio was Yukio's father.

'You idiot!' the father kept saying, and each time he said it he rapped Yukio on the head. Probably for that reason, Yukio was the only one among the many children who looked dejected.

Kosaku closed his eyes when they entered Shuku. People stood in front of every house, and he felt unbearably self-conscious at the thought that they might speak to him. At length they entered the old highway from the new one. He saw several men and women standing in front of the Upper House, all neighbours whom he was accustomed to seeing every day.

Kosaku's bearer carried him into the Upper House and set him down at the entrance. Kosaku again closed his eyes because so many people were looking at him. With his eyes closed, he said, 'Sugar water, please.'

It was Granny Onui who fetched the sugar water. 'Here, Ko-cha, it's sweet, sweet warm water,' she said as she handed him a teacup. She added, 'You're not to play with that stupid Yukio any more.'

Just as Granny Onui spoke, Yukio's father came in dragging his son. 'Now, apologize,' he said.

Yukio quickly bobbed his head.

'Apologize some more!'

Grandmother Tane brought some sugar water to Yukio, who, fearing another scolding, looked round at the people's faces before accepting the cup. Then he cast sidelong glances at Kosaku as he drank.

148

At near dusk, after resting awhile at the Upper House, Kosaku was carried to the storehouse. That night many people dropped in to enquire after his health. Their voices reached him from downstairs: 'My, that was dangerous. How fortunate he wasn't kidnapped and that he got home safely.' Or, 'Ko-cha, of all people, hidden by the gods!' Some of the women even came upstairs to peer at him before they went home.

Principal Ishimori also called. Kosaku trembled in his bed when he realized his uncle was there. Principal Ishimori came upstairs and sat for a time beside Kosaku's pillow, drinking tea and saying nothing. At last he directed a remark to one of the other visitors. 'If he's this delicate,' he said, 'he'll have trouble in the future. Even the tengu* will have nothing to do with him because he would not be good to eat.' He thereupon stood up and left.

Kosaku slept soundly until the next afternoon. When he awoke he heard the clamour of children's voices outside the storehouse. He wanted to go out, but Granny Onui strictly forbade him to leave his bed. When she went downstairs, he crawled out of bed and looked out the small latticed window upon an animated scene of children jumping around in the late-spring paddyfields. When one of them spotted him, he told all the others and they stopped playing and started shouting, gathering under the window. Yukio was among the group. They stared up at Kosaku as if he were something amazing and exotic.

'Yuki-cha!' As soon as Kosaku called out, all the children fell back and rushed away. Even Yukio dashed off, shaking his head and running with all his might.

Kosaku spent the whole day in bed in the storehouse. From time to time he gazed at the small window, his eyes turned towards the sun-bathed paddyfields that were in such contrast to the shady interior where he lay.

---

* See p. 136

6

One day at the beginning of May, the school janitor came into the classroom during a lesson and whispered something to the teacher. The teacher nodded vigorously and, as soon as the janitor left the room, called Kosaku and Mitsu and told them to go home immediately.

Kosaku and Mitsu had never been treated like this before. What could have happened? The other students started a commotion, saying, 'Their great-grandmother has died,' or 'The granny in the storehouse has died.' The only reason for any students going home during the day was that someone in the family had died, and Kosaku believed it must be as his classmates said: either Great-Grandmother Oshina or Granny Onui had met with an accident.

Kosaku left the classroom promptly and ran to the school gate to wait for Mitsu. Before long she too came running, carrying her furoshiki bundle of schoolbooks, and wearing an expression of grave concern. Kosaku thought she looked rather pale, but perhaps it was only by contrast with the young green leaves on the trees near the gate.

'I wonder if Great-Grandmother has died,' Kosaku said.

Mitsu shook her head decisively. 'Great-Granny would not die. It must be Granny Onui,' she said.

At her mention of Granny Onui, Kosaku felt the blood leave his face. Could such a thing happen? How could Granny Onui disappear and leave him? He shot Mitsu a glance of pure hatred. 'Great-Granny, who should be dead by now, has finally died. That's what's happened,' he said.

He had suddenly lost the desire to run to the storehouse, however, so he decided to go to the Upper House first. No one was in sight in front of the Upper House, but when he opened the front door he knew immediately that something was amiss. Several neighbourhood housewives were there.

It was Yukio's mother who saw Kosaku and Mitsu first. She said, 'Your great-granny is dying. Hurry up and say goodbye to Granny.'

Kosaku felt a rush of relief. It was Great-Grandmother, after all. It wasn't Granny Onui. Cheered by this realization, he went quickly upstairs. There he found Grandfather Bunta, Grandmother Tane, Sakiko and many other relatives, men and women, all looking solemn and peering into the face of the aged woman who lay there on the bedding. Kosaku and Mitsu seated themselves near Granny Oshina's pillow.

'You two take a good look at Great-Granny's face,' Grandmother Tane said. Kosaku took a good look. Great-Granny's face appeared much as usual, he thought. At the best of times it looked more like a small, wizened fist than a human face.

'Did she die?' Kosaku asked.

'She's dying now. My goodness!' Grandmother Tane exclaimed.

'Not yet. She should die pretty soon,' Bunta said.

Although everyone in the room wore a solemn face, no one appeared to be the least bit sad. Rather, they all seemed to be waiting impatiently for Granny Oshina to breathe her last. Kosaku sat in silence for about ten minutes. Just when he felt he could bear it no longer, one of the women said, 'She just drew her last breath.'

With those words the atmosphere changed completely. People began moving a little. Grandfather and Grandmother took turns looking at Great-Granny's face and feeling for her pulse.

'She's gone. It was a peaceful death,' Tane proclaimed at last. Several people then stood up and went downstairs.

Kosaku found it hard to believe. In the span of a moment, his great-grandmother had passed from life to death. He also went downstairs and as the house grew noisier with the arrival of more and more neighbours, he soon went outside. He had intended to tell Granny Onui about Granny Oshina's death, but she was not at the storehouse. She had probably gone to the Upper-House kitchen and he simply had not noticed her.

Because of Great-Grandmother's death, he found himself with unexpected time on his hands. All his friends were still in class, and he could find nobody to play with. He sat on one of the stone steps at the storehouse and stared blankly for a long time. He knew that none of the adults in the crowded and lively Upper House would pay any attention to him.

After an extremely boring period in which he sat bathed in the gentle warmth of the May sunshine, he decided he should go and look at his great-grandmother's face once more in order to see with his own eyes that she was really dead. He went to the Upper House again. In the short while since he had left, many visitors had come to express their sympathy and offer their help, and the place was in turmoil.

Kosaku found Mitsu among the adults and said, 'Let's go and look at Great-Granny.'

Mitsu was uncharacteristically compliant. She nodded, and he preceded her upstairs. There they found things totally different from before. The Buddhist altar had been set up and covered with a white cloth, and smoke from numerous sticks of incense filled the room. Like the adult mourners, Kosaku and Mitsu removed the white-cloth covering from Great-Grandmother's face and moistened her lips with a piece of cotton. Granny Oshina now definitely looked dead. Her face had taken on an earthy colour and her lips were pressed together tightly.

After a while Kosaku said to Mitsu, 'Shall we go and play at my house?' Mitsu again nodded compliantly.

Kosaku returned to the storehouse with Mitsu running after him as if in pursuit. It had been some time since the two had played together. Until a year before, they had played every day, but around last summer that had changed. Since then Kosaku had played only with boys and Mitsu only with girls. Even before, however, they had not got along well and Kosaku thought everything Mitsu did was mean. Kosaku's life with Granny Onui had created a barrier between the 'Rear House' and the Upper House, and Mitsu's attitude towards Kosaku was a reflection of the hostility between the two households.

For some reason it was different on this day, though. When Kosaku suggested they transplant nandina plants, Mitsu quickly responded by fetching the hoe from the side of the storehouse. Together they dug up many young nandinas from the garden of the main house and replanted them in a corner by the water-wheel shack. Thereafter they played peaceably until Yukio and Kosaku's other friends came by after school. Mitsu did not argue with Kosaku, and Kosaku did not poke or push Mitsu.

The village children were rather buoyed by the death at the Upper House. They spent some time mimicking exchanges between the adults. 'The funeral will be on such and such a date,' they said, or 'Manju cakes will be given out at the reception,' or 'No, not manju cakes but sweet rice cakes.' They gathered by the storehouse to play, and from time to time someone went to the Upper House to check on the festivities.

At weddings, children participated in the eating of party food, but at funerals the adults only drank sake at the reception and the children were ignored. Therefore a funeral was not as appealing as a wedding, but it was better than no activity at all and enough to enliven their spirits. Besides, the funeral procession that carried the deceased's coffin to the graveyard at Mt. Kumano was always a thoroughly captivating adventure. When the children learned that the funeral for the great-grandmother of the Upper House would be held the next day, they began counting the hours until then. And to fill the intervening time, they played the funeral game, running around outside the Upper House and chanting 'Jam-bon, jam-bon' in approximation of sounds they had heard at funerals in the past.

Kosaku joined in the funeral game during the day, but in the evening Granny Onui dressed him in his good kimono and sent him to the Upper House. There he found Mitsu in the confusion of the kitchen, and they went upstairs together to the place where their great-grandmother's body

153

lay awaiting the chanting of the sutra. The crush of people upstairs made movement all but impossible. Morinoshin Ishimori was among those present.

Kosaku and Mitsu squeezed themselves in among the adults and waited with solemn faces for the sutra readings to begin. But nothing happened for a long time. When the priest finally arrived and began chanting, Kosaku and Mitsu crept into the storeroom and lay atop a pile of cushions. The house was crammed with people and lively with their chatter. In time, Kosaku fell asleep. When he wakened after an indeterminate period, he heard the Buddhist sutra he had been waiting for being chanted by the old women of the village. Their voices filled the house with a flowing rhythm.

He listened closely for some time until, from somewhere within the chanting voices, the face of his great-grandmother floated towards him. He recaptured in succession a variety of impressions about the Granny Oshina who had sat immobile as a wizened statue and had rarely come downstairs. He recalled how she always took Mitsu's side, how when she toasted ginko nuts she always gave Mitsu two at a time and him only one, how she gave the thick cushion to Mitsu and the thin one to him. He had thought her a horrid granny, but now for some reason his resentment was gone.

Kosaku climbed down from the pile of cushions and left the storeroom. The sitting room was as confused as a battlefield, with neighbourhood women endlessly coming and going with plates of food or sake bottles.

'Ko-cha, where have you been?' someone asked.

He was told to sit in a corner of the first-floor living room to eat his dinner. He picked up a large piece of burdock root with his chopsticks but found he had no appetite.

The housewives who had come to help also took seats and began to eat. As they ate, they talked about Great-Grandmother in terms that were neither criticism nor praise.

'There was no one as fortunate as Great-Granny. She came as a bride with halberds and a red-lacquer bath basin.'

'She could make only miso soup and she lived her whole life like a bride. Even so, she had a peaceful death.'

As Kosaku listened, he felt a great welling of sadness. It

154

was not quite a sadness about his great-grandmother's death, but without question it was a sadness somehow related to her death. He left the room and returned to the storeroom, where he remounted the pile of cushions. Soon he burst into tears, no longer able to stifle the sadness in his heart.

Presently, his crying became audible and Mitsu, who had been sleeping under the mountain of cushions, woke up.

At the same time, Sakiko peered into the storeroom and asked, 'What's wrong, Ko-cha? Did you have a nightmare? You had a nightmare, didn't you? Don't be so foolish.'

Kosaku cried even louder. A woman neighbour came into the storeroom and seconded Sakiko: 'You probably had a frightening dream.'

Granny Onui then arrived and said, 'Now, Ko-cha, let's go home so you can sleep.'

The mild night breeze of May was blowing in the street when Kosaku and Granny Onui left the Upper House to return to the storehouse. As they walked along the road, Granny Onui whispered, 'She was a good granny, but she finally died.' Then, after a silence: 'It is very painful.'

She stopped on the way and looked up at the stars twinkling in the velvet-black late-evening sky. Her back must have hurt, for she reached behind her and repeatedly thumped at her waist.

Kosaku could not know that this day had been one of the most painful of Granny Onui's life. True enough, she had taken Tatsunosuke away from his legal wife Shina, the woman who had died that day, and thus she had been a persecutor and Shina a victim. But when she followed custom and joined the other women working in the kitchen of the Upper House on the day of her victim's death only to feel the critical stares of many villagers – that was a source of deep pain to Granny Onui.

When they returned to the storehouse, both of them went to bed immediately. Granny Onui promptly began to snore, but Kosaku remained awake. He still felt some sadness about the death of his great-grandmother, although he had thought her unkind while she was alive.

Next morning when Kosaku awoke, Granny Onui was

155

preparing breakfast. She wore her best kimono with its sleeves tied up with a sash, and she told him she had already been to the Upper House and done some work.

'Your mummy's coming today,' she said.

'Mama?' Kosaku suddenly felt both elated and bewildered. Until this moment he had not even thought about his mother in connection with the death. 'Why is Mama coming?'

'She's coming for the funeral.'

Realizing he would see his mother that very day, Kosaku felt his chest swell mightily. He completely forgot about his lamentations of the night before and thought that since his mother was coming for the funeral it was a pity Granny Oshina had waited so long to die.

Kosaku stayed home from school again that day. He felt strangely self-conscious at staying home so openly while his friends still had to go to class. He even told Granny Onui that he wanted to go to school, too. She was greatly distressed.

'Who ever heard of a child going to school when his great-grandmother has just died! Today you'll wear your good kimono and you'll participate in the funeral,' she said with finality. Then she ordered him to stay and take care of the house until it was time to attend the funeral.

It was indeed a special day for Kosaku. It was the day of his great-grandmother's funeral and also the day that his mother was coming. He had to join in the funeral procession, and he also had to see his mother. Kosaku felt important and busy – so busy, he thought, that even if he had many bodies they would not be enough. Even so, the time dragged and he found himself spending a long while doing nothing. He played in front of the storehouse. From time to time he went to peek into the Upper House, which was now even more crowded with people than on the previous day. But no one there spoke to him, and when he realized that the situation would not change – that he was being shunned by the adult world – he turned back to the storehouse. Around noon Mitsu came with a nest of lacquer boxes filled with food for their lunch. They ate happily together, sustaining the atmosphere of mutual affection from the day before.

At about two o'clock, an hour before the funeral pro-

156

cession was to start, Nanae suddenly appeared. When she came, Kosaku and Mitsu were in front of the storehouse playing menko cards. Since the game was a fad among the boys but not the girls, Mitsu played poorly and Kosaku enjoyed taking the cards away from her. He was thus absorbed when he heard someone call, 'What are you doing?' Only then did he notice the woman standing beside him. 'Oh, how terrible!' she said. 'A child brought up in the country learns this type of thing.' Then she looked hard at Kosaku. 'I wonder if you've grown a bit.' Her first remarks had sounded cold and unkind, but now, Kosaku thought, she was looking at him with a warmth only a mother could show.

At Nanae's sudden appearance, Mitsu had drawn back several steps. Now she turned and ran away. Her departure went unremarked by Nanae, who said to Kosaku, 'Well, now, let's go inside and get you changed into your good kimono.'

Kosaku went with his mother without hesitation. Upstairs, Nanae searched here and there in the chest of drawers until she found Kosaku's good kimono. She then dressed him briskly while he stood in front of her and offered no resistance. Granny Onui was gentler when she dressed him, and he was a little afraid his mother might by her manner be expressing disapproval of him.

She said, 'Turn round the other way,' and 'Keep your arms out straight,' and, when she was finished, 'Now don't get dirty. And don't play menko cards. Do you understand?'

'Umm.'

'Don't say "umm", say "yes".'

'Yes.'

The funeral, which had been scheduled for three o'clock, was delayed, so that it was almost four o'clock when the procession left the Upper House. Kosaku and Mitsu walked together behind Nanae and Sakiko. It was the most splendid funeral ever conducted in the hamlet. The procession was longer than any previous procession, and many more people held up artificial flowers.

As the slow-moving parade of mourners passed through the hamlet, villagers watched from both sides of the road

157

and Kosaku and Mitsu grew tense and began marching as they had been taught during physical-education class. The procession turned off the road near the base of Mt. Kumano to begin the ascent of the slope. As they started up the mountain road, many children joined them. Yukio, Yoshie, Kameo and others came to walk with Kosaku. From time to time the newcomers ran in front of the coffin or went round behind it. Kosaku wanted to join them, but he told himself he must behave that day and he continued his solemn progress beside Mitsu.

At the cemetery on top of the mountain the priest chanted the sutra, and after that the coffin, tied with ropes on all four corners, was lowered into a big hole. This was the first time Kosaku had seen anyone buried. Imitating the adults, he threw a handful of soil into the grave. Then, as the young men of the village took over to complete the task, the mourners started streaming back on to the road. Kosaku thought how quickly and efficiently his great-grandmother had been laid to rest in the earth.

'Is that the end?' he asked Sakiko and his mother.

That night Kosaku slept in the storehouse as usual with Granny Onui. He had anticipated that perhaps Nanae would stay with them overnight, but the hours passed and still she did not appear.

The next day Kosaku was told he had to stay home from school again, and that he could not go back to school for three days. Around noon Nanae took Kosaku and Mitsu to the communal bath in the ravine. Kosaku felt embarrassment at the thought of bathing with his mother. When she undressed, her body shone like marble and he could not look at her for long.

'What are you being so slow about? Hurry up and take your clothes off,' his mother said.

As soon as Kosaku undressed he plunged into the empty bathtub as if he were jumping into the river, sending up a great curtain of spray. This was the first time Kosaku had bathed with his mother since he had reached the age of reason. He went to one corner of the tub and stayed there, trying to distance himself as much as possible from her white body, trying not to look at her.

Nanae sank slowly into the tub and, in a swimming motion, pushed at the water with both arms a few times. Then she asked, 'Ko-cha, can you swim?'

He regretted that his mother did not know he could swim. 'Of course I can swim. Heibuchi is nothing to me.'

'Is that true? You're bragging!' Nanae said. She truly appeared to doubt his word, and he was hurt.

'Shall I show you how I can swim in the river?' Kosaku asked seriously. If his mother wished it, he was prepared to dive at once into the big river that ran past the communal bath.

'Don't be foolish. If you went into that river now you'd catch pneumonia and die right away.'

'But I really can swim. Isn't that true, Mit-cha?' Kosaku looked beseechingly to Mitsu for support.

'I don't know,' said Mitsu. Detestable creature.

The next instant, Kosaku kicked off from the bathtub frame and stretched out in the water. He'd show his mother how well he could swim! He started kicking and splashing water all about him.

'Stop it, stupid!' his mother shouted and stood up in the tub. Mitsu moved away quickly towards the washing area. At one point Kosaku felt his body brush against something exquisitely smooth and soft and realized he must have bumped into his mother's white body. Then he felt himself propelled away immediately. 'What you're doing is dangerous! My hair will get wet.'

When Kosaku stopped his swimming he saw that his mother looked really angry. 'Our clothes got wet, too!' she snapped. 'There should be a limit to your foolishness.'

Just as she said, the water had splashed near the clothes basket, for the distance between the tub and the dressing area was only about three feet. Kosaku was chagrined.

'Now, come here!' she snapped. 'Your neck is filthy. I never saw anything so dirty. Doesn't Granny ever wash you?'

His mother's face was still hard. He stood in front of her as directed. But now he was unaware of the lustre of that body

159

that had seemed too dazzling to approach. Now he felt only that he was entrusting his own nakedness to a cruel person.

'Sit down.'

Kosaku sat.

'You're a skinny thing, aren't you? It's not good for a boy to have a body like a praying mantis. Now, look here. See how much grime comes off. You're a regular lump of grime, aren't you?' Nanae applied a scrubbing brush to his neck with vigour, and Kosaku saw pieces of dirt fall away, just as she had said. 'Turn round the other way!' He turned his back and it, too, was scrubbed harshly until it hurt. He thought many times of running away from her, but he stood still and bore the pain. Eventually the scouring hand reached his ribs, where he was unbearably ticklish. This time he twisted his body and tried to escape.

'Don't move around so much. Now, be strong!'

Soon she slapped him smartly on the back and said, 'That's enough. No more washing for you. Mit-cha, come over here.'

Kosaku was relieved at being released, but he felt rather dejected. She doesn't like me, he thought. When he came to the bath with Sakiko and Sakiko washed him, she was much gentler. Until they got out of the bath, Kosaku remained unusually quiet, hoping to regain his mother's esteem.

Nanae stayed in her home village for ten days after Great-Grandmother's funeral, but in all that time she did not spend a single night at the storehouse. At first Kosaku thought she would surely come. But as the days passed and his expectations were betrayed, he grew resigned.

'Why doesn't Mama come here and stay overnight?' he asked Granny Onui.

Her response was always the same. 'Why should she come and stay here? She says the storehouse smells mouldy and she doesn't like it.'

This was the first he had heard of Nanae's not liking the storehouse because it smelled mouldy, but he had no doubt she had said so to Granny Onui. Nanae was notoriously fastidious and hard to please, and it was very much in character for her to say such a thing. And yet as long as his mother's visit lasted, Kosaku went to the Upper House, where his mother was, instead of going directly home to Granny Onui. The Upper House held more appeal for him because of her presence.

Nanae wielded great authority at the Upper House. Sakiko, Daizo and Daigo were all intimidated by her. Even Tane, who was Nanae's mother, deferred to her. So did Bunta. 'You say that, but . . .,' or 'Even if you nag like that, Nanae . . .' was about all Bunta said in response to her hectoring.

Kosaku heard his mother rail at his grandparents many times: 'You don't manage your affairs well,' or 'You're too soft as parents and that's why your children don't turn out well,' or 'You think you are still the great family of the past and you live too extravagantly.' She also berated Sakiko, Daigo and Daizo.

At such times Grandmother Tane put on her martyred expression and said, 'It's all my fault. Father and the others are blameless.' And each time Nanae took her to task, saying, 'I don't need you to tell me you're to blame.'

Kosaku did not fully understand why those in the Upper House should be scolded so by his mother, but even in his child's mind he had a general idea. The Upper House had suffered a decline and no one there had taken measures to deal with the situation. Nanae could not bear to see what was happening, and that was the reason for her disdain.

Kosaku once overheard a sharp exchange between Nanae and Sakiko in the family room.

'Things don't always go as logically as you say they should, Elder Sister,' Sakiko said. 'I feel sorry for Mother and Father, the way you bully them.'

'You keep quiet. It's not your place to speak up,' Nanae replied.

'I have the right to speak up if I wish.'

'My, how big you talk! It's because of the likes of you that the family is having financial problems. Since you're married now, why don't you move out and live with him? How long do you plan to stay with your family? In principle I was

161

opposed to that marriage, but since you have a child it's too late. You're such a wanton!'

Only then did Sakiko raise her voice. 'It's none of your business whom I married. You, of all people, talk big – you, who have no understanding whatever of the family situation yet feel free to come home and carp whenever you please. The funeral is over, so hurry up and go back.' Sakiko's face was pale and her voice trembled.

'Please, please, you two! Please don't shout at each other. You were both such gentle children, I don't know how you got this way. It's so frightening, so frightening.' Tane, flustered, went and stood between her daughters. Kosaku steadily watched all three of them. He thought his mother probably had good reason to say what she did, but he felt more sympathy for his grandmother and Sakiko. The reason he felt sure Nanae was right was that when she was not there he had heard Sakiko tell Bunta and Tane the same things. But even so, the way his mother talked seemed too harsh. He thought she was not at all inclined to listen to another point of view.

Kosaku saw his grandmother go out to the yard to take in the laundry after she had quieted Sakiko and Nanae. He noted that his grandmother was still agitated and wished he could comfort her.

He walked shyly to where she stood and said, 'Mama was wrong. Isn't that so, Granny?'

Tane stared at him a moment in surprise. Then she stretched her back and said, 'Not at all, not at all. Ko-cha's mummy is a good mummy. It's all Granny's fault.'

Kosaku had never seen his grandmother look as sad as she did then. His heart ached for her. Granny Onui stood up to Nanae and even spoke ill of her behind her back. Not so Grandmother Tane. Whenever anything went wrong it was because of her own shortcomings. It actually seemed as if she had been born believing that.

On the day Kosaku's mother left to return to Toyohashi, the yellow globeflower at the side of the storehouse was in full bloom. Kosaku received permission from his teacher to leave school during the lunch break to bid farewell to his mother. That day his grandparents, Sakiko and Granny Onui all put on their smiles and came to the carriage stop to see Nanae off. Many neighbourhood housewives gathered as well.

A middle-aged man wearing western clothes was taking the same carriage as Kosaku's mother, and because many people were seeing him off, too, the carriage stop was unusually thronged with villagers. This man, whose name was Kiyo, was a former villager who had gone to Tokyo and found success as a watch-shop owner. After Kiyo-san greeted Nanae, he said to Kosaku, 'You must feel sad at parting with your mummy.'

Kosaku did not respond; he was too busy looking at the pipe in Kiyo's mouth.

'What is that?' Kosaku asked.

Kiyo-san took the pipe out of his mouth. 'You mean this? This is called a peppermint pipe.* Want to try it?'

Kosaku accepted the offer. He put the pipe in his mouth and puffed, and the refreshing taste of mint filled his mouth. What wonders there are in this world, Kosaku thought. No doubt such a stylish, elegant thing was available only in Tokyo and even there no average person could acquire it. It must be very expensive.

Kosaku kept the pipe in his mouth and looked round at the adults. Only his mother's eyes glittered with disapproval. Flustered, Kosaku took the pipe out of his mouth and unthinkingly inserted it in his obi sash. He thought probably his mother was reproving him for putting something into his mouth that had been in someone else's mouth. To avoid her glare, he edged round behind the adults.

At length the carriage was ready and Roku-san, the driver, blew his trumpet resoundingly. Kiyo-san bade farewell to the villagers and got in first. Nanae followed, and the carriage started off immediately. The villagers all stood watching the departing carriage in a manner suggesting they had just said a last goodbye to loved ones. Kosaku saw his mother lean out a little way and wave. He clearly felt that she

---

* That is, a smoking pipe filled with peppermint leaves

was waving at him. He had decided that since he was the only child there that day, he would not chase after the carriage when it left. But when he saw his mother's gesture, it was as if a signal had been given, and he started running after the carriage without thinking. He ran to the edge of Sunoko Bridge before he stopped. His mother still waved.

When the carriage disappeared into Ichiyama village, Kosaku returned to the carriage stop, where the villagers still lingered.

'Well, she's finally gone. What a relief!' Granny Onui said.

Apparently Sakiko found Granny's comment amusing, for she smiled and agreed. 'That's right. What a relief.' Everyone around her laughed.

Tane thanked each person who had come to see her daughter off, then turned to Kosaku and said, 'Now you must go to school.'

She bent to retie his obi sash. Just then Kosaku saw a small object fall at his feet. The peppermint pipe! He picked it up quickly and thought, What a terrible thing! He should have returned it to Kiyo-san, and instead he had stuck it in his obi sash and forgotten about it. And Kiyo-san must have been too distracted by his well-wishers to get it back.

What a terrible thing he had done! Holding the pipe in his hand, Kosaku left the group of people and walked alone on the new highway towards school. He put the pipe to his lips once more and puffed. Just as before, that indescribably fresh, cool tang spread in his mouth.

But his pleasure died with the daunting thought that he had become a criminal. At that very moment Kiyo-san might be remembering the boy who had taken his pipe, and might be causing a great commotion about it in the carriage. He thrust the pipe back into his obi sash. He must not show it to anyone. He was concealing a stolen item. This guilty knowledge caused him great uneasiness all the time he was in school that day. He thought the teacher might approach him at any moment and say, 'You have the pipe, don't you? Now, give it to me.'

Even out in the playground he did not join his friends but stood in one corner alone. From time to time he put his hand to his obi sash to make certain the pipe was still there. Yes, it was definitely there. He had no idea what he might finally do with it, but he knew for sure he did not want to lose it. And much of the time he found himself doing battle with a desire to put the pipe in his mouth and inhale once more.

The memory of that refreshing taste at last became unbearably enticing and Kosaku ventured round behind the school. Ascertaining that no one was near, he stealthily pulled out the pipe, put it in his mouth, and took it out again. After that he breathed in and out many times and decided there was nothing quite so wonderful.

After classes were over he usually played with his Kubota friends, but that day was different. He avoided Yukio and the others, went to the paddyfields alone and sat in the shade of a strawstack. There, as he puffed on the pipe or played with it, he felt a complexity of emotions: guilt at keeping a stranger's possession and joy in its value and the pleasure it gave. Loneliness at parting with his mother also entered into his musings. From the place where he sat by the strawstack he could see the terraced fields sloping down towards the ravine, and beyond, the white Shimoda Highway on which the carriage had that very day taken his mother off into the distance. While she was here in the village, he had not been particularly attracted to this somehow cruel woman, but now that she was gone he missed her and felt a sense of loss. The image of his mother waving from the carriage remained particularly vivid. When he thought of her waving hand he felt a desperate longing. He had never before felt such a longing for his mother.

Kosaku played alone by the strawstacks until dusk and returned to the storehouse only after the sun had completely set. By then Granny Onui had stopped at each neighbour's house, searching for him, and had herself just returned home.

'Ko-cha, where have you been?' was her first remark, delivered in a slightly irritated tone. Then she heaved a great sigh and sat down at the entrance, weak with relief at his safe return. 'Granny was worried. I thought you were hidden by the gods again.'

165

After a bit she rose and thumped the small of her back. 'I have to go round the neighbourhood and let them know you've come home,' she said. Kosaku followed her as she did the rounds of every household in the neighbourhood, and at each one they found the family was in the middle of dinner.

'Ko-cha is safe. I'm sorry to have troubled you. Unlike that of your eldest son, Ko-cha's disappearance would be a cause of great concern,' Granny Onui said at each house.

One neighbour replied, 'We were worried too. If Granny, who *should* be hidden by the gods, is *not* and Ko-cha *is*, that would indeed be a catastrophe.' Another said, 'Granny, you of all people should be careful. Ko-cha had his turn and got through it safely. Next it will be your turn.'

When they returned to the storehouse Granny Onui complained of dizziness and said she was going upstairs to lie down. Kosaku lit the lamp with a match and went to fetch water for her. Back upstairs, he suddenly remembered the mint pipe.

'Here, Granny, take a puff of this.' He pushed the pipe into her mouth.

'What is it?' she asked, feeling the slender stem.

'If you smoke that, you'll feel better,' Kosaku said. She did as he said and kept the pipe in her mouth.

The next instant she sat up and asked, 'Goodness, is this mint?'

'Granny, you feel better, don't you?'

'Yes, I really do.'

'Wasn't I right?'

'How strange. My chest feels much better!' Granny Onui grasped the pipe with wrinkled fingers and held it under the lamp where she could examine it carefully. Then she popped it back into her mouth. 'Truly, it's refreshing.' Just as Kosaku had done, she began breathing in and out deeply. Soon she announced that she felt completely well, and to prove it she got up and made dinner, all the while puffing on the pipe.

Kosaku and Granny Onui ate their simple dinner together. For a while after Great-Grandmother's death a few side dishes were brought to them every day from the Upper House, but now that Nanae had gone home they were again

166

reduced to the fare that Granny Onui prepared. She had placed boiled bamboo shoots and bracken in a large bowl and they picked from it with their chopsticks. They both ate only the tender part of the bamboo shoots. All of Kosaku's teeth had cavities, which Sakiko claimed were the result of the sweets Granny Onui fed him in bed every morning.

Granny Onui disagreed. 'I never heard of such a silly thing – that teeth would get bad from eating sweets,' she scoffed. 'Why, when I was a child I was raised sucking sugar drops when I went to bed, and when I woke up I sucked on them again. And I don't have a single cavity. The reason for Ko-cha's poor teeth is that his mama didn't eat fish when she was carrying him.'

This Granny Onui said, and this she firmly believed.

That night Kosaku and Granny Onui slept with their bedding side by side as usual, Kosaku with the pipe by his pillow. When Kosaku awoke the next morning, the first thing he thought of was the pipe. But when he looked for it, it had disappeared. He got up and went immediately downstairs. There he saw Granny Onui making miso soup – with the pipe in her mouth. He took it away from her and put it in his own mouth.

That day he took the pipe to school again and Yukio found out about it, so they began sharing it. At school the pipe passed back and forth many times between Kosaku and Yukio, and at home it passed back and forth between Kosaku and Granny Onui. That night Kosaku again went to sleep with the pipe by his pillow.

The following morning when he awoke Granny Onui said, 'Ko-cha, the pipe is not as refreshing as it used to be.'

Kosaku took the pipe from her and put it in his mouth. As she said, the pipe was not so refreshing as before. The minty taste was gone.

About a month after his great-grandmother died, Kosaku went with Sakiko to the communal bath in the ravine. Of late, Sakiko had been carrying her baby with her everywhere she went, but this time, for once, she entrusted him to Tane

167

and went off to the bath unencumbered. Thus for the first time in a long while Kosaku had Sakiko to himself, just as before. And as before, he held the metal basin with her bathing articles high above his head, accepting the role of her attendant.

As they left the road and went down the hilly path towards the ravine, Sakiko sang a high-school song. Seeing her like this, he thought she did not look like the mother of an infant son.

But when they got into the tub, Kosaku saw that Sakiko's body was waxy pale and disconcertingly thin. She had been so plump before, and fairer and heavier than his mother. But now she looked like a totally different person. She sat on the frame of the bath and again sang the song she had sung on the way. Kosaku also sat on the tub frame, and listened to her sing. He was somewhat concerned about her appearance, but his happiness at having this time alone with her outweighed all else.

'You sing something, Ko-cha,' she said.

'I can't sing,' he replied.

'Don't be so timid, Ko-cha! You're a man, aren't you? Now, sing.'

'But I can't sing.'

'That's impossible.'

'Well, okay, I'll sing.'

Since he felt he had no alternative, he quavered into a song called 'The Mountains of Hakone, the Steepest in the World'. Kosaku was born a poor singer, and from time to time his voice slid far off the melody. Whenever he got particularly off-key, Sakiko took over and sang for him.

When he had finished the song Sakiko said, 'Ko-cha, you're tone-deaf, aren't you?'

'What's tone-deaf?'

'It means you sing off-key. Maybe you're right, it would be wiser for you not to sing when people ask you. But you can sing in front of me,' she added. 'I'll correct you a little at a time.'

'Well, then, I'll sing one more song.'

Kosaku was not particularly embarrassed about singing off-key after Sakiko's remarks. During music lessons at school he

168

could never bring himself to sing solo, but strangely enough, in front of Sakiko he felt willing to sing anything. He was happy. He felt that it was like a dream to be spending time like this with Sakiko.

It was shortly after the day at the bath that Kosaku heard the rumour from other children that Sakiko had tuberculosis. The children's gossip was evidence that the adults were saying the same thing. Now when the children passed the Upper House, some of them ran and deliberately held their breath until they were beyond the property line. Kosaku detested the friends who did this.

When he reported what he had heard to Granny Onui, she said, 'Sakiko is sick, and therefore it might be safer for you not to go to the Upper House. But don't you tell your granny what I said.'

But there was no need to disclaim Granny Onui's warning, for those at the Upper House would not allow Kosaku to play there. Whenever he approached the stone steps in front of the entrance, Granny Tane came out and said, 'Go and play over there.'

He felt he was being chased away. Even if it was true that Sakiko had tuberculosis, Kosaku wanted very much to see her. Their trip to the bath together had been her last outing; since then, she had not left her room on the second floor. The villagers were saying she was confined to her bed, but Kosaku did not believe them.

One day Kosaku went to the Upper House and found no one around. Taking advantage of the situation, he slipped upstairs and entered the room at the end of the corridor. He heard Sakiko's voice asking from the adjoining room, 'Who is it?'

'It's Ko-cha,' he responded.

'Ko-cha! You mustn't come here. Go downstairs. Why in the world have you come here?'

'I came to see the baby,' he said quickly.

Sakiko did not respond immediately and for a while there was silence from the next room. Then she said, 'The baby's not here. He would catch my sickness, so I placed him

169

outside with some other people. Now, Ko-cha, go down-stairs.' This was the first Kosaku knew of the baby's absence from the Upper House. Sakiko spoke again. 'You're so obstinate! I told you to go home, so why don't you go?'

Her tone was scolding, but somehow lacking in force. Kosaku was undecided as to whether or not he should try to enter her room. He knew if he let this opportunity pass he would not soon have another, but he also sensed it would be a grave crime to intrude upon the privacy of the tubercular Sakiko. At last he put his hand on one of the four sliding doors and tried to slide it open. But the panel did not move.

'No, you may not.' Unexpectedly, Sakiko's voice came from just the other side of the thin paper panel. It was no longer the scolding voice; it was the soft, breathless, sweet voice that had tantalized him so many times before when they bantered together.

'Open the door!'

'No.'

'Open it! Open it!'

'You mustn't.'

The next instant the door slid open a crack and Sakiko's white arm flew out and lightly tapped Kosaku's head. Then, quickly, the arm was withdrawn and the door slid shut again. Kosaku tried to guess which of the four sliding doors would yield to his touch. He tried them all. He could not tell how she was holding them, but not one of the doors would budge.

'Go home.' Now Sakiko's voice was changed. Her tone was firm, and left no room for argument.

Resigned at last to the fact that he would not see her face, Kosaku went downstairs and let himself out by way of the veranda, still carrying in his mind the vision of Sakiko's thin white arm as she reached through the crack between the sliding panels to tap him on the head. He felt unusually contented. He was happy that he had gone upstairs and talked to Sakiko, happy that she had tapped him on the head, happy that they had stood facing each other with only the paper of the door between them. Happy, too, that in their contest over the doors he had detected a hint, however slight, of gaiety.

At night, after dinner, Kosaku told Granny Onui he had gone upstairs in the Upper House that day. She was aghast. 'Don't tell anybody else about that, Ko-cha,' she warned.

Then she urged him down the stairs, poured some salt into a cup and hustled him outside to the edge of the moonlit stream. There he was forced to gargle many times with water and salt.

'Is that enough?' Kosaku asked after a while.

'No, you must do more. You must gargle some more,' Granny Onui responded.

'I have to do more? I drank some,' Kosaku said.

'Drank some?' Again Granny Onui was aghast. 'If you drink it, Ko-cha,' she said in a biting voice, 'you'll get tuberculosis. You'll get thinner and thinner and turn as pale as wax, then finally you'll die.'

'I won't die.'

'My goodness.' Looking extremely dismayed, Granny Onui straightened her back and strengthened her voice. 'When people get tuberculosis, they die. It's always so!'

'They don't die.'

'They do.'

'They don't.'

'My goodness!'

'They don't die.'

'Stop arguing and gargle some more.' By now Granny Onui was getting angry.

But Kosaku was even angrier. If everyone who contracted tuberculosis died, that meant Sakiko would die. How could that happen? Kosaku couldn't bear it if Sakiko died. The mere thought was frightening.

'They don't die,' he repeated stubbornly.

'They die. They die,' Granny Onui said, just as stubbornly.

This was the first time Kosaku had ever really argued with Granny Onui. Usually he deferred to her. It was not like him to rebel and insist that he was right and she was wrong.

Granny Onui finally flew into a rage. 'Very well, you obstinate, stupid, good-for-nothing Ko-cha! Go ahead! Drink a lot of the gargling water and get tuberculosis and die!' With

171

that, she left him and stomped back towards the storehouse. When Kosaku turned to follow, he saw her standing in front of the storehouse. She was still angry, but she seemed to be waiting for him.

'They don't die, they don't die.' He was repeating these words as if they were a magical incantation as he brushed past Granny Onui on his way into the storehouse and quickly mounted the stairs alone. Presently, as he lay in his bed, he heard Granny Onui coming up the stairs, too. But tonight, instead of her usual chant of 'Dokkoisho, dokkoisho' to mark time, she was saying, 'Stu-pid, stu-pid'.

After a while Granny Onui came and stood by Kosaku's pillow. 'Ko-cha?' she said tentatively.

Kosaku remained silent. Who would answer *her*? he thought spitefully.

'Are you asleep?' She bent down and brought her face close to his own.

'Don't bother me, Granny.' He opened his eyes and brushed aside the arm she was resting on his quilt. It flew to one side, virtually weightless and totally without resistance. Kosaku was startled.

'Ko-cha, are you still angry?' Granny Onui asked, apparently thinking nothing of his rude rejection. Once again the arm that had been brushed away rested on the bedding.

Kosaku realized that Granny Onui's arm was even thinner and weaker than that other arm he had seen that day. For all its fragility, Sakiko's arm was still white and beautiful, but Granny Onui's was only skin and bones and without saving grace, like a withered shaft of bamboo. Kosaku felt a surge of pity.

'Granny. . . .' He spoke the name gently.

'Do you want something?' she said eagerly. 'Do you want something? Tell me, tell me.' Then, like one suddenly infused with new life, Granny Onui stood up light-heartedly and went to the cupboard where the box of sweets was stored.

7

In early June it was decided that Kosaku would go with Granny Onui to stay two nights in Numazu, at the base of the peninsula. Two of Granny Onui's relatives, a couple named Senda (he was a contractor who had gone to Manchuria and prospered), were coming to Japan for the first time in years and would be stopping in Numazu. Granny Onui was to go there to meet them.

Granny Onui was obviously overjoyed at the prospect of seeing the Sendas again; once plans for the Numazu trip were settled, she talked to Kosaku about the Sendas every night until the day of departure.

'You never can tell when a person's luck will change,' she said. 'When they left for Manchuria I gave them money, but now they are really well off. They've built three or four storehouses in Mukden.' Or, 'He was a good-hearted soul but a ne'er-do-well who didn't know how to make money. But as soon as he went to Manchuria he started to get smart. Now he's got many people under him, but he certainly doesn't look the type to be boss.'

It was hard to tell from her remarks whether she meant to praise Mr Senda or to disparage him. For his wife, however, she had only the highest praise. 'Mrs Senda is such a wonderful woman. She has a fine character. She's kind, she's intelligent and she's much too good for Mr Senda. Ko-cha, you watch them carefully. You'll see that Mrs Senda is far superior.'

173

After listening to stories about Mr and Mrs Senda every night, Kosaku felt he knew exactly how they both looked in face and form, for he had created a vivid image of each.

Not surprisingly, Kosaku's trip to Numazu was seen as a problem by those in the Upper House. Grandfather Bunta was opposed to the plan to take Kosaku out of school. Sakiko, who was confined upstairs, was also against it.

But in this situation, as in so many others, Granny Tane mediated. 'Don't make things more difficult,' she told them. 'Let Granny Onui have her way. Ko-cha, you go with Granny.'

Kosaku didn't particularly relish the thought of taking time off from school either, but he definitely felt happy about going to Numazu. Although he had stayed there overnight at the inn in front of the station on his way to Toyohashi the previous summer, he had seen only the inn. He did not know the city at all. He had not seen the famous Thousand Pine Beach* nor the big Onari Bridge.

Granny Onui spread the word to everyone she met, so that Kosaku's trip to Numazu quickly became a topic of conversation among the students.

Some of the older boys jeered at him. 'Going to look for a bride, Ko-cha?' they asked. Or, 'You'll be kidnapped, Ko-cha, and Granny will have her tongue pulled out and you'll have your belly button cut out.'

On the day they left for Numazu, Kosaku donned his good kimono, put on a new pair of wooden clogs, and rode in the horse carriage for the first time in ten months. Yukio and the others were at school and could not see him off, and only Grandmother of the Upper House and two or three neighbourhood housewives came to say goodbye to Granny Onui, so it was a quiet send-off for them both.

The carriage swayed wildly as it travelled along the gravelly Shimoda Highway. Inside, Granny Onui and Kosaku, the only passengers, fell off the small seats many

---

* Thousand Pine Beach, named for its famous pine grove, is situated on Suruga Bay and has Mt. Fuji as its landward backdrop. It is a spot well known for its scenic beauty.

times. Each time Granny Onui was jolted from her seat she criticized the horses, just as on the previous trip.

'Such undisciplined horses! I never saw such horses!'

'So sorry you find them so undisciplined,' Roku-san, the driver, shot back.

'They're probably taking it out on us because you don't feed them. They're living creatures, after all, so it's a pity you won't feed them.'

'That's right, I haven't fed them for two or three days to make sure they'll bounce Granny right out of the carriage.'

With the driver and Granny Onui thus trading barbs, the horses ran until they reached Ichiyama, Roku-san whipping them on even through stretches where they normally walked. When they slowed down, Granny Onui straightened up, looking relieved, and began retrieving bundles that had fallen from the seats. Kosaku was never particularly bothered by the horses' galloping. He was concerned, however, at the mounting virulence of the exchange between Granny Onui and Roku-san.

But after they had rested and drunk tea in Deguchi, midway between Yugashima and Ohito, Roku-san and Granny Onui were too tired to talk any more. The horses also appeared to be weary, for they no longer ran but only walked slowly. Roku-san actually dozed off from time to time, and Kosaku's concern now was that he might go to sleep and fall off the driver's seat.

When they reached the rail terminal at Ohito, they boarded the train. Kosaku enjoyed riding on the small, toy-like train again after so long a time. Once aboard, Granny Onui said she felt ill and lay down on the seat, taking up two spaces. Each time the train stopped at a station she raised her pale face and asked, 'It's Mishima, isn't it? Is it Mishima yet?'

When they reached Mishima they transferred to the Tokkaido line. The next station from Mishima would be Numazu. Though the distance was not great, Granny Onui enlisted the aid of other passengers to put her bundles on the luggage rack and then to take them down again.

After they alighted at Numazu station they booked into

175

the same inn where they had stayed en route to Toyohashi the previous year. From now on, Granny Onui, perhaps recalling past glories, seemed to acquire a new dignity. She dealt graciously with the innkeeper's wife and the maid who came to greet her, and Kosaku thought how admirably self-assured she appeared.

They bathed and had some tea, and by then dusk was closing in. Kosaku was gazing down from the window at the busy twilight scene in front of the station when he heard activity in the room behind him. He turned and saw the head clerk and the maid bringing many bundles into the room, and in their wake came an ill-matched couple in their fifties. The man was short, sallow and undistinguished looking, and the woman was tall but oddly spoken and strangely coiffed. They were the Mr and Mrs Senda Kosaku had been hearing about every night. They were totally different from what he had imagined.

Kosaku disliked Mr Senda immediately.

'Whose kid is this?' Mr Senda asked Granny Onui, gesturing with his chin towards Kosaku.

'He's the very, very important sonny,' Granny Onui replied.

'Oh, the Eldest Son. Gad, what a puny-looking pup.'

By comparison, Mrs Senda was a bit more attractive. 'Oh, so this is sonny,' she said. 'He has a girl's face. I'll hold you between my legs and sleep with you tonight,' she laughed. Kosaku thought, Nobody's going to let you hold *me* between your legs, but he had heard warmth in her words. Besides, Mrs Senda resembled Granny Onui. In fact, when she smiled she was the living image of Granny.

All through dinner Kosaku was virtually ignored. Probably because they had not seen each other for so long, the adults were absorbed in incessant conversation to the point where he wondered how anyone could talk so much. Actually, it was not all three adults who talked, but only Granny Onui and Mrs Senda. Mr Senda sat silently drinking sake most of the time and only now and then interrupted with a brief comment. From time to time he turned his pale face towards Kosaku and said things like, 'Don't spill any rice,' or

'You eat that fish from its head.'

Kosaku felt that his trip to Numazu was being ruined by these two intruders. He wished they would hurry up and go home.

That night Kosaku went to bed before the others in the next room. He was tired after the jostling in the horse carriage and he fell asleep immediately. He wakened once or twice in the night, got up and peered through the sliding door, and each time he looked he saw Mr Senda drinking his sake alone and the two women still chattering.

Next day when Kosaku awoke, Mr and Mrs Senda were nowhere in sight. They had left on the first morning train to Tokyo. He was happy to be alone with Granny Onui once again. Because she had stayed up so long, however, Granny Onui slept late and Kosaku ate breakfast by himself.

After breakfast the maid took him to a large house called Kamiki, on Uwomachi Street, as Granny Onui had instructed her to do the day before.

'They're your relatives, sonny,' the maid said on the way to the house. 'You can play there until I come and get you at dusk.' Kosaku had heard many times about the house called Kamiki. It was the home of Grandmother Tane's elder sister or cousin or somebody – anyhow, a close relative. At the first mention of Kamiki, Kosaku felt himself tighten up. He had heard somewhere that this was one of the wealthiest business families in Numazu, that their lifestyle was extravagant and their children spoiled rotten.

The distance to the Kamiki house was about a ten-minute walk. Kosaku felt self-conscious and insignificant walking on the busiest street in Numazu with a young maid.

The Kamiki house proved to be a two-storey structure facing the street. It had a larger, more imposing entrance than any other house in the neighbourhood. Since Kosaku knew the family had a business, it crossed his mind to wonder what items they sold. But when he stepped inside the earthen-floored entrance and looked into the wooden-floored room that faced it, he failed to see a single thing that looked like a business commodity. He saw only beautiful, darkly gleaming polished wood.

177

Down one side of this shining room, the earthen floor continued back to the kitchen. The maid from the inn continued on in that direction and left Kosaku waiting at the entrance.

After a short time a woman about his mother's age appeared and said, 'So you're Ko-cha of Yugashima. This is a lovely surprise. My, how you've grown!'

Kosaku stiffened to attention and bowed politely. It was the lady who had visited them at the inn on their way to Toyohashi the previous summer.

'I'm so glad you've come. This is the first time you've visited my home, isn't it? Please come in.' Her manner was incredibly welcoming, and she seemed genuinely pleased that he had come. Kosaku thought he had never heard such a clear, beautiful voice. His mother's voice, and even Sakiko's, seemed somewhat vulgar by comparison. Not only was her voice beautiful, he thought, but her face, her form, everything else about this lady seemed somehow superior.

These thoughts were interrupted by the maid returning from the kitchen area. 'I'll come and get you towards evening, so you play till then,' she said, and left immediately.

Kosaku followed his hostess past the wooden-floored room into a back room. There he sat down beside a wooden brazier and was treated to tea and cakes. The teacup was presented on a coaster, and the cakes were aligned precisely on a piece of white paper. They were red and white rice cakes. Encouraged to help himself, Kosaku picked up a morsel and tasted it. Just then an old, bent-over woman about Granny Onui's age appeared and said, 'I heard that sonny from Yugashima had arrived. Let me see, let me see your face.' She sat in front of Kosaku and he again stiffened and nodded politely. The old woman, still seated, now pulled herself towards Kosaku and peered into his face.

'Indeed, you look very much like Nanae-chan. Just like her, in fact. I wonder if you have as strong a personality as your mummy. Since you're a boy, it's all right if you have a strong personality.'

Then the younger woman said, 'When your mother was a young girl she came to this house and learned etiquette and

178

had koto* lessons from this granny! Did you know that?'

Kosaku had not known. He shook his head.

The old woman said, 'Have your auntie here feed you lots of goodies. Your playmates will be home from school soon, so you play nicely with them. You mustn't fight!' Then she rose and, resuming her bent-over stance, made her way to the other end of the corridor and disappeared.

Kosaku liked these two women. He decided that wealthy people were different, after all. They were not at all petty and their speech and behaviour were serene and composed. Also, they wore fine kimonos.

'What do you like to eat, Ko-cha?' the hostess asked.

'The licking food,'† Kosaku replied.

'Do you mean the licking miso?'

'Umm.'

She showed her white teeth and laughed as if this were a very funny remark. 'What do you like for a feast?' she asked.

'Grated yam,' Kosaku replied.

'Ah. How about tempura?'

'I never ate such a thing.'

'Don't tease me. How about sushi?'

'I don't like it.'

'Oh, too bad. How about broiled eel?'

'I don't like it.'

'How about steamed eggs on rice?'

'I don't like that.'

'I'm more and more perplexed. Well, do you like chawan-mushi?'‡

'I don't like it.'

'How about sashimi?'§

'I don't like it.'

'How about fried eggs?'

'I don't like it.'

---

* A five-stringed instrument played with a plectrum
† Kinzanji miso (see p. 20)
‡ Steamed rice mixed with various titbits
§ Raw fish

179

Kosaku was agitated because he had never heard of most of the foods she was naming. He thought under the circumstances it would be best to tell her he didn't like anything.

Finally she said, 'Well, then, I'll think of something you might like. Your playmates will be home from school soon. Until then you can play on the veranda.'

Kosaku, relieved, stood up and did as he was told. From the veranda he saw a garden abloom with red azaleas. He sat down and began turning the pages of a picture book the lady had given him.

As he was thus occupied, he heard a high, piping voice: 'Tadaima. . . . Tadaima. . . . I said tadaima.'* The voice grew louder. 'I said tadaima, Rei-cha is home. Tadaima. Ta-da-i-ma.' And finally a bellowed, drawn-out 'TA-DA-IIII-MAAA!'

Apparently the mother and the maid had gone somewhere, for there was still no reply from within the house. Now the owner of the voice fell silent and Kosaku heard only the rustle of footsteps approaching on the tatami. He looked towards the house and saw through the crack of the shoji door a small girl with a Dutch bob, a child perhaps two or three years younger than himself. Then she spotted him. She stopped short and stared, clearly startled.

'Who are you?' she asked rather petulantly. Kosaku knew immediately that she was Reiko, the second daughter of the house.

'I'm Ko-cha,' he responded.

'I don't know anyone by the name of Ko-cha. Whom did you come with?'

'I came by myself.'

'Where did you come from?'

'Yugashima.'

Her eyes lit up with comprehension. 'Oh, then you're that country boy, aren't you?' Kosaku was irritated by the patronizing tone in her voice.

'It's not the country,' he said.

---

* See p. 12

180

'It is too the country. I never heard of such a thing. Yugashima is in the country, isn't it? It's a place where grass grows and there's a graveyard. It has mostly paddyfields and only a few people. I've been there.' She turned and went into the kitchen.

Kosaku got up from his place on the veranda and followed her.

'Don't, you stupid child! I won't play with you,' Reiko said. She glared malevolently.

Kosaku was astonished. He had not suspected until then that she felt such violent enmity for him, and for no reason that he could determine.

Just then he heard another voice, obviously that of another girl. 'Ta-da-i . . .,' the voice said. The phrase was incomplete – not 'Tadaima', just 'Tadai. . . .' The voice came again: 'Is anyone there? Hurry up and bring me a rag.' Then, after a few seconds, 'All right, don't bring it. I'm coming into the house just as I am.'

Next he heard loud footsteps and the sound of a weight being dragged across the floor.

When Kosaku saw her he knew she must be the elder daughter, Ranko – the one known among the relatives as the spoiled, totally undisciplined daughter. Like her sister Reiko, Ranko at first simply stared at Kosaku. She stared at his face long enough to bore a hole, then she abruptly turned away and totally ignored him.

'I'm starving,' she said. 'I think I'll have some sweets.' She delivered the last remark as if it were a pronouncement. She then took a box from a cupboard and placed it on the table, lifted the lid, took something from the box, popped it into her mouth, and munched with great deliberation.

Kosaku felt a strong antipathy towards this Ranko. What a conceited brat, he thought.

At about that time the lady of the house returned. She took in the scene and said to Ranko, 'Ran-cha, Ko-cha has come from Yugashima.'

'Hmm,' Ranko replied.

'Play with him, please.'

'No.'

181

'Why not?'

'He's a bore.' Now Ranko's enunciation was clear and crisp.

'You shouldn't say such things. After all, he's a guest come to visit. Please play with him. If you do, I'll take you to the cinema tonight.'

Ranko yielded slightly. 'I'll play only a little bit with him,' she said grudgingly. Then she looked straight at Kosaku. 'I'll play with you, so come over here.' She said it as if issuing an order.

As Kosaku approached she said, 'All right, I'll play with you, I'll play with you. So what do you want to play?' Pause. 'Well, hurry and tell me! What do you want to play?' Kosaku saw that Ranko's face, too, was filled with a hatred he could not understand. 'Well? What do you want to play?' she continued. 'Tell me! You do want to play, don't you?'

Kosaku decided this was about the most horrible girl he had ever seen.

And by contrast, even in this situation her mother was gentle. 'Go and look at the ocean,' the mother urged in her thin, beautiful voice that sounded like a bell. 'The ocean will be novel for Ko-cha, so why don't you all go to the Thousand Pine Beach?'

'No!' This time it was the younger sister's voice, coming from the kitchen.

'You shouldn't say such things,' the lady said. 'All of you can have Kane-san take you.'

At this enticement the two horrid but beautiful sisters shouted with pleasure. The younger one, Reiko, dashed in from the kitchen and the elder, Ranko, threw the slice of cake she held in her hand up towards the ceiling, where it broke into several pieces before falling on the tatami.

'Now, now,' the mother said, but without real reproach. Then she raised her sweet voice slightly and called, 'Kaneki-chi, Kanekichi.' Almost immediately a young man wearing a kimono with wide vertical stripes appeared from the rear section of the earthen-floor area. He was a youth of about sixteen or seventeen, with a lumpy head. 'Kane-san, take them to the Thousand Pine Beach. You can use the bicycle,

182

but give them turns so they won't fight,' the lady said.

Kane-san disappeared outside immediately. Ranko and Reiko rushed after him, scampering down to the earthen floor and then outside.

The lady accompanied Kosaku to the road, where he found Ranko and Reiko arguing violently beside a bicycle with a luggage rack attached. Each wanted to ride first on the luggage rack, and neither would give in.

'Now, now.' Their mother waved her slender hand from the entrance, but Kosaku thought the hand looked ineffectual and powerless.

'I'm going to hit you! If I say I'm going to hit you, I'll really hit you!' Ranko's shout was followed by a loud slap. True to her threat, she had delivered a staggering slap to Reiko's cheek with her right hand.

'Now, now.' The mother waved again, but she did not appear to be particularly perturbed by their fighting. The sound of a second slap resounded as Ranko hit Reiko again. This time Kosaku took his eyes from the woman saying 'Now, now' and watched the two sisters, realizing that something very odd was happening. Reiko, who had been slapped, was glaring at her older sister with eyes filled with hatred but not a single tear. Ranko's eyes, on the other hand, were brimming with tears, and before long she started sobbing loudly. When the sobbing began Reiko smirked at her mother as if to say, See? I won again. At any rate, Reiko was clearly the victor in this fight.

Reiko directed one more venomous glance at the wailing Ranko, then took Kane-san to task. 'Kane-san, what are you doing standing around like that? I told you to put me on the bike, so do it!' Kane-san lifted Reiko up to the luggage rack and immediately started to pull the bicycle.

Kosaku turned to Ranko and said, 'Shall we go?'

Ranko stopped crying abruptly, stiffened her tear-stained face, and said haughtily, 'Of course I'll go. Next, it's my turn to ride. After that it's Reiko's, then mine again, then Reiko.' Kosaku thought, Who'd want to ride on that stupid bicycle anyway?

Ranko and Kosaku followed the bicycle and Kane-san

pulled. Both sides of the street were crammed with shops and swarming with pedestrians. Kosaku felt extremely embarrassed to be in the company of two girls wearing beautiful kimonos. He felt all the passers-by were looking at him.

When they had gone about fifty yards Ranko said, 'Now it's my turn.' Reiko compliantly got off the bicycle and Ranko got on. When they came to the end of the main road and arrived at the entrance to the Thousand Pine Beach, the ground became sandy and Ranko got off the bicycle and said, 'Now, it's your turn.'

'No,' Reiko said. 'Next is Ko-cha.'

Reiko's words came as a surprise to Kosaku. 'I don't want to ride,' he said.

'You don't have to stand on ceremony,' Reiko said pertly. 'Get on.'

'I don't want to ride,' Kosaku repeated. He shook his head stubbornly and ran towards the pine grove ahead. As he ran, he felt bad about rejecting Reiko's friendly overture. He stopped at the edge of the grove, turned round and saw Ranko and Reiko coming towards him. He was surprised to see not just one but both of them on foot and running after him.

He waited until they caught up, then turned and bolted into the grove. Ahead he could see, between the trunks of the trees, the gleam of water.

'Yeah! I see the ocean!' he shouted impulsively.

This was the first time he had seen the ocean close up. On his way to Toyohashi he had seen it from the train window, but the ocean he saw then was totally different from the ocean he saw now peeking through the pines. The ocean seen from the train window had looked static, like a bolt of indigo cloth spread in the sun, but the ocean he saw in front of him now was rocking and noisy and alive with white crests.

'Yeah, the ocean! Yeah, the ocean!' He shouted again and again.

Apart from shouting, he knew no appropriate way to express the feelings erupting inside of him. Paying no heed to the two sisters, he raced through the trees towards the

184

water. Beyond the stand of pines, the sandy beach stretched in a gentle incline to the water's edge. There the white waves rolled in one after another, then scattered on the beach and receded. Ranko and Reiko followed him to the tideline.

'Yeah! Yeah!' Kosaku continued shouting. Astonished by his excitement, even Ranko and Reiko remained silent for a while.

Then Ranko asked, 'Ko-cha, don't they have the ocean in the country?'

Kosaku was surprised to hear Ranko use his name. 'We have no such thing,' he replied.

'Is that right? You have no sea? Then this is the first time you've seen it?'

'Umm.'

'Is that so? The first time you've seen the sea. My goodness, I'm surprised. You're seeing the ocean for the first time? Is that right!' Ranko stared at him with a look of mingled wonder and contempt. 'How disgusting!' she said at last. 'Country bumpkin!'

Kosaku's antipathy for Ranko returned.

Then Reiko said, 'If this is the first time you've seen the sea, you've never ridden on a boat either, have you? You poor thing, it's better you don't tell other people. They'll laugh at you.'

Kosaku felt antipathy for Reiko, too, although for a minute there on the other side of the grove he had begun to feel a bit friendly towards her. He decided he had best be on guard with these two or who knew what might happen? Without responding to her remarks he went to the water's edge, took off his clogs, and after a wave broke and receded, put his feet in the water. Ranko and Reiko trailed behind him and did the same.

Kosaku would have liked to stay on the sandy beach and play for ever, but Ranko began saying she wanted to go home, and when she persisted he decided it was time to leave. They returned to the edge of the pine grove to find Kane-san seated by the bicycle, which was rested against a tree. Again Ranko and Reiko argued about who would ride. Finally Ranko pushed her sister aside and jumped on to the

185

luggage carrier. However this time, instead of pulling the bicycle Kane-san pedalled it, and for that reason Reiko and Kosaku were left far behind in a matter of moments.

When it was just the two of them, Reiko became quiet and no longer treated Kosaku like a country bumpkin. After they had walked about a hundred yards along the main street, Reiko said, 'I want some pop. Do you have any money?'

'Uh-uh.'

'You mean you don't have even one sen?'

'Umm.'

'You poor thing. Well, then, I'll treat,' Reiko said. Kosaku did not understand this word 'treat'.

Reiko went into a sweet shop, bought two bottles of pop, and handed one to Kosaku.

'I don't want to drink it,' Kosaku said. He was in fact quite thirsty and would have liked to drink the pop, but somehow he felt it was wrong to be drinking such a thing with Reiko in such a place. Besides, that word 'treat' sounded sinful.

'You don't *want* to drink it? Strange child! If you don't drink it, I won't play with you,' Reiko said.

'Well, then, I'll drink it,' Kosaku said. He had already brushed aside one friendly overture from her; it wouldn't do to insult her again. He brought the bottle to his mouth and the two of them drank. It tasted good.

Reiko went back into the shop and spoke to the lady again. 'Give me tangerine juice!' She received two bottles and handed one to Kosaku. This time he drank it immediately. Having already drunk the soda, after all, he could hardly refuse the tangerine juice.

When Reiko finished her juice she went back into the shop and said, 'Give me some peanuts.' She was given two triangular bags of peanuts and again handed one to Kosaku.

They started walking and eating peanuts, and in no time at all they had finished them.

'I think I'll get some sweets,' Reiko said and went into another sweet shop, smaller than the one before. This time she returned empty-handed and said, 'They have tokoro-

186

ten.* I'm going to have some. Do you want some?'

'Umm.' Kosaku nodded. He had never eaten anything called tokoroten, but he decided this would be a good chance to try it.

'All right,' Reiko said. 'You stand guard first while I eat and then I'll stand guard while you eat.'

Kosaku nodded. By way of standing guard, he looked here and there on the road while Reiko sat on a stool in front of the shop and ate tokoroten. He wasn't sure what he was standing guard for, but he had an idea he should signal Reiko immediately if he happened to see her father or mother.

At length Reiko tapped him on the shoulder and said, 'Now it's your turn.' Kosaku then sat on the stool, just as Reiko had done, and watched as the old woman in the sweet shop scooped up the mysterious concoction known as toko-roten and pushed it into a bowl with something that resembled a water pistol. In Kosaku's view this thing called tokoroten turned out to be not particularly tasty, but because he thought he should not leave any, he ate it all.

They made their way home at a leisurely pace. Along the way Reiko looked into every shop on both sides of the street and supplied titbits of information. 'This shop is expensive,' she told Kosaku. Or, 'This shop will give you a discount.' And, 'At this shop the wife is said to be domineering, so you can see that the man is quite meek.' Undoubtedly she had gleaned this knowledge by listening to adults, but as she spoke it sounded as if she had arrived at these conclusions and judgements through long first-hand observation.

When they returned to the Kamiki house, the mother was in the kitchen making oshiroko† and Ranko was sitting at the table in the family room pouting.

'Where have you been? What were you doing? You're very late. The oshiroko has boiled down to nothing,' Ranko said.

Reiko and Kosaku seated themselves and soon the maid

---

* A gelatinous confection made from seaweed. It is eaten cold, with vinegar and soy sauce.
† Rice cakes in sweet-bean soup

brought in the oshiroko. Reiko picked up her chopsticks, but immediately set them down. 'My stomach hurts,' she said. The pallor of her face would have been noticeable to the dullest observer.

Speaking of stomachs, Kosaku's didn't feel so great either. He forced himself to eat a bowl of oshiroko since the lady had taken the trouble to make it, but as soon as he finished eating he felt sick.

Reiko's mother and the maid meanwhile rushed to set down Reiko's bedding while Reiko lay on her back on the tatami clawing at her chest with both hands. 'Oh-h-h, I feel terrible,' she moaned. Kosaku wanted to lie down on the tatami too, but he forced himself to remain seated.

As Reiko was being carried to her bed, she stopped to vomit from the veranda into the inner courtyard. Hearing her groaning and retching, Kosaku suddenly felt his own gorge rise. He ran frantically to the kitchen and vomited on the earthen floor. Kane-san and the maid ran to his aid. The lady also came, and the next thing he knew Kane-san was carrying him into the room where Reiko lay and placing him on bedding next to Reiko's.

He had felt terrible until he vomited, but after that he gradually improved. Apparently the same was true for Reiko, for she started talking when the others left the room.

'Don't tell them we ate tokoroten.'

'Umm,' Kosaku agreed.

'Or the tangerine drink.'

'Umm.'

'Or the pop.'

'Umm.'

'Or the peanuts.'

'Umm.' But Kosaku was not at all sure he had the character to remain silent to the bitter end about what they had eaten. Indeed, he thought if anyone at all should ask, he might very well tell everything.

'The doctor is coming, but don't say anything.'

When he heard the word 'doctor', Kosaku felt desperate. How could he lie to a doctor? 'Is a doctor really coming?' he asked.

'Kane-san just went to fetch him.'

Kosaku was up off the bed in a twinkling. 'I'm better already,' he said.

Just then the lady of the house entered the room. 'You mustn't get up,' she admonished. 'Now lie down. You two might die. I feel sorry for you, but there is nothing I can do. You ate peanuts and tokoroten, so you're probably past saving. Perhaps I should have called the Buddhist priest instead of the doctor.'

What a catastrophe! Kosaku thought. Reiko closed her eyes and feigned sleep. Apparently the doctor arrived immediately after the lady left the room, for Kosaku heard several people talking outside. Reiko continued to feign sleep. She would not respond even when Kosaku spoke to her.

The doctor came in carrying a black bag and sat between Kosaku's and Reiko's pillows. He checked their pulses, took their temperatures, had them open their mouths and peered into their throats, then pressed and probed at their abdomens.

'I believe I might just barely save your lives this time,' he said at last. 'But if you should ever again secretly buy and eat things outside without permission, something dreadful will happen. Do you understand?' He then stood up and went home.

As soon as the doctor had left, Reiko stuck out her tongue and asked, 'Ko-cha, are you better?'

'Umm,' Kosaku replied.

'Me too.' Then she added in an impish voice, 'It was fun, wasn't it?'

But Kosaku had begun to think about Granny Onui, and he wanted to return to the inn in front of the station. He hesitated at the thought of leaving the bed, though, and remained lying on his back on the bedding until the white summer dusk closed in outside. Then he was bored and wanted to talk to Reiko, but she was sound asleep. At about that time Reiko's mother looked in and told him that Granny Onui had sent someone to fetch him, but 'I sent her away, telling her you were sick.'

'I'm better!' Kosaku jumped up, rattled.

'Oh no, we can't be sure yet. The doctor said you must rest quietly at least overnight.'

'I want to go back to Granny,' Kosaku blubbered. He thought it would be terrible to be left alone in such a place.

'Well, you'd better sleep here tonight. Granny says she'll come to get you before she leaves on the train tomorrow.'

Kosaku and Reiko ate a dinner served to them in bed. It was a simple fare of rice gruel and pickled plums. Reiko screamed for fried eggs, but her mother stood firm. This gentle woman, who let her children have their way in everything else, proved strict in dealing with invalids. Reiko insisted that she felt better and would get up, but her mother simply would not permit it.

From time to time, Ranko came into the sickroom carrying a dish of sweets from which she selected some and deliberately ate them with exaggerated enjoyment.

'You'd like to have some of these delicious sweets, wouldn't you?' she said.

Next she brought fireworks to the veranda and said tauntingly, 'I'm going to light some fireworks for you, but you just watch. You mustn't get up. If you do, I'll tell Papa.'

Kosaku lay on his stomach on the bed and looked out towards the veranda, where Ranko held a lighted sparkler in her hand, and watched the twinkling shower with rapt attention. Her face looked clever and pretty at that moment, very much the face of a city child. He didn't like her when she talked, but when she was silent and watched fireworks with that serious expression he was quite taken with her. She looked just like a girl on the cover of a picture magazine.

The father appeared once. He sat on the veranda and drank beer while his wife and a young maid massaged his shoulders. The label on the beer bottle was made so it could be peeled off to reveal a smaller label – a picture of a geisha. He took that label and pasted it on the floor of the veranda.

'This geisha is the most beautiful in all Numazu,' he said, 'and the second most beautiful is our Ranko.' Kosaku had heard rumours that this man played favourites with his own two daughters and was affectionate only towards the elder

190

daughter, Ranko. It appeared the rumours were true.

The next morning when Kosaku awoke, he heard the lady of the house talking with someone who sounded very much like Granny Onui.

Yes, that was definitely Granny Onui saying, 'Oh, my,' and 'Our Ko-cha did that?'

As soon as he got out of bed he went directly to the sitting room. It was Granny Onui, all right. She had tucked a white handkerchief round her kimono collar at the nape of the neck and she was bent forward drinking tea, seated across the table from the hostess. The maid led Kosaku to a well at the rear of the house so he could wash his face. He thought it novel to wash his face with water in a washbasin.

After breakfast Kosaku and Granny Onui left the Kamiki house. Ranko had gone to school and Reiko was still in bed. Kosaku felt bad about leaving without saying goodbye to the girls. Kane-san, who had taken them to the Thousand Pine Beach the day before, loaded Granny Onui's luggage on the bicycle rack and transported it to the station.

8

When Kosaku returned to Yugashima his memories of the day at the Kamiki house in Numazu seemed strangely unreal, and he felt almost as though Ranko and Reiko, their mother and father, and Kane-san were not living people but characters from a dream. Yet every night when he went to bed he thought at least once about Numazu and wondered what those spiteful but undeniably beautiful girls might be doing.

The Numazu trip had an enormous impact on him. Until he went to the Kamiki house in Numazu, he had never imagined that such girls could exist in all the world. Such nastiness, such wilfulness, such lavish spending, such daring, such opulence – all these things were strange and wondrous to him. And the parents of the girls – they, too, were of a type Kosaku had never before encountered. How great is the variety of mothers and fathers in this world, he thought.

About ten days after his return from Numazu Kosaku suddenly woke up in the middle of the night to find the lamp lit in his room and Granny Onui retying her obi as if she were preparing to go out. He thought it must be morning, but somehow it did not feel like morning.

'Granny?' he called.

Granny Onui turned to him and said, 'It's still night-time. You sleep some more and have a good dream.'

'Where are you going?'

'I'm not going anywhere,' Granny Onui said. Then she corrected herself. 'No, I'm going to see someone off. But I'll be right back. Now go to sleep. Go to sleep.'

'Who are you seeing off?'

'Never mind. It doesn't matter.'

'Who?' Kosaku persisted. He could not understand why she would be seeing someone off in the middle of the night. 'Please, Granny – who are you seeing off?'

Granny Onui hesitated. She lowered her voice. 'Elder Sister Sakiko. She's leaving tonight.'

'Where is she going?'

Again she hesitated. 'To where her baby is.'

Kosaku sat up quickly. Sakiko was leaving Yugashima? How could this happen? 'I want to go too.' He scrambled to his feet.

'Oh, my word, I thought I'd keep it a secret but you find out everything,' Granny Onui said. Then she added, 'If you really want to see her off it's all right. But don't tell anyone. She's leaving quietly so the neighbours won't know.'

Kosaku was into his kimono and down the stairs before Granny Onui could say another word. There was no light downstairs, and it was pitch-black inside until he pulled open the heavy front door. Then moonlight flowed on to his feet and made all the surroundings bright.

Kosaku stood by the persimmon tree in front of the store-house until Granny Onui emerged from the doorway, unwilling to dash to the Upper House alone. When they arrived together in front of the Upper House, they found two jinricksha waiting, light streaming from the house, and every sign of a great stir within.

As Kosaku started up the stone steps a stranger came out the door. Granny Onui asked the man, 'Are you leaving already?'

The man grunted, then murmured as if to himself, 'Poor thing has got so thin.' It was clear he was talking about Sakiko. A second stranger emerged, and on his heels came

193

Grandmother Tane clad in her good kimono and carrying two kerchief bundles.

Grandmother Tane paused in front of Granny Onui and murmured politely, 'Thank you for coming to see us off at such an hour.'

'Not at all,' Granny Onui said. 'You must have her healthy again.' Then she added, 'I kept it a secret, but Ko-cha woke up and found me leaving. I can't keep anything from clever Ko-cha.'

Grandmother Tane's face softened. 'So you came too, Ko-cha.' She briefly patted his head.

Just then Kosaku saw Sakiko. She passed in front of him and continued towards the jinricksha standing in the street. But halfway there she paused, apparently only then having registered his presence.

She spoke his name. 'Ko-cha.'

'Yes?' he replied tensely.

'You study, now. You're different from other children, and when you grow up you must go to the university.'

'Yes.'

'Well, then. . . .' Sakiko nodded briefly towards Granny Onui, then resumed her course and stepped up into the jinricksha.

Mitsu, Daigo, Daizo and Grandfather all came outside to see off the two jinricksha, the one in front carrying Grandmother Tane and the second one carrying Sakiko. Kosaku watched without blinking as the two jinricksha rolled away. He knew why Sakiko was leaving in the middle of the night. She did not want anyone to see her so ill and wasted. That was why she left with only family seeing her off.

Kosaku could also understand, to some extent, why Sakiko wanted to join her husband at his post on the west coast. In fact in his mind that seemed rather a good thing for her to do. Perhaps her health would improve if she moved to another place; and if the opposite should prove true – if as people said her illness was terminal – it seemed right for her to spend the life that remained to her with her husband and baby.

As the jinricksha gradually drew away into the distance,

Kosaku became aware of a mounting sensation unlike any he had known before, and he knew it was because of this sensation that he had not said more to Sakiko or tried to chase her jinricksha. The jinricksha soon disappeared from view and all that remained was an empty street shining in the moonlight.

Granny Onui talked quietly for a while with Grandfather from the Upper House, but presently she ended the conversation.

'Well, Ko-cha, let's go home to the storehouse,' she said.

Kosaku heard, and started walking. Then, without warning, a sadness welled within him like a massive surge of water and he wanted to cry out with a loud voice. But he controlled the impulse and willed himself to overcome it. I will not cry, he thought. I will not cry, but tonight is the saddest night of my life.

When they were back on the second floor of the storehouse Kosaku asked, 'Will Elder Sister Sakiko get well?'

'We certainly want her to. She has the child. . . .' Then Granny Onui said, 'I wonder why it is that the good people have such bad luck in this world. Take those two sisters, now. Compared to Ko-cha's mother, Sakiko is so gentle.'

'I thought you didn't like Elder Sister Sakiko, Granny,' Kosaku said.

'In the past she was quite aggravating – when I met her in the street she was rude and antagonistic. But since she got sick she has become a truly sweet woman. Not long ago when I went to see her, she asked me to take good care of you. And do you know what else she said? She said, "Granny, watch what you eat and live a long life."'

The window was open and the late-evening moonlight poured in. Granny Onui stood by the window with the tobacco holder in her mouth, her features distinct yet seeming to float in space.

'Is that why you began to like Elder Sister, Granny?'

'Umm.'

'I like Big Sister, too.'

'Of course you like her. Why, she became a teacher, so that tells you she cared about children,' Granny Onui said.

195

Then she added musingly, 'Well, it seems that child was the kindest of all at the Upper House. When they get a kind one up there it always turns out this way.'

'I like Elder Sister,' Kosaku repeated. And feeling those words were not adequate, he added, 'I like Elder Sister Sakiko *best*.'

'Naturally. There's no other person at the Upper House that you could sensibly like,' Granny Onui said.

'I like Elder Sister.'

'I know. I know.'

'I like her better than Granny.'

'Who?'

'Elder Sister.'

Granny Onui frowned and pouted. 'Stupid,' she said. 'There are many just like her if you go to Tokyo.' She paused. 'Still, she was kind. She told me to have a long life.' Granny Onui seemed extremely pleased that Sakiko had told her to have a long life.

Kosaku could not sleep. Granny Onui noticed and offered to paste some pickled plum on his forehead.

'No, I don't want it,' he said emphatically. He was in no mood that night to have anything to do with pickled plum.

When Granny Onui said, 'Very well, but it will be hard for you if you can't sleep,' Kosaku became very cross and refused to listen to her at all.

After the summer holidays began Kosaku half expected that he might be invited to Sakiko's new home. He thought if she didn't ask him to come alone he might be invited along when someone from the Upper House went to see her. He heard that Sakiko's condition had worsened after she left Yugashima, and he knew that people at the Upper House took turns visiting her. But no one invited him to go. He felt totally forgotten.

Meanwhile his mother wrote to Granny Onui inviting them to come to Toyohashi, but Kosaku preferred not to go there. He knew from the previous summer what kind of place Toyohashi was, and furthermore he knew that life with

196

his parents was extremely confining. He decided he would rather spend his summer holidays in Yugashima. In this he encountered no objection from Granny Onui. 'I'll tell them Granny doesn't feel well and we won't go,' she announced to Kosaku in a manner suggesting that they had talked it out and were in complete agreement.

It was in the midst of the unspoken negotiations about Toyohashi that the dreaded news about Sakiko reached the Upper House. Mitsu came to inform Kosaku. When she came, Kosaku was by the streamlet washing himself in a wooden bathtub filled with warm water.

'Elder Sister Sakiko just died,' Mitsu said matter-of-factly, as if she were speaking of a stranger.

'Died?'

'She stopped breathing.'

'Who did?'

'Elder Sister Sakiko.'

'Hmm.' Kosaku could not quite comprehend the sense of this message. He had heard Sakiko's condition had worsened and knew everyone was worried, but he could not connect all that with the idea of Sakiko's death. He only knew that he wanted to protest at what Mitsu had said. There was no reason why he must believe her. 'She wouldn't die, stupid!' he said as he stood up in the tub.

'But she *did* die,' Mitsu said.

Just then Grandmother Tane arrived and informed Granny Onui, who was cooking in the kitchen. 'Sakiko has passed away,' she said. Apparently Grandmother had been round to all the households in the village where her family had friendly ties, for she was breathing hard.

'Oh, my goodness.' Granny Onui stretched her back and stood facing her visitor. When she spoke again her tone was uncharacteristically subdued. 'A person who has died will never come back,' she said. 'Granny, please don't lose heart.'

Granny Onui's enigmatic words of comfort seemed to release something pent up inside Kosaku's grandmother, for she reacted by sobbing and bringing her kimono sleeve to her face. Granny Onui also began to cry then and so did

197

Mitsu, who was still standing beside the bathtub. When they all started, Kosaku understood at last that something terrible had happened, something having to do with Sakiko . . . what Mitsu had said . . . Sakiko. Elder Sister Sakiko was dead.

That night and the following day, Kosaku shut himself up alone in the storehouse. All the residents of the Upper House had gone to the village on the west coast and Granny Onui was housesitting for them. Kosaku was left to look after the storehouse by himself. Yukio and the others came there to play, but Kosaku did not want to be with his friends the day after he learned of Sakiko's death. Instead, from early morning he sat at his desk by the window, studying. He recalled how Sakiko had told him to study as she was leaving Yugashima, and since then he had not studied at all. Now it was probably too late, but even so, he would study. From time to time Yukio and the others climbed the stairs to the second floor of the storehouse to gaze at the strange sight of Kosaku poring over his books, then they put their fingers to their lips and said 'Shush' and tiptoed back down. They came to look many times, and each time they left without disturbing the student.

Kosaku went to the Upper House only during meal times and stayed just long enough to eat his meal with Granny Onui. Then he returned to the storehouse and his studies.

When Granny Onui learned of Kosaku's sudden dedication to scholarship she said, 'Don't study too hard. Your health is your wealth. You can do well without studying. If you study too much, you'll get too clever and make life hard for the teachers.'

To Kosaku the entire village seemed changed. It was strangely silent, and he concluded this was because everyone was mourning for Sakiko. Actually, quite a number of villagers had gone to the hamlet on the west coast to attend Sakiko's funeral. No one invited Kosaku to go along. He was mildly resentful at being treated as someone inconsequential in Sakiko's life, but he did not really want to go.

By the day of Sakiko's funeral Kosaku was satiated with studying and ready to go and see the tunnel at Amagi Pass

198

with Yukio and some other friends. Yukio initiated the plan, but it was Kosaku who translated it into action. The talk of a hike to Amagi Pass spread among the children of the village in no time, and an unexpectedly large number of them turned out to participate. A party of twenty left the village shortly after noon and headed south towards the Amagi Highway. Kosaku walked at the front of the line with Yukio. Yoshie, Kameo, Shigeru and Heiichi were also present.

Kosaku, seized by the feeling that on this day he must assign himself some sort of painful task, decided they should all walk the whole distance without resting. Yukio suggested a break many times, but each time Kosaku warned, 'If we stop nobody will want to start again,' and kept his own feet moving.

When the other children got the message that there would be no resting, they decided as with one mind not only that they would keep walking but that they would go naked. Off came their kimonos, to be tied with obi sashes and held in various ways. Some put their kimonos on their heads, some on their hips. Some held them in their hands, some tied them to their backs like luggage. Each child did with his kimono as he saw fit. Three boys among the twenty walked both naked and unburdened, having either hidden the kimono bundle by the side of the road or tied it to a tree.

Now and then the children met an adult or two. The adults always asked, 'Where are you going like that?'

'To the tunnel,' someone would reply.

'You can't go through the tunnel naked. It's cold even in summer.'

Then, like as not, the adult would mutter something like, 'Good-for-nothing brats!'

As he walked, Kosaku kept his eyes on the white clouds that hung on the ridges of Mt. Amagi. His body was wet with sweat; dust clung to the sweat, which became black beads that rolled down his nude body and dropped on to the dust beneath his feet.

Once Kosaku said to Yukio, 'Elder Sister Sakiko died.'

Yukio responded, 'I know.' Then he suddenly raised his voice and, imitating a Buddhist sutra chant, cried, 'Namu

199

maida. Namu maida.'* The strange band of children following him took up the chant. 'Namu maida. Namu maida,'
they wailed, harmonizing with Yukio.

Kosaku felt no anger at their chanting. He knew they were
not making fun of Sakiko's death, but meant rather to mourn
her. And indeed to every one of them Sakiko had been a
teacher at one time or another.

When the children tired of chanting they began to sing one
after another the many songs Sakiko had taught them, with
no one in particular leading. When one started a new song
the others chimed in and harmonized.

Kosaku walked far ahead of the singers. Devout in his
self-assigned mission, he plodded from pass to pass without
pause. Now and then a vision of Sakiko cold in death
flickered in his mind, and each time he securely retied the
kimono bundle on his head as if to extinguish the thought.
Then he thundered, 'Hang on!' to those behind him.

The first autumn wind of the year blew on the slope of Mt.
Amagi that day. Intermittently, the undersides of the leaves
on the trees glittered silver in the sunlight, revealing the
direction of the wind.

---

* A childish mispronunciation of the Buddhist chant for the dead